MW00775538

DELTA

The K9 Files, Book 23

Dale Mayer

DELTA: THE K9 FILES, BOOK 23
Beverly Dale Mayer
Valley Publishing Ltd.

Copyright © 2024

All rights reserved. Except for use in any review, the reproduction or utilization of this work in whole or in part by any electronic, mechanical or other means, now known or hereafter invented, including xerography, photocopying and recording, or in any information storage or retrieval system, is forbidden without the written permission of the publisher.

This is a work of fiction. Names, characters, places, brands, media, and incidents are either the product of the author's imagination or are used fictitiously. Any resemblance to actual events, locales, or persons, living or dead, is entirely coincidental.

ISBN-13: 978-1-778862-98-4
Print Edition

Books in This Series

About This Book

Welcome to the all new K9 Files series reconnecting readers with the unforgettable men from SEALs of Steel in a new series of action packed, page turning romantic suspense that fans have come to expect from USA TODAY Bestselling author Dale Mayer. Pssst… you'll meet other favorite characters from SEALs of Honor and Heroes for Hire too!

Delta is always eager to help animals in need, especially when the request comes from Kat and Badger. Learning the animal is a retired K9 dog, now serving as a comfort animal for other injured dogs, Delta's determination only increases. However, arriving in town, Delta's contact has now vanished, and Delta discovers the War Dog is missing as well. Although Delta had looked forward to dinner with the woman he'd spoken to frequently on the phone, he now finds himself entangled in a disconcerting theory that extends beyond just one War Dog.

Rebecca has always had a soft spot for animals, and retired War Dog Gracie has effortlessly found a place in her heart. However, Rebecca's attempts to adopt her from the center are consistently thwarted. As Rebecca seeks a solution, she stumbles upon something far more sinister, and soon realizes she is out of her depth.

All she can do is hope that Delta comes through for both her and Gracie … before it is too late.

Sign up to be notified of all Dale's releases here!
https://geni.us/DaleNews

PROLOGUE

B ADGER WALKED INTO the dining room, finding his wife, Kat, sorting papers into folders. He stopped, his hands on his hips, and stared at the documents, but, upside down, he couldn't read clearly what they were.

When she looked up, she gave him a smile and said, "More work."

"What kind of work?"

She chuckled. "Four more K9 files."

His eyebrows shot up. "Seriously?"

"Yes, they just came in this morning. Commander Cross did phone ahead of time, and he asked if we were up for it. Of course I said yes, and he was extremely grateful."

Badger added, "We have had amazing successes in doing this War Dog work."

"Commander Cross has also told several other people in his department how well we have done with it all. I guess we've made a name for ourselves, without expecting to."

Badger rolled his eyes at that. "Not sure that's a good thing."

"Of course it is," Kat said, with a laugh. "Anything that we do to help these animals and to give the department other options for helping these War Dogs is a good thing." She tapped the file closest to her and then slid it toward him.

Badger shook his head. "We're out of men."

"Nope." Kat laughed. "I know that you think so, but I also know that each dog has a rescue out there. And it's important we find the right ones to pair up with each War Dog."

"I agree," Badger murmured, "but that doesn't change the fact that we have nobody to call on for help right now."

"I'm not so sure about that," she said, as she slid the file to him again.

Badger looked down at the file and shrugged. "So, you have somebody in mind?"

"I do," she murmured. "I was thinking about somebody I was working with today. Delta has consistent ankle problems, and I've seen him regularly over the last couple months. However, we think we've got his ankle joint sorted. He has a lot more weight on the outside of his right leg than he has on the inside." Seeing the look on Badger's face, she laughed. "That's the technical stuff I've been dealing with for him. Just a pressure joint adjustment."

Badger smirked. "So that would be good, if Delta's ready."

"It would be, and I was talking to him. He absolutely loves dogs and was considering doing canine training, potentially to work in the police department or a sheriff's office or in some other capacity. And I mentioned how we had done all this work with the retired War Dogs coming out of the military, and he grew quite excited. He worked with several War Dogs while he was overseas and loved everything about it. He's a big fan of the department and what they were doing. Hated to see any kind of animal mistreated. And was a big advocate for the animals. He did a lot of first aid work on them as well."

"So he's a vet?" Badger asked.

"No, but he was a vet assistant, before he went into the military. He was contemplating going to veterinarian school, but I think just the amount of years involved was a deterrent for him back then, and particularly now with his health. However, he's getting better, and I would say he's probably fully capable of doing something like these War Dog cases."

Badger nodded. "Lots of years to invest in becoming a veterinarian, and Delta, with his military service, is now probably already in his late twenties or early thirties, right?"

"Delta's thirty-four, not married, not engaged, doesn't have any attachments."

Badger's eyebrows went up at that.

She nodded. "Of course I guess he had somebody, but she broke up with him when he was deployed." Badger frowned at that. She agreed. "I know that you and I have a hard time with that. However, a lot of people have been through that experience, and it hasn't stopped them. Delta's moving forward with his life."

Badger asked, "And did he say he would like to do something like this?"

Kat nodded. "I told him that, at the moment, we didn't have a War Dog file, but I would consider him, if I got one." Again she motioned at the table and the file she kept sliding toward Badger. "And that would be the file."

"And why this file? Why would Delta be the right man for this job? What about this case screams *Delta* to you?"

Kat nodded, as she pulled her chair away from the dining room table to situate it closer to Badger, where she relaxed, facing him. "Yes, Delta Granger is the man for this file."

"And that's his real name?"

"Yes, that's his real name."

"Okay, and what about this War Dog?" Badger asked.

"What matters is this dog was used as a comfort dog for the injured War Dogs."

He pulled out a dining room chair, sat down across from her, and studied her features. "Seriously? I didn't even know something like that was possible."

"It is, and it's not common, but it should be common in a vet clinic. If you have injured animals, another animal—particularly one of the same species—can often give comfort to the injured ones. There was a military veterinarian on staff who used several comfort dogs to help with the injured animals. So this War Dog, now a comfort dog, whose name is Gracie, was one of those. She was injured, and she's missing her back leg and some of her tail, plus the muscles in between are damaged." Kat looked at her own missing limb.

Badger couldn't help but stare down at his as well. "I can't even imagine what the pain would be for a dog to go through that. … Of course, that would make Gracie one of ours."

Kat chuckled. "It absolutely would."

"Well, I'm game if you and Delta are," he murmured. "You're a better determinant of character than I am."

"I'm not sure that is true," she murmured. "I might have luck in pairing relationships, but not to the extent you do." She picked up her phone. "I'll call him. He was just here earlier today. In fact, you've met him. Remember the guy who did the patio stonework at Jager's?"

Badger smiled. "He did good work."

Kat chuckled, holding the phone to her ear. "He did do great work," she said, listening to it ring. "Delta, it's Kat. Can you come over tomorrow? Let's talk about something we might have available." She smiled, looking at Badger.

"The file just came in. … That would be great. Thank you." She smiled as she ended the call. "He's coming tomorrow."

"Perfect," Badger murmured. "Now what's up for to-night?"

She laughed. "Our *kids* coming over to enjoy the pool, as usual, maybe some barbecued steak."

He grabbed her hand, giving it a kiss. "With you, I'm game for anything."

CHAPTER 1

DELTA GRANGER DECIDED that a road trip was in order when his destination was a small town, probably with no airport at all. It would entail a few hours, but it would be easier to have his vehicle than it would be to fly and then deal with a rental. Besides, he was more than ready for a chance to get out and about. He needed time away. After multiple conversations over the phone with Rebecca to discuss Gracie, the War Dog turned comfort dog, Delta decided this was a perfect escape.

He eventually arrived outside the K9 training center. This private company provided for both the training and medical needs of these dogs for later placement within the military or police and sheriffs' departments, or even at banks and other locations that hired security guards. As he parked in the huge parking lot, he was amazed at the sheer size of the building. He understood a rehab center was also attached, which was fascinating to consider. The fact that he was coming in to evaluate Gracie's position here, as a retired War Dog, currently working as a comfort dog for other War Dogs after surgery, just blew him away.

Yet he absolutely loved the concept. Just like everybody else, when a War Dog was injured and hurt, they needed comfort too, and another dog—usually another animal of the same species as them—seemed to calm them down and to give them that extra ability to detach from what was happening around them and to adapt a little better. Any animal that could adapt better always healed faster, so that made a lot of sense to Delta.

As he stepped out of his SUV, his ankle kinked. Not really his ankle but the same pin joint that Kat was having trouble with. He looked down at his leg and shook it out. Not that it would help, but it made him feel better. He took a couple steps, wincing as the joint didn't work as well as it should have, impacting his stump. "Damn it," he muttered. "I should have gone in for another adjustment before I left."

He slowly made his way into the building and the front desk in the lobby. When he walked in, the woman at the reception desk looked up at him, but, instead of smiling, she frowned.

He studied her features for a moment and then asked, "Am I interrupting something?"

"I don't know," she replied briskly. "What do you want?"

He looked down at his phone. "I came to see ... Rebecca."

"She's busy." The woman dropped her gaze to her computer. as if the conversation were over.

"Yeah, I'm sure she is, but ... I'm here anyway."

"That's nice." She sat back, studying him. "And what's your business here?"

"I'll discuss that with Rebecca," he stated, giving her the same brisk responses he was getting.

"I told you, she's busy."

"That's interesting," he murmured. "I'll just make a note here that the company is uncooperative. It'll get back to the war department soon enough, though I might as well file the report right away."

Immediately she froze and asked, "What are you talking about?"

"None of your business," he declared, as he turned to head back out again.

His attempt at a smooth exit was marred by his inability to make that turn as easily as he should have. He kicked his leg out again, looked down, and then frowned, but he took several more steps, with more of a limp than he wanted.

She called out to him, "What are you doing here?"

"None of your business," he repeated. "I told you who I needed to see. That's as much as I'm telling you."

And, with that, he stepped out of the building and headed toward his car. He was the most amiable of people, if he got cooperation, however, when he was served up an attitude, you could bet his own mirrored what he was getting. He didn't have any reason to be upset at the receptionist, but neither did she with him, so they were left in a stalemate.

Back at his vehicle, he slowly got in his car, watching the performance of that ankle, then quickly sent a text to Kat. Arrived. Uncooperative. Front reception stated Rebecca is busy and would pass on the message. Haven't found this Rebecca person. Ankle not functioning great.

He got back a sad face emoji with a quick note, saying the new part wasn't in yet but hopefully soon.

He nodded in understanding. Kat was one of the few people he knew of who custom-designed prosthetics to fit what was needed because, where prosthetics were concerned, every person had a special, unique circumstance. There was no one-size, one-part-fits-all concept, so she was constantly creating new parts for various people. Then she had to get them made, even though she was a hell of a good machinist herself.

As Kat would say, time had demanded it, but these parts also had to be made of a special material. So she now had experts she worked with to create most of them.

Delta managed to get his leg back into the car, shut the door, and turned on the engine. As he backed out of his parking spot, he found an older woman standing there, her arms across her chest, glaring at him. He wasn't sure what the hell was going on with this place, but some serious attitude issues were evident. He stopped his car, turned off the engine, and watched to see what she would do.

She walked closer to him and leaned in to speak with him. "I understand there's a problem."

"When somebody can't walk inside and get a civil response from your front desk clerk, I would say that you're the ones with the problem."

She shook her head. "We've had some issues."

"Yeah? Well, I guess you'll probably continue to have issues, with that attitude."

Again she glared at him. "What is it you want?"

"To speak with Rebecca." When her expression cleared slightly, he wondered if that's who this lady was.

"She's not here right now," she stated in a calmer tone.

"That would have been nice to know up front. Too bad your receptionist didn't say that instead of just pissing me off."

She frowned. "That's not what she told me happened."

"Of course not. Why am I not surprised?" He snorted. "No point in even speaking with you either."

"She mentioned something about the war department." Her gaze was intense.

"Yeah, what about it?" he asked, refusing to give an inch. She frowned again. He waited but got no response. "You stated Rebecca's not here, so when is she coming back?"

She hesitated and then shrugged. "Honestly, we're not sure."

"What do you mean, *you're not sure?*" he asked in exasperation.

She looked around, as if to see if anybody were listening, and then continued. "Look. We've had some problems, potentially serious problems. I don't know if you're part of the problem, part of the solution, or neither. However, I know that Rebecca is in the midst of the problem."

He shook his head at that. "I don't even know what the hell that means. I came to talk to her about Gracie."

At that, she stared at him in astonishment. "Gracie? The comfort dog?"

"Yes, the retired War Dog," he snapped. "What is so hard to swallow about that?"

"But she's not here."

"I know that," he replied patiently. "That's why I came to talk to Rebecca." This unidentified woman shook her head, and he could see that she had no clue what he was even talking about. "Is Rebecca coming back or not? And, if she is, when is that likely to be? A straight answer, please—"

"I don't know," she said. Then she sighed, looking defeated. "The cops have been here all morning, and we're all on edge."

"What are you talking about?"

"Rebecca's disappeared. We don't know why or how."

"What do you mean by *disappeared?*"

She shook her head. "Rebecca didn't show up for work today."

"And you were expecting her?" he asked.

"Yes, we were expecting her," she confirmed, looking at him shrewdly. "She was due in early, like *early*-early. She didn't show up. I called her but got no response, which is also very unusual." Then she frowned and added, "I shouldn't even be talking to you about this."

"Actually you probably should," he declared. "Now I need to know exactly what's going on."

"But it's none of your business," she pointed out briskly, as she took several steps back.

"Then I'll go to the sheriff's office," he stated.

She pivoted toward him, as she had been in the process of walking back to the building. "Do you know Rebecca?"

He nodded. "Yes, I know her." Honestly, he didn't really know her well at all. Days ago he'd left a message to introduce himself to her, and she'd called back, followed by a little more phone tag and a few text messages in between. He had even checked out her online presence. Yet, without any personal face-to-face interaction, he had felt … a connection. Just thinking about something happening to her already hurt him in his soul.

"I don't know what to say to you because we don't know what happened."

"Well, you're certainly not making things any clearer with your cryptic responses. Did anybody go to her apartment?"

"No, as a company representative, I don't think so, but she wasn't answering her phone. We contacted the cops about it, and they offered to do a welfare check."

"Did they get back to you?"

She shook her head. "No, they didn't. I tried to follow up, but apparently there was some other incident."

"So, you haven't had anybody go to her place and check if she's there?" he asked incredulously. "You're all just sitting here, waiting for somebody to do something?"

"You don't understand. … Well, maybe you do. If you know Rebecca at all, she doesn't like people in her space. She's … different."

"We're all different," he replied, staring at her. "That's no excuse for not following up to ensure she's okay."

The other woman flushed in anger. "That's why I called the cops," she snapped. "I don't know what else you expect me to do. If something's happened to her, I really don't want to be the one who finds her."

"Finally some honesty." He had to give her points for that. And, if there was a problem, nobody wanted to get involved to begin with. Not him though. That just made him feel more concern for the poor woman. "Does she drive to work?" he asked. "Any chance that she's been involved in an accident?"

The other woman shrugged. "We don't know, and that's why I called the sheriff."

"The fact that nobody's gotten back to you is interesting," he murmured. He tapped his hand on the steering wheel. "I'll talk to the sheriff."

"Yeah, you do that," she muttered, taking several steps backward. "I just don't know what else to tell you."

He nodded and turned on the engine again. "I'll see what I can find out."

She gave him a tentative smile and then called out, "If you could let us know something?"

He frowned. "Do you have a card?"

She pulled something from her back pocket and handed it to him. "Yes. Contact me here."

He took it and then watched as she quickly walked away. It seemed she was almost escaping. She was an older woman, mid-fifties maybe, which nowadays was surely the new thirties. She was well-preserved, wore minimal makeup, but was well-dressed. It went along with the massive building behind her—older but well-maintained. She certainly was a little friendlier compared to the first woman he'd met, but not by much.

As soon as he pulled out onto the main road, he hit the GPS, looking for the local sheriff's department for this small town. It took him a few minutes to navigate through the myriad of left and right turns, before he pulled up into a small parking lot.

As he parked his vehicle, he saw two deputy cars alongside the small building. He hopped out and walked slowly, worrying about the ankle joint more than he should, but reminding himself that Kat was on it. Meanwhile, once he got back in town, he would have her at least adjust this one, while he awaited his final product.

As he walked into the building, two deputies stood off to one side, each with a cup of coffee in hand, just chatting. They looked over at him, and the younger one raised an eyebrow. Delta frowned and announced, "I'm Delta Granger, and I'm here looking for Rebecca Postal."

The two men just stared at him.

Delta tilted his head ever-so-slightly. "I believe you were contacted because she didn't show up for work and has been reported as missing."

The younger deputy shrugged. "She's an adult, and she has the right to leave and to not show up for work."

"Did anybody do a welfare check at her home?" Delta asked, trying to control his muscles, already tightening with each passing moment, due to that internal knowing that something was wrong.

The same deputy nodded. "We did, and no one answered the door. We aren't allowed to go in just because she didn't show up for work a few hours ago."

Delta pondered that. "I see. So, when is it that you'll take action?"

"Tomorrow," the younger deputy replied curtly.

"So, you don't check up on her phone or GPS on her vehicle or anything like that in the meantime? By tomorrow, when you can do something, you could discover that she's dead. Is that your procedure here?" Again that same old fury was building up inside, yet Delta knew it wasn't fair because they were supposedly following the rules, and it wasn't personal.

Both men stared at him, but now the older deputy asked suspiciously, "Who are you?"

"I already told you who I am. I drove here to meet Rebecca this morning, and she didn't show up for that meeting."

"Maybe that's why she went missing," the younger deputy muttered under his breath.

Delta shot him a glance, pulled out his phone, and brought up his Notes app. "What did you say your names were?"

Both deputies frowned, as one stood a bit straighter, and asked, "What are you talking about?"

Delta eyed him and repeated, "I'm asking for your names." Delta read the name tag on the nearest guy's uniform. "Are you Deputy Halvorson? And you are Deputy Sal Patton?" Delta quickly wrote down the two names and turned and made his way outside.

It took a little bit to coordinate the failing ankle joint on the front steps. Delta would have to grab his screwdriver and adjust it again. Back in his car, he left the driver's side door open, while he grabbed the screwdriver and quickly adjusted the joint. When he sat back up again, Deputy Halvorson glared at him. Delta raised an eyebrow. "You got a problem?"

"Yeah, we got a problem," Halvorson snapped, his tone hard. "We don't want no strangers around here causing trouble."

"No, you probably don't," Delta agreed in a smooth tone. "I would think you also wouldn't want a well-respected woman to go missing or have something bad happen to her, simply because you guys were too lazy to put down your coffee cups and look for her."

The deputy shook his head. "That's not fair."

"If you haven't done a welfare check, if you haven't done anything to see whether her vehicle is missing or there at her home—"

"We didn't look," he admitted.

"Exactly. You followed the rules you are required to work under but completely ignored all the other things you could have done to locate her or to gather data that would be invaluable, should she still be missing come tomorrow. You must know that the first twenty-four hours are crucial. So I will go over there and have a look myself."

Delta didn't have her address, but he was hoping that he might bluff somebody into revealing where she lived. He would also need the license plate and the make and model of her car, but he wasn't past asking Badger for that kind of help either.

Halvorson shoved his hands in his pockets, as he looked around, frowning. "Maybe I'll take another drive over there," he said reluctantly.

"You probably should," Delta agreed. "You don't want anything bad to happen, only to have it come back later as being uncaring and incompetent."

At that, Halvorson glared at him again but then turned and stormed back inside and came out a few minutes later, his hat on and keys in his hand. Delta sat here, as if still working on his ankle joint, waiting until the deputy hopped into a vehicle and pulled out. Right behind him, Delta followed the patrol car to Rebecca's home.

When he pulled up to a small townhome in a small complex, the deputy parked out front and hopped out. He was talking on his comm system for a minute and then quickly hung up and walked to the front door of unit 3. Immediately Delta walked up behind him.

Deputy Halvorson glared at him, as he knocked on the door. "I told you that we already checked."

"Yeah, you did, but how much did you check? Did you go around back?" Delta noted the unit number, and, while the deputy was knocking at the front door, Delta headed around to the back, where he found more parking and a vehicle in her numbered spot, but that didn't mean it was her car. He walked up to the back door and knocked, hard. The door wasn't even latched and readily slid open.

He walked through and called out for her, "Rebecca, are you here?" He gingerly opened the front door—not wanting to disturb any existing fingerprints—and faced the deputy, who once more glared at him. Delta shrugged. "The back door was open."

"Why would you do that? He snapped. "If something was wrong, you'll have your fingerprints all over the place."

"The back door was barely even latched," he shared. "All

17

I did was knock, and it popped open. Also I came straight through, calling out for her. The only set of prints for me will be on the inside of this front door."

The deputy shook his head and sighed.

Together, the two of them did a full search but found no sign of her.

"A vehicle is parked in her allotted slot, but I can't guarantee it's her car." Delta frowned. "I don't remember what she drove."

The deputy headed out to the car, walked around to the back of it, and wrote down the license plate. He then proceeded to call somebody. He came back a few minutes later and told Delta, "It's her car."

Delta nodded. "So, she either left with someone, voluntarily or has been taken. I'll search her home again and see if anything's missing."

"How will you know if anything's missing?" the deputy asked in a hard tone.

"Not so much what's missing but whether she left in a hurry. I'll look for a suitcase, a purse, makeup, things out of place like that." Delta shrugged, as he walked back to her unit.

The deputy called out behind him, "You realize we shouldn't even be in there."

"Her door was ajar. She didn't show up for work, and she missed a meeting. She's not here, yet her car remains here. That's suspicious circumstances to cover you," Delta explained, shooting him a look. "I would rather err on the side of trying to help a woman in trouble than have nobody know or care." That just earned him another dirty look.

With the two of them going through Rebecca's bathroom and her bedroom, taking a closer look, Delta pointed out to the deputy, "Look. Her makeup's here, her tooth-brush, her hairbrush. … It's all here."

The deputy nodded and added, "Her purse, with her driver's license and her charge cards, are all here too."

At that, Delta muttered, "Which means she didn't pack and didn't have a chance to take anything important with her."

They opened closets, which were all stuffed with cloth-ing. "So, we can't tell if she took anything from here either." Delta frowned, as he looked at the bed, which was made. "It's all very clean, neat and tidy," he noted, "and my concern now is that she didn't sleep in her bed at all last night."

Deputy Halvorson swore at that and nodded. "I think you're right. In which case did she leave work on time yesterday? Where did she go after that?"

"Nothing like the present to find out," Delta replied, as he pulled out his phone. He quickly phoned the company where Rebecca worked and spoke with the receptionist, once again identifying himself. "We're at her townhome. When did Rebecca leave work yesterday? And, if you're wondering if this is an official request, Deputy Halvorson is right here with me."

The woman's tone changed after that. "I can check when she logged out," she muttered.

In the background, Delta heard keys clicking. "Does she have any pets?" he asked her.

"No, but she was pretty partial to the one dog here at work."

"Right. We're talking about Gracie, aren't we?"

"Yes." Then she asked, "How do you know that?"

Having to blend the lies he'd already told this rude

woman and the deputy and the unknown woman in the parking lot earlier, he replied, "Rebecca told me when we were discussing Gracie."

"That sounds like her. According to the security system, she logged out at ten minutes after six o'clock last night." But an odd note filled her tone.

"And what's wrong with that?"

"Well, she's off at five. She does stay and work late quite often, but the system also says that her security key logged in again at seven, then left at seven-thirty."

"So, it's possible she left something at work and came back for it?" Delta looked over at Deputy Halvorson, who was writing down notes.

"Well, it's possible," the receptionist replied, "but it would be unusual."

"Is anything missing?" he asked.

The deputy looked at him sharply, and an audible inhale of breath could be heard over the phone. "You need to talk to my boss," she stated. "Just a minute. Hold on please." He looked over at Deputy Halvorson. "So, something *is* wrong."

The deputy frowned and nodded, reluctantly adding, "Something's not right, let's put it that way."

When another woman came on the phone, Delta realized it was the one he'd spoken to earlier in the parking lot. She asked sharply, "There's no sign of Rebecca?"

"Not at her townhome. Her car is here, and it doesn't look like she even slept in her bed last night," he shared. "Now, I understand from the receptionist I just spoke to, that there are some concerns over her coming and going last night, after logging out."

"Not necessarily. For instance, if she forgot something and had to come back for it, that wouldn't be a concern. Maybe she just left her phone here or something," she explained, yet sounded doubtful. Then she added in a brisk tone, "I can't really help you. We don't have any issues here."

"So, no break-ins, no security leaks, and nothing's been stolen? I am here with the deputy, so please remember you're on the record."

At that came a sharp sucking in of breath, much like her coworker. Then her tone turned completely sour. "Now you're making it sound like I might need a lawyer."

The deputy's eyebrows shot straight up, and he reached out a hand for Delta's phone. Delta handed it over. "This is Deputy Halvorson here. Are you telling me that you feel you need a lawyer because there's been some criminal activity you're afraid of being accused of?"

Dead silence followed.

Delta hid a smile, as he waited to hear what the woman would say.

"There have been no issues here at all," she snapped. "There's no reason for any concern except for the fact that she didn't show up for work today."

The deputy replied, "I'll need a list of all known associates, a list of any work issues and current cases. You should know that I am prepared to go through appropriate legal channels with the district attorney, should there be any resistance to supplying us with the requested information. This is now officially considered a missing person's case. She was last seen at work and, in an unusual move, left her workplace, but then her security card was used to enter the facility again, but that doesn't mean that *she* reentered that building," he snapped.

The older woman added, "No, hang on, hang on. We

have no reason to suspect it wasn't her."

Delta leaned forward and stated, "Therefore, we'll also need immediate access to the security camera video at your facility. Do we need to get a search warrant for that, or will you cooperate? And you should know we can easily expand the parameters of the search warrant, if need be."

With the older woman blustering, the deputy declared, "We'll expect a timely response as to when and how we can access the videos."

"Since time is clearly of the essence," Delta quickly added, "we'll need to see them within the next hour."

And, with that, the deputy hung up and handed Delta's phone back. "You're pretty good at that stuff."

Delta nodded. "I did two tours in the military and then came back due to an injury, but, before that, I was in law enforcement."

"Why the hell did you go from law enforcement to the military?" he asked, shaking his head.

Delta had heard that comment before.

Halvorson shrugged and added, "You know you can't go with me to see the video camera footage, right?" Delta glared at him, but the deputy shook his head. "We can't allow that."

"Maybe I presently can't go with you to see the video," he noted. "However, are you fully staffed? Unless you're full up on deputies and have the manpower to do this, I suggest you deputize me to assist in this case to help you find her."

The deputy studied him, one eyebrow raised.

Delta continued. "Look. I have experience, and right now you're obviously short-staffed. And, if word gets out that this kidnapping got missed already and that we have a lack of cooperation on the search for this poor woman, things are bound to get ugly."

REBECCA SAT CURLED up in the corner of a ten-by-twelve bedroom. A blanket and a flat mattress sat off to the side, along with her ever-present companion, Gracie. Rebecca smiled, as she placed a hand over Gracie's hip. Immediately the dog's partial tail thumped on the floor.

"At least you're with me," she murmured. "Although I don't think the guy we were supposed to meet will appreciate that we didn't show up."

Not that she'd told anybody about him. She was hoping for some sort of compromise as to Gracie's future. Gracie was family. Gracie had been her special pet. Rebecca was a little worried what Delta would think, once he heard how this special dog had gone missing earlier, with no sign of her since.

After being kidnapped, Rebecca found Gracie at her side. That had filled Rebecca with joy, but the knowledge that both of them were captive now was difficult and made no sense.

She had no idea why she was here and had yet to see anyone.

She noted the closet and the window in this room, but the window had plywood over it. Not that it needed it because it didn't appear to be broken, not from what she could discern. Surely if the window had been broken or was missing, she would feel the breeze, hear more birdsong, feel the weather seeping inside. Just enough cracks were around the edges of the board that she could see it was daylight outside.

Why she'd been kidnapped, she didn't know, but would really like to. She didn't know what day it was or where she was. And she certainly had no idea why Gracie was here, but it seemed they'd both been taken by the same people.

However, Rebecca was absolutely overjoyed to have Gracie with her. The dog had arrived at her worksite for medical treatment but had been such a good source of comfort for the other animals that Rebecca had shifted Gracie's role to being a comfort animal herself. Also, Gracie's missing leg seemed to have given the other animals a sense of acceptance that they were in the same boat. In a weird way it gave them all the chance to recover a little bit easier.

Animals were much like people. They could accept and understand others like them, but it was harder if they were very different. As long as the animals coming out of surgery or being treated for various infections had recovered from the effects of the anesthesia, the other animals would generally accept them.

But often you had to watch out for the reaction of animals when one animal came in that was of a different species or that smelled different. Animals could attack if something was deemed strange or abnormal. But, in Gracie's case, she didn't have any temperament aberration and accepted everybody, making her the perfect animal to help other dogs going through similar experiences to what Gracie had already been through.

Maybe it was the fact that she had been through her own experiences that made her so good at what she did.

One day Gracie went missing from work, yet nobody had any explanation for where she was. The doors to the building had been locked and supposedly were all night.

And yet, even though Gracie was an essential part of the

work they were doing here, not everybody agreed with keeping an extra animal for the sake of the others. For some people, it was all about budget. Somehow the cost of keeping one extra animal was too much for them to justify. For Rebecca, it was all about the animals, which just made her even more unpopular in some quarters.

When she'd woken up on the mat with Gracie's nose nudging her gently, Rebecca had spent a good twenty minutes hugging the dog, trying to control her emotions, as she tried to ascertain what had happened. She'd been home, having dinner last night. At least she thought it was last night.

The last memory she had was picking up dinner and getting into her place. But now, as she thought about it and her empty stomach, she realized that chances were, she didn't have a chance to eat. As she tried to focus and to remember, she had some dim memory of walking out to her car and returning to work ... or maybe not. It was all very hazy. She checked for her purse, which held her wallet and her company card. It wasn't with her. Another hazy memory surfaced of probably somebody else using her card. Rebecca had watched from a vehicle, and she wondered if they just wanted her card—in which case whoever did this wasn't likely to be part of the company. But that made no sense either. Why Gracie? Anybody who knew anything about Gracie knew she was part of the company.

Then Rebecca had to wonder if something else was involved, maybe someone with even more ulterior motives. Rebecca had gone to her boss a few weeks ago, sharing suspicions about something going on at the company that made her worry, only to be told it was garbage and that such a thing couldn't happen here.

Now as she lay back on the cheap mat, she wondered if this could be a result of that earlier accusation raised by Rebecca. She didn't know who was involved in her earlier suspicions or her current kidnapping, but she believed something very suspicious was going on about the surgeries at the animal center. She groaned as she rubbed her eyes. "You should have just kept your mouth shut. That's what you should have done," she whispered to herself.

But it wasn't in her to do that. Not if they were hurting animals. Yet she didn't have any proof. All she had was suspicion. She didn't have access to the surgical areas. It wasn't her field. But, as far as Gracie went, this animal was all heart, and Rebecca would do anything to give Gracie a better life, which is what Rebecca thought she was doing when she had talked to the company about keeping Gracie— especially considering people were unhappy that Gracie was even still with them and all that fuss about the budget.

As Rebecca checked over the dog, she realized Gracie was walking with a different prosthetic. Rebecca frowned at that. It wasn't one of their prosthetics. And Rebecca would know, as that was her field. The light wasn't bright enough for her to establish exactly what the difference was though.

When the door opened suddenly, she jolted and looked up to find a stranger staring at her.

"Good, you're awake," he stated in a hard tone. "Now maybe somebody can make some damn decisions."

She didn't know what to say to that but asked, "Could I have some water, please?"

He stopped for a moment and then nodded. "That's a reasonable enough request, so yes. ... I can see you're not terribly enthralled with your current situation, but you might get out of this, if we can figure out what to do with you."

"I don't know who you are or what you even want with me," she replied, her tone raising in pitch.

He just glared at her.

She had tried to modulate her tone, but it was hard when she was staring at a man who had likely kidnapped her from her own home. "What do you want with me?" she asked, keeping her tone as low and as calm as she could.

"As long as you're polite and you keep that squeal down, we can talk. The minute you get out of control, I'm out of here."

She swallowed, but her throat was very dry.

"I'll get you the water." And, with that, he walked out.

She stared at the door, wondering what her chances were of escaping, of the door being unlocked. She hadn't heard it *click*, but that didn't mean her captor wasn't there, waiting on the other side of the door for her to try something. And, if that were the case, it wouldn't go well if she did try to escape. After all, Rebecca would have Gracie with her.

Her captor returned a few minutes later and nodded happily, when he saw her still on the mattress. "That's good. You're a fast learner."

She didn't say anything. There was plenty she wanted to say, but she didn't think he would like any of it. He walked over and tossed a bottle of water on the mattress beside her. She immediately opened it and drank, finding it hard to swallow at first. She knew certain drugs could leave that parched feeling and would also explain the headache and wooziness in her stomach.

"How's your stomach?" he asked, even as she thought about it.

She shrugged. "Upset. Nauseated."

"Well, don't bother throwing up. I ain't cleaning up that

shit. You puke, and you'll be lying in it."

She winced at that. "It's the side effect of the drugs."

"I know. I've seen it before, but it still doesn't matter. I ain't cleaning it up." And, with that, he turned and walked back out again.

She shared her water with Gracie, knowing that they both had to ration it and that they couldn't guzzle too much water without vomiting also. She collapsed back down onto the mattress, her hand still on Gracie. Hearing her whimper, Rebecca rolled over ever-so-slightly and hugged her. Gracie inched closer, her front paws coming down on Rebecca's belly, and Gracie tucked up close.

"I'm so sorry, sweetheart. I don't even know what this is about, and neither do you, of course, but somehow we got crosswise with somebody."

Rebecca closed her eyes and rested. Maybe it was the drugs, but it seemed she'd drifted off a little bit, before suddenly waking up again. She sat up, looking around her room, noting nothing had changed, then threw herself back down on the mattress. Gracie was still here, stretched out beside her. Rebecca pondered that.

When the door opened again, she looked over at her captor and asked, "When does Gracie get to go to the bathroom? Or me for that matter? We both need it."

The man glared at her, then looked down at the dog and nodded. "She does, considering she's been in here with you all night." He tossed her a leash. "Put it on her."

She quickly buckled Gracie up and slowly made herself vertical. He glared at her. "I didn't say you could go."

"It would be easier if I just walked her outside," she suggested in a low tone. "Fresh air is always better for prisoners too."

He laughed at that. "I'm not a fool, and I don't want you taking off on me."

"I can barely walk," she pointed out, as she took a few unsteady steps. "So, I certainly won't sprint off anywhere."

He considered that for a moment and nodded. "Good point. At least it would be one trip and not two. Bring the damn dog."

His attitude toward the dog worried Rebecca. Was Gracie in danger here too? Rebecca knew she should be focused on herself, but Gracie had become a very large part of her family. Hence the reason she had contacted her boss, asking if it was possible to keep the dog.

The fact that her captor was looking after them both but hadn't even taken Gracie out for a morning pee was troubling. He led her down a stairway and out to a very small fenced-in garden, but still, it was fresh air, and she was grateful. Gracie walked to the first bush and emptied her bladder. It was such a long pee that even the man was surprised.

"She really did have to go to, didn't she?"

Rebecca looked over at him and nodded. "First thing in the morning for sure," she shared. "And we don't want any messes, so the easiest thing is to just keep taking the dog outside, so she has a chance to do her business."

He shrugged. "I've never had any pets, so I wouldn't know."

She felt sorry for him because being raised without pets often left children with a limited amount of love and caring. Having pets really showed people that it was not just about them but about others, and learning to look after somebody that gave so much love in return was very healthy. Having a pet was good for children and adults alike. Seniors blossomed when they had a chance to have a pet, as did children.

He watched as she walked the dog around a little bit more. "What are you doing?" he asked suspiciously.

She turned to him and replied, "Seeing if she needs to go to the bathroom."

"She just did," he pointed out.

She nodded. "Yes, but she might have to poop." His lips curled into a grimace, and she shrugged. "It's normal. Every morning most of us get up and empty both our bladder and our bowels, plus other times during the day so we have no pressure building up there, and she needs to do the same."

And, sure enough, as if realizing she might not get another chance, Gracie found a spot in the far corner, which was still only about ten feet away, and proceeded to do her business. Rebecca asked the man, "Do you have any poop bags?" He just stared at her. "So, I can clean it up."

He shook his head. "I don't have anything like that."

"I don't know if anybody has given you supplies or if you're going out, but it would make it easier to keep the space clean if we had poop bags for her."

No further answer came, and he just motioned at her to hurry up.

All too quickly she and Gracie were ushered back to the same bedroom.

Just before he went to close the door, Rebecca called out, "Is there any chance of food for me and Gracie?"

He just snorted and closed the door in her face.

She wasn't sure if that was a *Hell no* or a *Maybe later* or a *Somebody else's problem* type of response. Still feeling the drugs coursing through her, Rebecca sank back down onto the mattress with Gracie. Rebecca wondered what drugs she'd been given. Drugs that they used for the animals or something else?

She was still fully dressed, which she had to admit was a mild relief. Still, the fact that Gracie was here, after she'd been missing, really bothered her.

"What did they do to you, girl? And why did they want you?" She reached out and gently stroked the lovely Malinois's ears.

Gracie had been through hell and high water—her training, several tours of service, getting blown up overseas, multiple surgeries and recoveries, and still a never-ending cycle of further problems. Problems Rebecca had hoped could be minimized, if not alleviated altogether, by Gracie being at the center with Rebecca.

Gracie was a retired War Dog. She'd served her country and deserved the same kind of pension benefits that people got, at least in Rebecca's opinion. She knew most people would laugh her out of the room if they understood what she was saying. But still, she just didn't understand why they had to treat animals so badly, when the animal had done nothing but do what was asked of them.

Gracie had been doing so well that the other animals had been excelling too, due to Gracie's presence after each surgery. So, what the hell was going on, both at the facility and now here, with the kidnapping of both Rebecca and Gracie? Why did anybody care about Gracie now, and why in this way? The day droned on and still no response, no answer from anybody. Finally Rebecca fell back asleep, and, when she woke up to an odd sound, she heard the door closing. She called out, "Wait."

But the door slammed with a bit more force than necessary, and then she realized that Gracie had gotten up and was eating. Somebody, while she had been asleep, had delivered food. This made her wonder if she was on a camera and if somebody had known she was asleep and had used that opportunity to feed the dog without having to interact with Rebecca. Or was it just luck on their part?

Stifling a sigh, she got up, realizing something had changed. Frowning, she looked around and noted that she was in a completely different room. That bothered her more than anything. What the hell was going on? She stiffened, checking out a few of the areas, then realized this room had a bathroom.

With a smile, she made her way there. Again afraid she might be on camera, she checked out her surroundings. Determining that, as far as she could tell, it was free of videos or peepholes, she quickly used the facilities, realizing what a gift it was to have a bathroom attached to her allocated room. With that, she washed her hands and face, then checked out her appearance in the mirror, checking that nothing really looked any different. That was a good thing.

She followed her nose and headed over to a tray. Pleasantly surprised, she found a bowl of rice and a vegetable mixture off to the side, plus a bottle of milk and a cinnamon bun. She frowned at it, confused, thinking it was hardly prisoner food, but then who was she to argue? She quickly picked up the tray and settled herself against the wall.

Gracie seemed to have no problem with her dog food, and, when she was done, as there was no water, the War Dog headed to the toilet and had several drinks, then came and collapsed on the blanket beside Rebecca. The only thing that concerned her now was whether the food was drugged or not. She sniffed it tentatively, but it smelled fine.

Honestly there was no reason to suspect that they would keep her drugged, unless she was in a residential area, where her screams could be heard outside, if anybody lived close enough. However, if they thought she was trying to be difficult, she knew that the unpleasant encounter this morning with her captor would get a whole lot worse.

She had barely finished her tray when the door opened again, and this time she stared in shock, as she recognized the young man before her.

CHAPTER 2

REBECCA CRIED OUT as Benjamin was pushed farther into the room, and the door slammed behind him.

He walked over to crouch in front of her. "Hey." He tentatively held up a hand. "Before you ask, I'm a prisoner too."

She blinked and shook her head. "What?" She racked her memory to recall what had happened with Benjamin at work lately. He'd been gone from the company maybe one week ago, but the details were hazy. She had heard how he'd walked out in a huff and right afterward had been terminated for being a no-show. She sagged back against the wall. "You too?" she asked faintly.

He nodded.

"Why?" she whispered, staring at him and searching his face for any sign of what had happened.

He shrugged. "They haven't exactly told me," he muttered. "If I had answers, I would give them to you. I've been sent in here to tell you to cooperate, and, if you do, they'll treat you fine. If you don't, they won't."

She swallowed, as she stared at him. For a young man, he was amazingly calm in this situation. She found no sign of any injury on him, no evidence that he had been abused or starved in any way. "Based on how you look, I assume you've cooperated," she replied.

He nodded. "Yes, I have."

Just enough bitterness filled his tone to make her believe him. "Do you have any idea how long you have been here?"

"Four days. And, yeah, I keep looking for a way out." He again raised a hand. "But, no, I haven't found one."

She groaned. "Who are these people? What do they want? I don't understand."

"No, I don't either. I just know it has to do with work."

She slid him a sideways glance. "You left really quickly."

He nodded. "I got into an argument with Don, and then his boss got into it. I didn't like what he had to say, so I walked," Benjamin admitted. "It wasn't the best of circumstances, but I thought it was better to leave than to compromise who I am and what I believe in. So, there you go."

"What happened after that?"

"I moped at home for a day as two. The next thing I knew, I woke up here. I went to sleep in my bed and woke up here, as a prisoner."

"Have you seen anybody?"

"Just the guard. He likes to act as if he's the boss, but I don't think he is."

"But he brought you in here and let you walk in on your own?" she asked, trying to keep her suspicion at bay.

He nodded. "Yes, but he has a gun. And, even if I were to come in here under duress, what good would it do us?" he asked, with a shrug of his shoulders. "I want to get out of here just as much as you do, so the best way for us to do that is to cooperate."

"And yet cooperate how? You've been here for four days. Have you seen anybody else or have they talked to you about why you're here? What do they want from us? If they're hoping for ransom, I sure don't have any money or, for that matter, know anybody who would pay to get me back."

He shook his head. "No, it's not ransom." He hesitated and then shared, "Honestly, I'm afraid it has something to do with the company."

Her heart sank, as she stared at him. "I wondered the same thing," she muttered.

"Did you …" He hesitated. "Did you ever see anything that made you suspicious of the company?"

She grimaced. "Not so much anything that I saw, just something I was questioning."

"Yeah? I think *questioning* is the reason we're being held."

"And yet that makes no sense."

He looked at her with raised eyebrows, and his lips twitched. "Remember the talk about a big buyout?"

"Oh," she muttered and then frowned. "Do you think this is to keep us quiet until the sale is done?"

"I have no idea," he admitted, "but, if that's the case, what's to stop us from saying something afterward? And why would they keep us alive at all, if they would be worried about that?"

She stared off in the distance. "Kidnapping and murder are two very different things," she murmured. "Maybe they're just hoping we'll stay quiet afterward? I don't know." No way she was sure of that. Now this worry nagged at her.

"You're right," Benjamin agreed. "No need to keep us alive now if they think we could harm them later. But killing us?" He shook his head. "I'm not sure of that either."

When the door opened suddenly beside him, she watched a grimace cross his face, that sense of dread, and she realized that he really was telling the truth about being a captive here. He slowly straightened and repeated to her, "As I shared, cooperate and you'll be fine." Without another word, he walked toward the guard and stepped out of the room.

After a pointed look in her direction, still not saying anything, the guard closed the door on her. Just like that, he too was gone.

Rebecca sank back in a stupor, trying to sort this out. If this had something to do with the buyout, it would mean that the kidnappers didn't want either of them making any waves, meaning the waves would be big enough to stop the sale. She frowned. What could she possibly know to stop a commercial sale from happening?

The company was huge. Rebecca could imagine what it was worth. Taking a moment, she tried to calculate what was going on at the place and thought that, with the research they were doing and maybe some of the patents they had recently developed on their inventions, the company could be worth hundreds of millions. As she thought about that, she realized how much jeopardy she and Benjamin might be in, if they were deemed to have blown that buyout.

She groaned, then sat back and muttered, "They could have just asked."

Then she heard a man in the shadows laugh and say, "As if that would have worked."

Her captor had this room bugged.

DELTA GRABBED A room at the one and only motel in town, which did happen to be near Rebecca's home. He would rather have stayed in her place, just to get an idea and a feel of what the neighborhood was like. It looked safe, but that didn't mean it was safe. So he left his motel room and drove back there. As he walked around her neighborhood that evening, a man came out, eyed him suspiciously, and asked him what he was doing here.

Delta smiled and replied, "Thank you for keeping a watch on the neighborhood. I'm here because Rebecca's gone missing." Then he pointed out her unit. "She went missing last night, and nobody's seen her at all. Have you?"

The man frowned and repeated, "Rebecca's missing?"

Delta nodded. "I was supposed to meet her earlier today, but she was a no-show at work, and, since then, the deputies have come to believe she's been kidnapped."

The other man's face paled, as he turned toward his own place. "Good God, what the hell is this neighborhood coming to?"

"That's one of the reasons I'm here now, to see what the neighborhood is like. Is it quiet? Does she have many visitors? Are there any disturbances? Do you have drug problems or that sort of thing around here?" Delta shrugged. "You know what I mean."

"Yeah, but nothing like that," the older man stated, raising a hand. "It's mostly families, with young kids. Down the road, we've got a preschool and an elementary school. Rebecca is one of the few in this area without children. She was always really friendly and nice when I was around her. I've never had any problems here, with her or not, and there was certainly no need for the sheriff to be called to her place, as she was never any upset at all."

"Boyfriends?"

The older man stared at him and slowly shook his head. "No, not that I ever saw. She kept to herself. She's the kind who delivers cookies with little pumpkins on them to the schools at Halloween and then later drops off Christmas cookies in the shape of reindeer," he shared, his tone dropping in pain. "My God. Why would anybody kidnap her?" Then his gaze narrowed. "Unless it's connected to that damn company."

Delta raised one eyebrow. "Has she complained about her job before?"

"No, she never complains about anything. She's seriously sunshine and roses," he murmured. "It just makes it all the more horrible that somebody would treat her like that. But I know that she was looking a little more troubled recently. I did ask her about it, but she just smiled and said it was a work thing. I know she was trying to get one of the dogs from the office to stay with her. She'd fallen in love with her. Some dog named …"

"Gracie?"

"Yeah. I don't think I ever saw it, but Rebecca told me that Gracie was an injured War Dog. Then she mentioned something odd. Something about it being *unnecessarily injured*."

Delta stared at him and asked, "She didn't explain that?"

"No, I just figured it had to do with the fact that the dog had served time in the war and had done multiple tours and …" He shrugged. "Rebecca didn't really talk about her job much at all. We got the impression that she was there because she loved it, but maybe she loved it less as time went on."

"Some jobs are like that," Delta noted, turning to look around. "So, you haven't seen anybody lurking around the place? You didn't happen to see anybody carry her out of her townhome?"

The neighbor shook his head. "Good God, no," he said in a nervous fit. "She told me that her security lights had been smashed a couple nights ago. I offered to help her fix them this weekend." He stared at Delta, frozen for a moment. "Do you think that was done by whoever kidnapped her?"

"Seems to be pretty convenient timing, doesn't it?" Delta murmured. "Her vehicle's still out back."

"Yes, it's always there when she's not at work. Her place has more trees than mine," he added, "so, if somebody did carry her out, I wouldn't necessarily have seen it."

"Do you have security cameras?"

"Oh, yes, I sure do," he replied, then shook his head. "Why didn't I think of that? Still not sure you'll see much, but come on in. My wife has the kids at the playground anyway," he added, as he ushered Delta inside. "I wouldn't want her or them to hear about this."

"Maybe not, but still we don't know if this was some random attack either, so you do need to warn her," Delta reminded him.

"I will," he stated, "but I would rather do it when the kids are in bed."

The other man walked into a small room obviously set up as an office. "I work from home," he explained, motioning around the room. "I have ever since that virus ripped through the world. I lost both my parents to that damn thing. ... Something like that really reminds you what's important. So, I made the decision to stay at home and to be here for my kids, while I work. I have breakfast and lunch with them and coffee breaks." He smiled. "The kids love it too. Soon enough they'll be in school, and I'll lose that connection with them."

Because that was all too possible, Delta didn't say anything. He didn't have any children. In fact, no one in his family had any children, but there was always hope that one day such a thing would happen. His parents were hoping, but, then again, they were aging and not in the best of health. For them to enjoy grandkids, this event would need to be sooner rather than later.

"I am Mike, by the way." He went to play the footage on his laptop.

"And I'm Delta." He closed in, as Mike played the recording. "Stop."

Mike hit the Stop button and rewound it a few seconds. They both leaned closer. "You're right," Mike whispered in amazement. "You can hardly see him for the trees, but a man is on the other side."

"As long as we can be sure it's not her," Delta replied, leaning forward and studying it with a critical eye.

"No, that tree is pretty damn tall," Mike stated animatedly. "She wouldn't stand over it like that."

Delta nodded and added, "Look at the way his arms are, the way his neck is straining forward. He's carrying a weight he's not used to."

"That could be her," Mike said in a worried tone. "She's not very heavy. What is she? Maybe five two and 110 pounds soaking wet, but, when it's a dead weight, it's an unwieldy load."

"That it is," Delta murmured quietly, as he studied the screen. "Do we have any other cameras around this neighborhood? Do you know if anyone around here has cameras facing Rebecca's unit from the back?"

Mike thought about it and nodded. "The guy on the next street over might have one on his back side. He had a couple bikes stolen a few years ago, and he beefed up his system then."

"Are you up for coming with me? We can check with him."

"Absolutely," Mike declared, as he hopped up. He pulled out his phone and added, "Let me give Joe a call. That'll make it easier."

As they walked toward the neighbor named Joe, Delta listened in on the conversation, while Mike gave Joe a rundown of what was going on. Joe's excited words jumped through the phone at them.

"Come on over then. We'll check the cameras here. I'll meet you inside." Then he ended the call.

At that, Mike smiled at Delta and shared, "Joe's nothing if not excitable."

"Oh, excitable works, as long as it's on our side."

"No, I hear you. At least this guy's got something that might help. Doesn't mean we'll get lucky though." Mike grimaced.

"Anything is a help," Delta noted. "If we can confirm that she was taken from here, we don't have to wonder where else she might have been kidnapped from."

"Right. I hadn't thought of that," Mike muttered, "and that's important to know, isn't it?"

"It absolutely is. Were they casing the house? How did they know she was even at home? Did they follow her home from work? Did they know which car was hers? We need to figure out the answers to those questions. To figure out what the kidnapper wants, we have to know who the kidnapper is, then try to figure out why he would be interested in her."

Mike shot him a sideways glance. "Well, there could be many reasons. She's petite, brilliant, kind, and quite beautiful." Then he stopped and shook his head. "No, *beautiful* isn't the word, but she's really pretty cute. That sweet grin, curls. Just a real sweetheart, you know? My kids absolutely adore her. She always finds a way to make them feel special."

At Joe's house, Mike just walked right in and called out, "Hello?"

"I'm upstairs," Joe replied, his voice a bit muffled. "Come see this."

They raced up the stairs to see Joe sitting at his security system, much more advanced and elaborate than what Mike had. Delta was delighted to see that.

He pulled up behind the man sitting at the computer array, gave him a smile, and said, "I'm Delta."

"Got it." Joe eyed him and grinned. "Like one of those Alpha, Beta, Delta kind of Romeo titles?"

"Used to be," Delta admitted. "At one time but not for quite a while."

"Ah," Joe replied, with a nod. "That's what happens in life."

"It is." As Delta went to sit down, there was a *pop*, and he swore. Both men look at him. He shrugged and admitted, "I have a prosthetic. The ankle joint keeps going in and out on me." He pulled a little screwdriver from his pocket and bent down to adjust it. Both men were fascinated. As Delta straightened, he grinned. "You get good at doing things like this on the fly."

"Man, the stories you could tell," Joe replied enviously.

"Yep, I sure could," Delta agreed, "but not a one of them is nice."

At that, Joe winced. "Good point."

Delta turned to the camera. "Look at this vehicle. Does anybody know whose it is?" he asked, as he stared at the small Toyota pickup.

"No, I've never seen it before," Mike said. "You, Joe?"

"No, I haven't seen this one at all," Joe muttered, then sighed. "If I had checked my damn camera, we would have known earlier maybe, but honestly, I hadn't gotten to it today. I upgraded a while back and have been trying to review it daily, looking for trouble, but I've gotten kind of lax. You just get into that mode where *Okay, nothing's happened for a while, so it's all good.* And then *zap,* that's when they come and get you."

"What was it you had stolen?" Delta asked, as he studied the camera. Hearing Mike's reply, Delta tapped the screen. "Look. He's coming out of the house now."

And, sure enough, not only was he coming out but he was carrying something that looked like a bundled-up sleeping bag.

"Well, hell."

The three men pulled back and stared at it. "Do you really think Rebecca is in there?" Mike asked.

"I sure do," Delta stated grimly, as he stared at it. "Can we get a close-up on the guy's face at all?"

Joe fiddled with the controls. "He's not looking our way," he noted. "I don't have a really high-end camera," he muttered. "And right now I'm really regretting that I didn't put up the money for a bigger system."

"Well, you at least have something," Mike said. "All I've got is trees."

Joe looked over at him. "Right, you got that big tree bank in front of you, don't you? You couldn't see this from there." He turned back to his screen. "I'm trying to get a picture of that plate, but he's just not at the right angle."

"Maybe when he pulls away," Delta suggested, watching

the kidnapper as he dropped his load in the bed of the truck. The poor woman must have landed with a hard *thump*, as the whole vehicle just shook.

"Jeez," Joe noted beside him. "That wasn't very gentle."

"No, and I don't get the feeling that he cares much about his victim," Delta replied, "and that's a concern too."

"Yeah, you're not kidding," Mike agreed. "That would mean he didn't care whether she lived or died."

"But, if that were the case, why go to all the trouble to get her out of there?" Delta asked.

Joe nodded. "Right, it would have been far easier to just pop her in there and be done with it, than to try and get her out. She's not a big woman, but she is still a full-grown person and one hell of a risk to pack out like that," he explained, turning to look at both men.

"I'll need a copy of this video for the sheriff. Can you do that for me?" Delta asked Joe.

"Sure can," Joe replied, perking up at the idea of doing something along this line.

"It would be better if you can send a copy to your email, then forward it to me." Delta handed his card with this email address to Joe.

"That's a good idea," Joe said.

"I was with Deputy Halvorson earlier at her place. He's gone to look at the video cameras from the company's parking lot."

"Oh, that's a good idea, checking to see whether she had any issues in the parking lot or even inside at work even …"

"I also want to know who clocked in later with her key card," Delta muttered, as he straightened up. Both men turned to look at him with rapt attention, and he realized he probably shouldn't have mentioned that out loud. He just smiled at them. "You guys have been a huge help. Thank you."

Both men nodded. "Wish we could do more," Mike replied regretfully. "She's good people."

"She is, indeed," Delta confirmed. "I was coming here to see her about one of the dogs she's been working with."

"Ha." Joe added, "The only dog she ever talks about is Gracie."

"That's the one that I came to see," Delta confirmed.

"Well, if you were to take that dog away from her, I know she would be devastated."

Delta looked at the two men, and they both nodded.

"She loves that dog," Joe shared. "She was even petitioning the company to keep her."

"Well, I'm certainly not trying to take the dog away from Rebecca," Delta stated. "As long as Gracie is in good hands, I'm happy to leave her where she is. But we need to find Gracie first."

"What does that mean?" Mike asked, frowning at Delta. "What are you here for?"

He quickly explained about Gracie and how she had been kidnapped or disappeared from the facility and how Rebecca had contacted him and the war department. He told the guys how he was here to see if he could find the missing War Dog.

"You're here because of the dog?" Joe asked.

"I am, and now Rebecca," Delta shared, "but I guess, for you guys, that doesn't make any sense, does it?"

"Doesn't matter whether it does or not," Joe stated amicably. "We can appreciate an animal lover, particularly when we know how much Rebecca loved that dog."

"She didn't say anything to me about the dog being

missing, but she did look really sad," Mike noted thoughtfully.

"You shared earlier that she looked a little bit more ..." Delta hesitated. "Something about being more upset, more unnerved, something of that nature."

"Yeah."

Joe looked over at Mike and added, "I haven't seen her in a few weeks, so I can't really comment on that, but I do know she loved that dog. Every now and then she would mention how she was trying to get approval to keep her. But Gracie was like a company dog or something. Of course they had millions of dogs going through that place, so I can't imagine why they would allow Rebecca to keep one versus any other, but she told me that this one was special."

Delta smiled and nodded. Anybody who wasn't a dog lover wouldn't understand how different their personalities were and how one could be special to somebody versus another one. However, if you were an animal lover, you got it right off the bat.

Mike immediately shared, "She would have done anything for that dog, but I can't see that it has anything to do with this," He motioned at the video in front of them.

"No, I hear what you're saying there," Delta agreed, "but you do recognize that both Rebecca and the dog came from the company, so that can't be a coincidence. I have to follow up regardless."

"Are you skilled enough to do that follow-up?" Mike asked. "I'm not trying to insult you, man, but you've got a bum leg."

"Yep, and I got that bum leg doing what I do best."

CHAPTER 3

REBECCA GENTLY SCRATCHED Gracie once again. Rebecca couldn't imagine being held like this without having her constant companion and best friend with her. However, her captor also wouldn't hesitate to hurt Gracie if deemed necessary to make Rebecca cooperate, and she was such a marshmallow for pets that she absolutely would comply.

She understood that was a weakness as far as most of the world was concerned, but she was an animal lover through and through, and that just meant she could never do anything to hurt Gracie. The reality that other people could just blew her away. Where was the humanity? How could people even do something like that when Gracie was such a sweet girl?

But sitting here whining about it wouldn't change her circumstances, and, boy, did Rebecca need something to change. She was coming to in the darkness of her first night of captivity, awake this time, and she wasn't looking forward to it. When she heard a door bang, she stiffened. Immediately Gracie's head popped up, and she growled.

"It's okay, sweetheart," Rebecca murmured. "We can't have you attacking them, as much as I'd might like you to. We need a little more information first." She patted her. "No point in dealing with one guy only to go downstairs to find ten others with guns."

Then she considered Gracie in that light. She was military trained and had done a hell of a job on her missions, but she had also been badly injured, and that was an ongoing concern. Rebecca didn't want Gracie to do anything that would end up ruining her mobility.

She gave Gracie a reassuring hug and kiss. "We're okay. We're fine. Just stay put."

When her door banged open a few minutes later, she jolted and once again wondered how this guy could move so quietly that she didn't hear him approach before the door opened. A bag of fast food was dropped in front of her.

She smiled. "Thank you."

He just looked at her, shook his head, and turned to leave.

"Gracie needs more food too."

His footsteps stilled.

"And," she pushed home the advantage that he might be listening to her, "she needs to go out again."

She heard him mumbling, but it was true. A dog needed to go to the bathroom more than just once a day. She didn't think they could use puppy pads or anything like that for a full-grown dog, particularly not one Gracie's size.

But what did they expect? They had her locked up. It wasn't exactly something they could expect her to hold in all day long. Within a few minutes he was back with a bag of dog food.

He flung it off to the side and said, "You can dish it out as she needs it."

"That's a good idea," she replied warmly. "I'll make sure she doesn't starve."

He rolled his eyes at that, and she frowned, wondering

what end he could be anticipating for them if he was already so sour and cranky. Not knowing what else she could do, she added, "If you don't mind, she would probably be good to go out now before we sleep."

"Eat your dinner," he barked, as he shut the door.

Not sure how long he would give her, she quickly ate. It wasn't a whole lot of food, but it was enough to keep her alive, particularly when she didn't have any appetite to begin with. When he came back a few minutes later, Gracie had also finished eating.

He looked at them and nodded. "You can go out now." And, with that, he led her downstairs and out to the same back garden area.

She tried to glance around to see where she was, but it was too dark. Then it dawned on her. Of course it was dark. That's how he was arranging these outings and why he'd made them wait. On the other hand, it was kind of a *who cares* thing, since she couldn't escape with him around anyway. Yet he had no weapon, not as far as she could tell. Was she being foolish by *not* trying to escape? That was the one thing that worried her. Was she supposed to try? Is that what they wanted, so they could shoot her or something, or was it something completely different? She also didn't understand why they were holding Gracie.

She asked him quietly, "Have you ever spent time with K9 dogs like Gracie?"

"Don't like dogs."

She just nodded and didn't say anything. Of course he didn't like dogs. Liking a pet would be way-too-much niceness in his heart. Whatever. She wouldn't waste time considering his loss.

As she walked Gracie around, he turned and snapped at

her, "Come on. Hurry up."

"I can hurry up," she said, "but Gracie needs to find the right smell in order to release her bladder and bowels."

"Well, she needs to find that right smell sooner." He glared. "It's not as if I can stand out here the whole time."

She looked around at the small fenced-in corner and asked, "Does it matter if we're out here for a few minutes? It's not as if I could leave, and then you wouldn't have to wait on us."

He stared at her, glanced around, and shrugged. "If my boss found out, I would be in trouble."

"It's not as if I would tell him," she replied, with a note of humor, "and Gracie is in no position to tattle."

He studied her for a moment and then shrugged. "Doesn't matter if she could or not. They sure as hell won't listen to her or to you."

"So just leave us out here and go do your thing, and, when Gracie is done, I'll let you know." Then she added, "I don't have any way to contact you. So you can just come back and check on us, I guess?" she asked hesitantly.

He shook his head and shrugged. "Maybe," he muttered. "I do have other shit to do."

"I appreciate your looking after us," she said.

He rolled his eyes. "Being nice to your guard doesn't get you any brownie points."

She nodded, yet still smiled. "But it doesn't hurt to be human either."

"Your loss. Nobody'll be nice to you in this deal."

She winced and nodded. "You could be right, but I still can't change who I am."

He snorted at that. "Whatever." Then he went back inside, leaving her and Gracie outside.

Happily the two of them wandered in the fresh air amid the small space, loving the few moments of freedom while they had it. Who knew how long before he came back, yelling and looking for them again. After Gracie was done with her business, the two of them lay down and stretched out in the grass. Rebecca took several deep breaths, enjoying the fresh air before she lost her access to it. Then she heard someone and realized it was Benjamin again. She sat up and smiled at him. "How are you holding up?" she asked gently.

He crouched beside her and shrugged. "I'm doing fine." He looked around the fenced-in area. "It looks like you're doing okay too."

"I'm … holding up. It's all just very strange."

"Yeah, very strange." He nodded. "On the other hand, we're alive, and we're doing okay."

She smiled at his positive response. "I won't argue with that. It does feel a little on the strange side though."

"Oh? What does?" he asked.

"Just everything. There's no rhyme or reason to it."

"Oh, there'll be a rhyme or reason," he muttered. "We just don't know it yet. We aren't in on the secrets of it."

"Possibly," she agreed. "Still, it would be lovely if we had a way to communicate with each other and not just here. I presume you got dinner."

"I did," he replied, with a half laugh. "And you?"

"Yes," she murmured. "I did. Now we're just trying to enjoy some fresh air. Do they let you out here very often?"

"No, they really don't. In fact, this is the first time I've been out here," he shared, looking at her. "I figured it was because of you."

She shrugged. "Well, if it is, you're welcome." He laughed and nodded. Just then their captor returned. She looked over at him and asked, "Which one first?"

He glared at her. "Don't be so damned friendly."

She shrugged. "I can't stop you from doing whatever it is you're doing," she murmured. "So, no harm, no foul."

He pointed over at Benjamin. "Him first."

She nodded and waved goodbye to Benjamin and called out, "Have a good night."

"You too." He got up and walked amiably back toward the door. She wasn't sure if he was even checking out the surroundings, but she certainly was. Could the two of them overpower her captor? Supposedly he did have a handgun. She may not have seen it, but Benjamin had, so she had to consider that deterrent, but still, there were two of them. And honestly, she would cheerfully take a bullet, if it meant getting out of this place. However, she had to stay healthy enough to care for Gracie, even to carry her out of here if needed.

Surely, between the two of them, they could go over the fence. But, just like that, the opportunity was gone, and Benjamin was inside. Her captor returned a few minutes later—a very quick few minutes—so she wasn't sure where he had dropped off Benjamin.

Her captor motioned for her to get up.

She got up, walked over to him, and asked, "Bedtime?"

"Yeah," he muttered. "Bedtime." He led her up to her room and locked her in very quickly.

As she turned around to speak to him, the door slammed in her face, and she winced. "Okay, so I don't have any more questions," she muttered.

She gave Gracie a big hug and whispered, "We'll be fine, girl. We'll be just fine."

With a small *woof* Gracie snuggled against her, and the

two settled into an uneasy sleep.

SHOWERED, CHANGED, AND now crashed on the bed—his stump airing out, after being irritated from the joint all day—Delta stretched out with his laptop and quickly called Kat. He brought her and Badger up-to-date on the news, hearing a whistle at the oddness of the situation.

"Really? I wasn't expecting that," Kat noted.

"No, I wasn't either," Badger replied. "And yet it's an odd coincidence. You know how I feel about coincidences."

"Yeah, the same way we all feel about them," Delta said. "Anybody in espionage or investigative work knows that coincidences really aren't a thing."

Badger asked, "But the dog went missing? How long ago?"

"I need to check the file to confirm the date," Delta replied. "On top of that, now Rebecca's gone missing too. I spent some hours with Deputy Halvorson today, chasing down leads, then found a neighbor's security video which I have just sent you," he noted, as he hit the Send button. "It seems she had been picked up and carried outside in a sleeping bag, then tossed into the back of a Toyota. I'm wondering if you guys can get a close-up on the model of the Toyota, and preferably a license plate, so we could figure out who owns it and where it's gone from there. Do you have access to city cameras? I would really like to track down that vehicle ASAP."

"Hang on," Badger said. "I can do that. Just give me a few minutes to get it set up."

"The other thing," Delta added, his tone brisk, "any

chance these War Dogs are chipped?"

"Most of them are chipped," Badger shared, "but just for ID purposes, not location-wise."

"So, they don't have trackers on them?"

"No, but they're chipped, so, if they go to a vet or a shelter, they pop up," he explained. "That's how we find out about War Dogs that get moved or end up in different situations."

"Right. So, it's not something we can use to see where Gracie may have ended up."

"No, that's not how it works."

"Damn," he muttered, frowning, "So, I know it's an odd question, but, if Gracie has got some kind of chip, is there any way to reverse engineer something in that chip to maybe get some communication going with her?"

Badger was hesitant when he asked, "Communication? What do you mean by that?"

"Yes, what do you mean by that?" Kat asked curiously. "I really like the idea."

"Yeah, but I don't know that it's possible. It would depend on the software and the chip. It could possibly work if it was a tracker."

"But it's not a tracker," Badger stated. "It's more of a RFID chip... You get them from a vet. It's got where she's from, her number, the owner, that sort of thing."

"Right. But the war department and maybe this place where Rebecca works were doing very convoluted surgeries on these animals now, weren't they?"

"Yes," Kat agreed, "the military sure are." Then her voice rose with excitement. "And now that you mention it, they're also using a different kind of chip. They're testing out software that will allow them to check blood pressure, pulse rates, and things like that on the War Dogs while they sleep, so the military gets better health-related data into the computer database."

"Then the question is, does Gracie have any of that advanced software? Did she ever have surgery with this local company that we know of? Did they ever use her as a test subject for something like that?"

"I don't know," Kat admitted, "but that is one hell of a good point. I can't very well contact her employer and ask them, so we'll go around them. I'll get on that and research that company and see what we can come up with. We also have a few contacts of people who work in this particular high-tech field with specific applications for animals. We might tap that resource to see if they've got any kind of software that is more advanced."

"What I would really like to do, if we have compatible software in Gracie, is to *ping* a communication signal through that chip."

Kat started to laugh, softly at first and then louder. "Oh, I do like that. It's late, but these techies work all hours. So I'll see if I can get some answers tonight, and then I'll talk to you tomorrow."

Before Kat took off, Delta had a horrid thought. "*Uh-oh.*"

Both Kat and Badger simultaneously asked, "What is it?"

"I'm getting a scary thought, what with this massive technology-based company squatting in this tiny little backwoods town," Delta began.

"*Uh-oh,*" Badger echoed.

"Exactly," Delta agreed. "Is this company creating Frankenstein monsters out of these retired War Dogs in the lab or in the surgical suite? Or is it stealing intellectual property or patented ideas from its vendors or owners or just selling off these devices or what? This could be far-reaching too. So don't think Silicon Valley, but instead think China."

"Oh my God," Kat gasped. "Okay, I'll check out my American business contacts, along with some military ones I know too, while you guys do your worldwide secret agent stuff." And, with that, she was gone.

Badger and Delta shared ideas and suggestions, and each knew who would take responsibility for tackling these various items. It was all conjecture at this point, but it rang true in Delta's gut. Badger agreed. Then he went silent, staying on the line for a few more minutes, and Delta knew right away what to expect.

"How are you holding up?" Badger asked.

"Outside of the damn stump swelling up on me and the ankle joint in the prosthetic giving out at the most inopportune times," he muttered, glaring down at the leg in question, "I'm doing fine."

"That's because what you really want is your ankle back, and we can't give that to you, not 100 percent anyway," he shared, his tone matter of fact. "Now my wife is fixing your problem, so the next iteration should be better. Still, what you must learn to do is make peace with it. As soon as you do that, you will find out the kinks ease up."

"And how is that?" he asked curiously. "Is that what happened to you?"

"Yep, it sure is. We come into these situations with the same expectations that we put on our body, and these injured limbs can't always keep up. But the minute we ease up and relax, we can do a whole lot more because we're not putting the injury under constant pressure. Instead we allow the muscles and nerves to heal in a very different way."

"I like the sound of that, but I'm not convinced it's just more of that mumbo-jumbo bullshit."

Badger started to laugh. "As if I would do that."

"You absolutely would," Delta declared, "particularly if you thought it would get you what you want."

"That's everybody though, isn't it?" he murmured. "Everybody wants what they want, and they don't really care how they get it."

"That's how we end up with these problems," Delta said. "Just look at the politicians and the brass. That shit never ends."

"I think you're right," Badger noted, "but also we need people like you and me out there to keep things running smoothly."

"Do they ever run smoothly though?" Delta asked. "It seems to me that it's more of a false front than anything."

"Maybe, I'm not sure. … Anyway, you get some sleep, stay off that ankle, and we'll talk in the morning. I mean it, Delta. Your to-do list can wait until tomorrow. Spend some time healing first. Then you can get back to work at first light." And, with that, Badger hung up.

Delta sat here for a long moment, thinking about Rebecca, how he'd connected with her on the phone a few times, and also by text. He'd really been looking forward to seeing her and getting the chance to know her. He hoped to visit a little bit and to understand this woman who would take on a War Dog in rough shape, knowing there could be a lot of pain ahead. Yet, somehow she seemed to be totally okay with it.

You had to appreciate somebody with heart. Delta would do that, take on a War Dog like Gracie. He would do it instantly, if he had the chance. He wasn't used to seeing other people doing the same thing. His family, although he loved them dearly, weren't big on pets, and they weren't big on heart. They were pretty much just big on themselves. Only through Kat had Delta started to see another aspect because she came from her heart, and there was no way not to see that. It was just so obvious with her.

It had really helped Delta to see that so much more was out there. His family had been less than impressed with his disability, less than impressed with his prospects. To them it had been a failure to go into the military, only to come back wounded.

Not that they would ever say that. It was a silent judgment, something he recognized every time he was in their vicinity. Yet he didn't consider what he had gone through as a failure at all. It was simply part and parcel of the work he was doing to fight for freedom, to keep his family and untold others safe. Too bad his family didn't realize or even care, oblivious to what true service was all about.

Sadly it was the same for so many people in the world. They were completely unaware of what the military did for them, while they were happily sleeping in their own beds. Or for some, causing chaos in the world, while he and the others like him were out all over the globe, trying to keep the peace. Trying to keep others safe. Sometimes, despite their best efforts and intentions, the wrong people paid for all the wrong things, which is how Delta viewed his life right now. He'd paid the price. Not fair. And yet nobody cared.

He didn't consider himself *lost* as much as he was alone, and that was something he would have to work on, as soon as he got this damn ankle joint to work. And, with half a laugh, he rolled over, dropped the laptop down beside him, and went to sleep.

CHAPTER 4

REBECCA WOKE WITH a jolt, when Gracie jumped up, growling beside her. Rebecca sat up as the door burst open, and her captor stood there, glaring at her. She rubbed her eyes. "What's the matter?"

"I am finally getting rid of you." He sneered. "Get up. Let's go."

She rose, pointed to the bathroom, and said, "I need to go."

His glare deepened, but he nodded. "Make it quick, dammit. I've been waiting for the boss to come." He clapped his hands. "I don't want to be stuck here any longer than is necessary."

She winced at that and quickly raced to the bathroom. After she used the facilities, she washed her face. When he pounded on the door, she opened it. Drying her face, she explained, "I'm just trying to wake up."

"I don't give a shit," he snapped, as he glared at her. "Let's go." And, with that, he dragged her by the arm. Gracie growled, and he turned, pointing a gun at her.

Rebecca stepped between them. "It's fine, Gracie. It's okay."

"Jeez," he muttered, still waving the gun. "Stupid dogs. They should all just be put down."

"They serve a big purpose in our world." Now she glared

at him. "You don't need to threaten the innocent dog. If you're the one who kidnapped her, shame on you."

"Shame on me?" he repeated, staring at her. "Do you really think I give a shit what you think?" He motioned at her. "Go. Go, go, go."

As the gun slammed into her shoulder, forcing her to move faster, she jumped forward. As she got to the top of the stairs, she looked back at him. "Outside?"

"Downstairs," he muttered, glaring at her.

She nodded and moved downstairs, Gracie at her heels. When she got downstairs, she was shoved roughly in a different direction than she had gone before and walked into a small dining room to find two people sitting at a table. They looked at her as she came in. One man. One woman. Rebecca didn't recognize either one. She frowned, and they frowned right back at her. She groaned inside and tried to smile. "Hello," she said, trying to settle her nerves. "Maybe now I can understand why you had me kidnapped."

The man looked at her and shook his head. The woman gave a small smile. "According to Reggie here"—she pointed at Rebecca's captor—"you're being difficult."

She looked back at Reggie, who flushed. "He told me that I'm too nice," she muttered.

The unknown woman nodded. "And that he would consider to be *difficult*. He wouldn't know niceness if it reached up and bit him."

"Hey," Reggie growled. "Enough of that shit."

She laughed. "That's okay, Reggie. You're still very useful to us, so no worries there."

It was the *useful to us* that got Rebecca's back bristling. But oddly enough, it got Reggie's back bristling as well.

Rebecca noted the byplay in her head and asked, "What

can I do for you?"

"Now you see? That's the right attitude. We do like co-operation."

"Just get to it, will you?" her partner snapped.

The woman motioned at the dining room table. "Take a seat."

Rebecca sat down and kept Gracie close to her.

"So," the woman muttered, "we have a problem."

Rebecca waited to hear what that problem could be. She knew that her confusion would be clearly reflected on her face.

The other woman studied her and nodded. "You don't have a clue, do you?"

"No, I don't," Rebecca stated plainly. "I left work, and I went home, but that is where my memory ends. Next thing I knew, I was here and nothing beyond that."

"And yet you complained to somebody about the treatment of animals?"

She stared at her. "I suggested that the lab conditions could be improved," she replied cautiously. She had said a lot more than that, but Rebecca didn't know how much of her spewing this woman knew about.

"Right. So, a bleeding-heart animal lover," Reggie snapped, groaning.

Rebecca turned to Reggie and nodded. "Definitely an animal lover, yes. Who wants to see an animal abused?"

"Well, of course we won't abuse any animal," the boss lady declared, "but we also can't have any rumors going on."

Rebecca stared at her. "Has this got something to do with that buyout?"

"It's not a buyout. It's a sale," she stated, her tone hardening ever-so-slightly. "And we do want that sale to go through."

"Okay," Rebecca murmured. "That's your business, and you know it best. What does that have to do with me?"

The boss lady laughed. "You're not stupid, so please don't play it that way."

Frowning, Rebecca eyed the woman. "I don't know what you're talking about. I don't know anything about a buyout, sale, whatever, other than hearing the single word. I don't know anything about animal abuse at work. I was just commenting to my boss about how conditions could be improved to match the marketing of the company. If it ever got out among other animal lovers, there would be a lot of kickback over it."

That's where Reggie interrupted again. "Didn't I call it? Bleeding-heart animal lovers."

Rebecca kept her tone mild, as she tried to pick up her scattered thoughts. "All I'm saying is that treating the animals a little nicer would not affect the bottom line."

Reggie snorted, and so did the other man.

Rebecca shrugged. "And this is where you'll tell me that it absolutely *does* affect the bottom line. So why am I here? If you wanted to terminate me from my position, that is a minor issue compared to kidnapping."

"Yes," the woman agreed, "but so is terminating you and having you go off to the authorities over this."

"Good Lord," she muttered, sitting back. So Benjamin had been right in his assessment of what was going on. "So, you think that, if you fire me, I'll take off and report you to some sort of animal abuse organization?"

"Or worse," Reggie muttered. "Probably go right to the bloody social media BS."

She looked over at him and nodded. "That's not a bad

idea. Except that I wouldn't want any of the animals to get hurt in the process."

"*Right*," Reggie said. "I can personally guarantee that the bitch at your side will get the first bullet if you do anything."

She stiffened and glared at him.

The boss lady intervened. "Now stop, just stop." She motioned at both men to calm down. "We're not here to hurt anybody."

"You must be here for some reason," Rebecca stated, "because nothing I could say would cause your deal to go sour."

"You don't think so?" the boss lady asked. "Except for one thing …"

"What's that?" Rebecca frowned, still trying to get a handle on what all this was about.

"You have a very popular YouTube channel, do you not?"

Rebecca stared at her. "Not necessarily very popular, I'm afraid. I started it a while ago for animal lovers, and we talk about dog tips, traveling with your pets, finding pet-friendly hotels and B&Bs, and all kinds of pet-related things like that."

"Sure, but you're on all the social media sites, aren't you?"

Rebecca snorted and continued to frown at her. "Are you really thinking that I could cause a storm big enough to stop the sale of the company when I voice my opinions online?" she asked in astonishment.

The woman studied her and slowly nodded. "Absolutely you could, but you won't."

"No, of course I won't. I have never mentioned my employer online," Rebecca replied, astonished. "That's not who

I am."

"Well, it might not be who you are, but that doesn't mean it isn't who a lot of people are," she pointed out. "We couldn't take the chance."

"I see. So, when the sale does go through, then what?"

"Well, that is, of course, our challenge."

Rebecca nodded. "It sure is, but, by the same token, because I do have a social media presence," she shared, "obviously I haven't had a chance to post anything in the last few days," she pointed out, "and people will start to get worried very quickly."

"We can also understand that too," the boss lady replied cooly, with that same congenial smile that made Rebecca's skin crawl. "But the question is, how do we stop you in the future?"

"Once the deal has gone through," Rebecca replied, "what difference does it make? It's not as if your buyers will care. Anybody who is buying a company like this is looking to make a profit, and then wouldn't future marketing be their problem?"

"Yes. But that doesn't mean they will take it kindly that we were trying to silence you in the first place."

She winced at that usage of *silence*. "Well, you could try *not* to silence me," she muttered, then shook her head. "This is just too unbelievable. Whoever would have thought that my social media would have any part in this sale of yours? Plenty of influencers online have millions of followers. I'm not one of them. I just talk to people about dogs," she muttered.

"I know, and it is a curiosity for us too," the boss lady noted. "However, once that possibility came to our attention, it became something that we couldn't ignore."

In truth, Rebecca had quite a following on her videos for animals and pets. It was her pastime, a hobby. Sure, she thought that maybe one day it could be her full-time job, monetized enough to quit her day job, but now it was just for fun. That this woman was taking it this seriously was more than alarming. "Who knew, when I started it, that something like this would even be a consideration."

The boss lady nodded. "That's why you have to watch what you do in life," she declared. "Particularly with online shit like this that goes worldwide."

"People don't even know what company I work for," Rebecca repeated. "I deliberately don't bring it up, which you would know if you actually looked at my channel. It's all about keeping everybody safe when online, … not just me and the animals, but also the company."

The woman smiled knowingly at her. "You could have a completely crazed fan."

She stared at her in alarm. "Meaning?"

"Meaning, you could disappear, and it could be because of one of your crazy fans." She shrugged. "Nobody would be the wiser."

She swallowed. "Seriously? You think my hobby, my passion, is worthy of murder?"

"Well, no, not us, of course," she stated in that same odd tone. "That would be something we would never dirty our hands with. Still, I'm sure we could point some crazy fan out there in your direction."

Rebecca sat back, horrified, staring at the woman. She may not be a raging loon like the two bastards around her, but she was cunning as hell. "Wow," Rebecca muttered. "That's pretty cold."

"You know, it is pretty cold," her male associate confirmed, looking at the boss lady.

She smiled at him. "I knew you would like it."

He smiled. "I do kind of like it. It doesn't involve us, and it would be nice and clean." Then he frowned. "So, we just have to find a deranged fan."

"They're everywhere." The boss lady gave a wave of her hand. "You leave that to me."

"So this means that you'll let me go and then get some psycho to come murder me?" Rebecca asked, staring at these people in shock. "Murder by social media?"

"Sure, why not? What's that new phrase that's all the buzz these days? *Canceled*," she shared. "I think you're about to be canceled via social media."

DELTA WOKE TO his phone buzzing. Groaning, he reached over, his hand slamming into the phone as he hit Talk. "Hey."

Kat was on the other end. "You awake?"

"No, not really, but I'm up now. More like getting there."

"Get there faster," she ordered.

He snorted at that, sat up, and mumbled, "Yes, boss."

"Good," she stated sternly. "You've almost got that down pat. A little bit more effort and we won't have the sarcasm to go with it." At that, he burst out laughing. He heard the smile in her tone when she said, "There, ... that's better."

"What's better?" he asked, yawning.

"I contacted Stone," she shared.

"Stone?" he repeated.

There was a moment of silence on the other end. "Yeah, do you know him?"

"Are we talking Stone from Levi's team? Big badass Stone?"

She laughed. "Yeah. Big badass Stone, and, boy, would he absolutely love that choice of terminology," she confirmed, with a chuckle. "He's also a pretty big IT tech guy. More tech than IT though, for my specified purposes."

"How does one become more tech than IT?" Delta asked.

"Well, he's less about software, more about hardware. Put it that way. Anyway, I brought up the subject with him, and he knows somebody working at that company that Rebecca works for, and he called her for me on the sly. As it turns out, Rebecca left because of some stuff going on in the back that made her uneasy and wasn't something she felt was appropriate. Her coworker said that Rebecca wouldn't provide details, but she did say that the animals coming out of surgery were being tracked with new medical technology that they were testing for human use. And it was some sort of … monitoring, I guess. Recording their blood pressure, pulse rate, things like that. It was apparently tested on Gracie. She remembered Gracie and a couple other War Dogs had done well with the testing. Then she backtracked and wasn't sure if Gracie was one of those dogs, but she thought so. She vaguely remembered her."

"Interesting." Delta sat up on the edge of the bed, rubbing the sleep out of his eyes. Then he checked his phone and groaned. "You do know that it's only five-thirty in the morning."

"Yeah, and?" Kat asked cheerily. "You were up, weren't you?"

"No, but I am now."

"Good," she declared. "In that case you'll be ready to talk to Stone because he'll be calling you in about ten minutes." With that, she ended the call.

Delta stared down at the phone, shook his head, grabbed his crutches then headed to the bathroom, where he quickly brushed his teeth and followed through his morning ritual. He was mostly dressed by the time his phone rang. He smiled and answered, "Stone?"

"Yeah, who's this?" the man asked.

"Well, who do you think? You called me. Remember?"

"Yeah, I remember," he grumbled. "I once knew somebody named Delta, except it wasn't his real name."

"Actually it *is* my real name," he confirmed, "and, yeah, you guys always called me Delta anyway. What did you think? I made it up or something?"

Stone replied in horror, "It's really your name?"

"Yes, it's really my name," Delta repeated and burst out laughing. "How the hell are you, man?"

He heard the smile in Stone's reply when he said, "Marvelous. Better than you if you're stuck on one of Badger's missions."

"I don't know about *stuck*," Delta clarified, "but I got sent out looking for a missing War Dog and arrived to find that the woman I was meeting had been kidnapped. Not going to leave a damsel in distress."

Stone started to laugh. "Right," he agreed, still laughing. "That goes against the grain no matter who we are," he said cheerily. "So, what's this about tracking, or backtracking really, on some medical device?"

"Well, first off, so far, we can't confirm that this War Dog even has this updated chip, which is another problem. I think the woman has been kidnapped recently by the same people who took the War Dog Gracie earlier."

"Why the hell would you think that?" he asked. Delta quickly led him through the little bit he knew. "Well, it's an interesting theory," Stone noted, "but, if this woman is cute and tiny and an interesting conquest, then potentially anybody could have grabbed her."

"Yes, except that she was kidnapped from her town-house. And they also used her card and accessed her office after hours. It shows she was in and out in thirty minutes."

"Oh, now that's a different story. Somebody would have known where she worked, what department she worked in, what her card would have given her access to, and had some reason to take that kind of risk."

"Exactly," Delta agreed. "Hence my thinking that it's all related. Plus, just so you know, I have a wild theory that this might include theft of intellectual property that might come to light now that the facility is possibly about to be sold. Just rumors about the sale and this related supposition so far. Badger and I are still working that angle, while you and Kat try to get me backtracked into that device in Gracie's leg."

A few minutes later, after Stone typed furiously on his keyboard, he finally said, "Look. Leave it with me, and I'll see what I can find out about the type of software, what kind of messages and information it's receiving and transmitting. I'll get back to you."

Delta ended that call and quickly phoned the deputy, wincing at the early hour.

The deputy, realizing who it was, bypassed any usual greeting and said, "I got the home security video you sent, and we're analyzing it now. And, yes, we're running a search on the license plate. But, as you probably expect, it'll come back as stolen, in my opinion."

Delta didn't tell him that Badger and Kat were working on that as well. All Delta really cared about was getting any leads anybody could find from the video itself and the vehicle used to kidnap Rebecca. "What is there to analyze? Hopefully you don't dispute the fact that she was taken off her property, plain as day."

"I don't have an argument about anything," the deputy stated, his tone stoic, "but I'm not alone in this thinking within my department, and we need cooperation on both sides."

"All you have to do is look at the video and realize what happened to the poor woman. Unless of course there is some reason why somebody in your department wouldn't want a proper investigation."

"Whoa, whoa, whoa," Deputy Halvorson said, perking up. "Ease up there."

"Look. I found that video. You were supposed to be checking the video at the company offices, and, if you didn't find anything, that's another thing. Regardless, I did find something, and we need to follow it up."

"Remember who you're talking to," the deputy barked, his tone sharp.

"Yeah, but you better remember who you're talking to as well. I represent the war department's interests in a missing War Dog and its handler, who have both gone missing," Delta snapped back. "If you think I'll let this go because you guys are too slow at getting your asses in gear, you are sadly mistaken." And, with that, he hung up.

He wished he had some legal recourse to do something about it himself, but he didn't. At least he didn't think so. He quickly texted Kat, explaining what the problem was.

She called him back right away. "Right off hand, I don't know anybody in that area, but, if need be, we can certainly pull some strings to try and get you a little more leeway."

"You better do it now," he replied, "because this guy is … Well, let me put it this way. He was quite cooperative before, but I get the feeling that he got back to the office and found a whole different attitude waiting for him."

"And why do you think that would be?"

"Sheer economics, including paychecks and bribes would be my guess. I suspect that the company hires a lot of people locally, and everybody is probably connected to somebody who works there. Who knows? Potentially somebody who works high up in the company or something has connections with our local sheriff's office."

"Right," she muttered. "Nobody ever wants to rock the boat, particularly if there's no proof."

"Right. Except Rebecca has been kidnapped, and, whether it's related to the company or not, we do have a home security video showing someone carrying something out of her apartment."

"And yet anybody could say it may have just been garbage he was taking out to the landfill. Who knows?"

"Right. And, of course, that's what the deputy may well say, but we don't have time for that. She was picked up for a reason, and, whatever that reason was, her kidnappers won't keep her indefinitely."

"Unless of course that's exactly what this is about," Kat warned. "We've seen that happen with women time and time again."

"I don't think it's anything to do with human trafficking. Honest to God, I swear that Rebecca is with the missing War Dog."

After a moment of silence, Kat asked curiously, "I'm not even sure how to ask you this, but are you certain you just don't *want* them to be together?"

"I absolutely *do* want them to be together," he declared. "That would be wonderful comfort for her and likely for the dog too. Whether they're being mistreated, I have no way of knowing. But Rebecca's not at work, she's not at home, and her car hasn't been moved. I even checked her social media accounts, and there are no entries for the last two days, yet Rebecca is online every day. I did a quick manual check to get a feel for her activity level, and that's been her pattern for at least the past year. So anybody who's taken her has likely done so against her will, and, therefore, it's a big issue."

"I agree with you," Kat replied, "and I'm on it. Let me see if I have anybody around the area who could apply some pressure to the local sheriff's office and get us some cooperation or even some insider gossip." She ended the call.

Delta had to be satisfied with that. He got up, and, with his prosthetic adjusted and back on, he headed out to the closest restaurant to grab some coffee and breakfast. When he walked into the small café, several people looked around, half smiled, but most of them just ignored him. He was a stranger, after all. He was used to it, especially since he traveled a lot. He sat down at a table in the back, and the waitress came over with a coffeepot and the menu. He quickly scanned the menu and placed an order, while she still stood here, filling his cup.

She looked over at him, smiled, and asked, "Hungry, are we?"

He nodded. "You could say that."

While he was waiting for his breakfast, several other people turned to look at him, and he felt like it could be a growing movement, as if people were starting to understand who he was. Yet there was no reason for anybody to know him or his purpose here. At least not yet, even with a robust town grapevine. Delta wasn't here to bother anybody. He was here to help a woman and a dog, yet he was getting stonewalled at every turn. That was driving him nuts too.

When a man walked over and slid into the bench across the table from Delta, he just gave him a hard look and asked, "Can I help you?"

"We understand you're making trouble for the town."

"That's an interesting rumor," Delta noted. "I'm trying to find a woman who was kidnapped, and apparently nobody gives a crap."

The man's eyebrows shot up. "I'm sure she was just heading out to be with her friends."

"Without her vehicle, without letting anybody know?" Delta countered. "Not showing up for work or notifying them that she was taking time off?"

The other man frowned, as if not expecting to hear that.

Delta nodded. "So, whoever it is who's trying to cause trouble, maybe you should be looking at them. Maybe you should be wondering why they're stonewalling looking for a poor woman who was carried unconscious from her townhouse, which we have on video, including the vehicle that drove away with her," he shared, suddenly studying the guy more intensely. "By the way, what kind of vehicle do you drive?"

The man blustered and got defensive. "Hey, I just want to know—"

"Do you know anyone with a gray Toyota Tacoma with a bed big enough for him to dump an unconscious woman into the back?"

The other man paled slightly and sputtered, "Hey, hey, hey, I don't know anything about that."

"No, but you came over here to cause *me* trouble instead of thinking about why I'm here," Delta spat, looking at him pointedly. "I'm trying to help a woman who's gone missing, and it blows me away that nobody here seems to care."

"I care," the stranger replied, "of course I do, but I didn't hear anything about a woman missing."

"Yeah, and that's the next problem," Delta snapped, with a cold smile. "Very selective information seems to have leaked out ... to cause trouble for me, instead of to get help for her. You might want to think about that."

The other man shot him a hard look; then he got up and walked away. He sat back down with his buddies, and their heads bent together, talking and looking back and forth at Delta.

He wasn't sure what the outcome of their discussion would be, but Delta doubted it would slant on the side of the missing woman, and that was interesting too.

Her neighbors had been all about helping, but the minute anybody brought up the company, it seemed to be the complete opposite. That meant that the company must fund a lot of people's lives around here. Probably paid a lot of their wages, which meant every financial aspect was involved. Their paychecks, their access to housing, and perhaps a lot of social programs. Delta didn't know for sure in this particular town, but that's how companies frequently got a foothold and support from the locals, when they came into a new community.

When the waitress returned with his breakfast, she spoke low, keeping her back to the room. "Are you serious about a missing woman?"

He looked up and nodded. "Yes, I am. News travels fast around here." When she didn't say anything more, he continued. "Why? Have you heard something?"

"No, I just heard what you shared, but ..." She took a deep breath and added, "My boyfriend, ... I think he went missing too." Delta stared at her, and she shrugged. "Everybody seems to think he just up and left, but ... look. I can't talk here."

"Got it, and that's fine. When are you off work?'

"I had the early shift, so I'm done at ten," she murmured.

"I'll meet you outside?"

"Yeah, in the back parking lot," she whispered, "but we can't stay there either." She considered that for a moment. "No, maybe we should just meet down at the park." She quickly gave him directions, and then she took off.

He pondered that. What could it mean if there was in fact a second missing person, and a man at that? He ate his breakfast, paid without any further disturbance, then waited around until it was time to meet the waitress. He wandered the park a bit, looking around to see if the two of them would attract attention and whether that would be an issue or not. After that look around the park, he settled on a nearby bench, with some large bushes to conceal him a bit.

He couldn't imagine what was going on that somebody would cause trouble over his searching for a missing person and a War Dog, but he'd seen worse reactions, so wanted to keep an open mind. When he watched the waitress walk toward him, her head down, he waited until she got closer and then softly called out to her. She lifted her head, looked around casually, but didn't appear to be afraid, then raced to his side.

"Hey," she greeted him, sitting beside him. "Look. Maybe it's nothing, and that's what everybody keeps telling me, as if I should just forget about it."

"From the beginning, please."

"He quit, or was fired, from his job," she began, with an eye roll. "And then he just, … about a week ago, … he stopped responding to my emails, my phone calls."

"How long have you known him?"

"I've known him for ten years," she whispered, pushing back the tears. "We've been going out for about four or five months now."

"Is that unusual behavior for him?"

"Absolutely," she stated, "and, of course, everybody's just looking at me with pity, saying that he didn't know how to break up with me."

He nodded. "Where was he working?"

She looked at him, troubled, and whispered, her tone edgy as she replied, "At the company." He raised both eyebrows at that. She nodded. "That's why, when I heard you were looking for a missing woman? … Now you've got me really worried."

Delta stared off into the distance and murmured, "That's certainly an interesting point, isn't it? Now we have two people who worked at the company, and both of them went missing. Did he have a security card?"

"Yes, but they took it away from him. Of course, when he left, he had to hand in that stuff, and they would have revoked his clearance."

"Did he say why he quit or was fired or whatever?"

She shrugged. "He didn't like some things that were going on there."

"Which is also what happened to the woman, I think."

She looked at him, surprised. "Really?"

He nodded. "Yes. She went to one of the bosses, saying she had ethical concerns with some things going on inside."

"Oh my," the waitress said, as she shivered. "Do you really think something's wrong with Benji?"

"What's his full name?" he asked, pulling out his pen and notepad and writing it down. "Also I need to know, did you go to the sheriff?"

"Benjamin Raudings. I did, but they didn't seem to think it was anything worthwhile to investigate. They told me that he's an adult, and I guess, once you're an adult, you are free to do what you want, even if what you're doing isn't normal behavior for you."

"It's a problem," Delta confirmed, smiling at her. "On the other hand, if you've been close, you would think he would at least tell you it's over."

"That's the thing," she whispered, "we were talking about getting married, not ending it. I am so out of my mind right now."

"Right. I get it. The sheriff will likely think Benjamin just got cold feet, right? Young men being young men."

She stared at him and slowly nodded. "That's exactly what they told me."

"Any chance you have a key to his place?"

"I do, yes." She frowned. "I did go over there. I didn't think I was allowed, so I did it in a sneaky way, but nobody else seemed to care, since I normally would have gone over there anyway."

"What about his family and friends?"

"He doesn't have any family to speak of. He was adopted, and he's not close to his adopted family at all. He's grateful, but they're not close."

"And that's fine. We don't have to be close with everybody," Delta shared. "So, why don't we head over to your place and then let's go take a look at his."

Grateful to have something to do, she jumped to her feet, flashed him a bright smile, and nodded. "If you wouldn't mind."

"No, I don't mind at all," Delta said, "and it sounds as if it's quite possibly connected to my missing woman, Rebecca. You may know her."

She nodded. "If it's the same Rebecca, ... I know who you're talking about. She was always nice, quiet, but friendly, you know? I followed her on YouTube also. I don't think I've seen any recent posts from her." Then she burst out impulsively, "What's so weird is that she was apparently popular enough around town, until she went missing. Now suddenly nobody cares. It's kind of a hard world right now," she murmured. "It's too much like, after the quarantine, when we didn't know how to relate anymore or even what we're supposed to do."

"Maybe so," Delta conceded, "but looking out for one another should never be something we forget how to do."

CHAPTER 5

ONCE AGAIN IN the backyard, after a simple breakfast of toast and water, Rebecca sat outside, letting Gracie explore, while wondering how to change the circumstances she and Gracie found themselves in. When Benjamin joined her a few minutes later, she looked up and smiled. "It does help a lot to have this," she admitted.

He nodded but didn't say anything.

She could tell he was a little less centered and calm about the whole thing today, after that unknown couple's visit yesterday. "Are you okay?" she asked him.

He shrugged. "It's an odd feeling to think that you can just be wiped out because of somebody else's decision. Something you really have nothing to do with and have no say in the outcome. This is happening, but is there even anybody looking for us?" he burst out, looking over at her.

She shrugged. "I would like to think so, but we certainly won't know right now either way. The town seems protective of everybody at the company."

"Too protective," he snapped at her.

Not having seen this side of him before, she wasn't sure what to say.

He groaned, closed his eyes, then added, "I'm sorry. I shouldn't be mad at you. I'm just ... frustrated. I'm worried that Hannah thinks I just walked out on her."

"Hannah, Hannah, Hannah," Rebecca muttered. "I don't think I know a Hannah at work."

"That's because she doesn't work there," he shared, with a sideways look at her. "The world does not revolve around the company, you know."

Her lips twitched, and she nodded. "Oh, a really cute Hannah works at the coffee shop though, if I remember correctly."

He flushed and nodded. "Now that is my Hannah."

"So would she not have raised the alarm?"

"Sure," he replied, chewing on his words. "I'm sure she would try. I just don't know that anybody would listen. I'm an adult, so I can just imagine, if she tried to report it, I'm sure they would just assume that I was either upset from having lost my job or ... who knows." He raised his hands in frustration.

"Nobody's looking for you, so don't worry about it," Reggie stated from the corner.

She glanced over at him. "How is that even possible?" she muttered. "We have lives. There are people in our world."

"Not really," Reggie argued, staring at her, as if some irritation in his life. "You don't even have a boyfriend. You live alone. You were a piece of cake to just pick up and walk out with. You're so small that you couldn't have even fought me, if I'd given you the chance to," he gloated, with a smirk. "Some people just lose in the genetic lottery, and believe me. You lost."

It was like a sucker punch to the gut. She'd never even considered the idea that life was a lottery, or that there were winners and losers. Yet, according to Reggie, she'd already lost in a big way. "So, that's what you do? You just go around and kidnap people for fun? I thought it was because of the company."

"You can think whatever the hell you want," Reggie replied, glaring at her. "It doesn't matter to me because I've got nothing to do with it."

"No, but you just all but admitted that you're the one who picked me up and hauled me out of my home. How is that even fair?"

"I really don't care about fairness," he said in a bored tone. "So, go cry me a river. Besides, if you had lived with somebody or at least had a boyfriend, maybe you wouldn't have been such an easy target."

"And yet my size wasn't the reason you kidnapped me," she declared, looking at him intently. "It had nothing to do with that."

"No, it didn't," he agreed, with a smile. "That doesn't mean my point's not valid."

"What about Benjamin here? Why did he lose the genetic lottery?"

"Oh, he didn't lose the genetic lottery. He was just another nosy body at the wrong time, wrong place."

Benjamin stared at him. "I didn't even have anything to do with the company. I walked."

"Sure, you did, but you didn't walk far enough, now did you?" And, with that, Reggie turned and headed back into the house.

She turned toward Benjamin, who had such an astonished expression, it was clear he didn't know what Reggie was talking about. With a sigh, she muttered, "I gather that made no sense to you."

"No sense at all," he muttered. "What the hell's going on here?"

"It seems that you're right, and it's the sale or something of the company. They just want to ensure that we're silent until the sale is done. The problem is, what will they do with us when the deal has gone through?" she asked, shivering inwardly. "That's the part that concerns me. That boss lady threatened to get in touch with someone to take care of me."

He nodded slowly. "You and me both, including Hannah too. It makes no sense that we would be in trouble for whatever we did, especially since we don't even know what that is."

"That's the problem, isn't it?" she asked. "They apparently think that my animal lovers channel is some terrible risk. They're hoping we can stay quiet. However, if they didn't think we could before the sale goes through, how would they think we could now that they've kidnapped us? How the hell do we stay quiet after this?"

"Well, we have to," he muttered, looking at her in shock. "Otherwise …"

She stared at him grimly. "Otherwise, what? They'll come after us?"

Benjamin nodded. "And Hannah."

Rebecca frowned. "I don't understand. We are clearly missing some major information here. If the buyout deal has come this far, I highly doubt that even kidnapping us will stop it at this point. And depending on who it is that they're selling the company to, how do we know it won't end up worse? The new owners could be way worse."

"God, that's a thought, isn't it?" Benjamin asked. "Can you imagine?"

"Unfortunately I can," she shared. That didn't bear thinking about. "How could somebody even find us," she muttered, as she looked around at the secluded backyard garden.

"You better watch what you say," Benjamin warned Rebecca. "Obviously they can hear us."

"I know," she muttered. "Not that it's doing us any good."

"Nope."

Just then came a commotion inside the house, and she hunkered down even lower. "I suppose that's the company bosses again."

"I can't understand why. … We've already been warned. We can't do anything since we're stuck here as prisoners."

She nodded but didn't dare take her gaze off the house. "If one of us were to escape, they could go get help." She smiled over at him. He was young but looked game. "Any chance you can bolt over that fence when Reggie's distracted?"

He stared at her. "I've been thinking about it, but …" Then he smiled. "You know what? There may never be a better chance than right now." And, with that, he took a few steps, and, just at the corner that was the most hidden from view, he bolted and jumped over the fence in one very smooth movement.

"And that," she whispered to herself, "was the genetic lottery in action." She was ecstatic for him. When your legs were long enough to lift you up and over, escape was possible, even easy, versus with her. Rebecca would probably need a stack of stuff to stand on even to get a look over the fence, much less vault over it, and then what about Gracie?

Luckily Benjamin was safely gone.

She closed her eyes, leaned back, and whispered, "Godspeed."

"SO, HANG ON a minute," Delta barked into the phone. He had a three-way Zoom call going on with Kat, Badger, and Stone. "You're saying that they've been doing advanced experimentation, and one of the chips that they have was potentially for war purposes? To what end, for transferring messages?"

"Not necessarily. Not so much for transferring messages, but it's built like a bug, able to transmit and receive," Stone explained. "For example, if the War Dog got close to the targets, they could overhear the conversations."

"Oh, good God," Delta said. "All you had to do was get close to an enemy with the dog, which … isn't exactly an easy thing to do."

"No, but people tend to ignore animals and don't initially see them as a danger, depending on how they are presented. So, if a dog was equipped with an embedded transmitter and receiver, chances are, nobody would know."

"Whoa, whoa, whoa. Transmitter *and* receiver?"

"Exactly," Stone confirmed, with a big fat smile. "I've been into the guts of the software, and while I'm no expert—"

"Oh, please." Kat snorted. "Who are you trying to kid? You are my expert, and you're damn good."

He chuckled. "I'll take that as a compliment. Especially coming from a woman who everybody thought was crazy to try to use an app for some of the robotics you make."

"Well, not everyone is as forward-thinking as I am," she stated, with half a laugh.

"That's true enough."

Delta's head kind of swam at that idea. "An app for robotics?"

"It was more for robotic help," she clarified in a casual tone. "Such as, I could see whether the oils were good, whether the mechanism was operating at 100 percent or 30 percent. So just data," she shared. "I love data."

Delta shook his head at the thought. "Well, sign me up," he declared, a bit more quickly than he realized. "Anything that works and is better than what I've got."

She protested, "Hey now, you're getting your new one. It's coming."

"I know. I know," Delta muttered, "but so is Christmas, dammit."

Badger snorted. "Can we get back to the topic at hand?"

"Yes, that would be a good idea," Kat agreed, with a pat on her husband's arm.

"Anyway," Stone continued. "I think we could possibly send out a short signal on Gracie's collar and potentially some sort of message."

There was silence as everybody digested that for a moment.

"Well …" Badger started, then stopped. "That could work. I just don't know what would happen if the wrong person was there with her. We're assuming she's alone, but there's really no way to know that."

"Actually I'm no longer assuming that Rebecca and Gracie are alone, and I need to bring you all up-to-date on this," Delta added. "I spoke to a girl by the name of Hannah. She works at a local café, and her fiancé also worked at the same company with Rebecca and Gracie. He has gone missing as well, so it's likely all three of them are together."

"Were you able to go to his house?" Badger asked.

"We went to his apartment complex, but we didn't go inside. I contacted the sheriff and asked for permission to enter, but he told me to leave it all alone."

"Right." Kat sighed. "Let me contact him." And, with that, she left the Zoom screen.

Delta stared at Stone and Badger. "So, Stone, even if we could get a message to Rebecca through Gracie, what we really need is for Rebecca to talk to us."

"We don't know if that's possible yet," Stone admitted. "It's all a bit preliminary. I need to see if I can hack the software enough to write some code and make it do what I need it to do."

"Well, while you work on that," Delta stated, "I'll work on the good old-fashioned way of dealing with this kind of stuff."

Stone laughed. "That would be a great idea. You do that." Stone now exited the Zoom call.

That left only Badger on the call. "I'm surprised you contacted the sheriff."

"I only did it because Benjamin's neighbors were watching," Delta admitted, with a half laugh. "I'll go back tonight with his girlfriend. We'll get into the apartment and have a look."

"That's a good thing," Badger noted, "but I know I don't have to warn you to be careful."

"Oh, I'll be careful," Delta replied.

Badger nodded. "Because something is seriously rotten about that company. We were able to pull the financials and are looking into what could possibly be going on. At first glance, there's activity we weren't expecting from basically a R&D setup. Plus, we have confirmed some talk of a merger or a buyout happening, and that might have something to do with all this coming to a head right now."

"I don't know why it should," Delta murmured. "If

they've got a merger going on, it should just make them bigger, right? The sense I've gotten is that everybody around here in town is pro-company all the way. To the extreme really. As a matter of fact, I got a very chilly reception at the café from some of the locals."

"It's understandable in a way. The company provides their paychecks and pays for their mortgages. At heart, people are very simple," Badger explained. "They just want security. They want to know they'll be okay tomorrow and every other tomorrow in the foreseeable future."

"Well, the problem with that kind of thinking," Delta pointed out, trying hard to keep the bitterness out of his tone and failing miserably, "is that life happens. And, when it does, it never gives us a heads-up. It's up to us to land on our feet and to move forward."

"One leg or two?" Badger asked, with a laugh.

"It doesn't matter. You've still got to get up and to get going because nobody else will hold your hand for you."

"That's true," Badger confirmed, "and not all of us are lucky enough to have access to Kat."

"Are you kidding? You have no idea how jealous I am that you've got her full-time," Delta shared, with a smile.

"I know. I get to test out all her prototypes." Badger chuckled. "Anyway, keep doing what you're doing, and we'll all keep working on our end. Let me know if you find anything tonight."

"Will do."

When he was sure the call was over, and nobody else came back on the Zoom connection, Delta disconnected and texted Hannah. **I plan to go back to his apartment tonight, when nobody's around.**

Her response was immediate. **I'm coming with you.**

He hesitated, and then sent her a thumbs-up. **Ten o'clock, and we meet outside his apartment. Stay in your vehicle. Remember. Something serious is going on here. I don't want you getting hurt.**

And, for that, he got a thumbs-up in return.

Still a lot of time remained in Delta's day, but he wanted to set up his notes and to see if he could find some more information. Just as he was working on his to-do list, he got a call from the deputy.

"Just wanted to let you know," Halvorson stated, "that we did a search for the young man who went missing, but our information is that they'd broken up, and she took it really badly. He's the one who did the breaking up, so this is more or less him trying to hide from her."

"I'll believe that when I talk to him," Delta replied briskly. "I come from too many years of experience where people say all kinds of things to get the authorities off their backs, and it doesn't mean any of it's true."

"Well, that's what we were told."

"Who told you that?" Delta asked, frowning into the phone. "Somebody reliable?"

"Of course it was somebody reliable," Halvorson said testily. "It's not as if we're in the business of making shit up."

"Listen. Lots of people are in the business of making shit up," Delta declared. "The question is whether you can tell whether the shit is made up or whether it's not."

"Look. I was just trying to do you a solid and to let you know."

"I appreciate that, thank you. When I bring the kid into the sheriff's office after he's been rescued, you can tell him the same story." And, with that, Delta hung up.

His phone rang a moment later, and, sure enough, it was

Deputy Halvorson calling back. "You really think something is wrong, don't you?"

"Yeah, I do, and that's years and years of instincts, even if we don't have the proof to convince you guys," he said. "I just wish it wasn't so hard to get a helping hand for these people who need it."

For a few long moments, silence once again came from the other end. "Look. I'll admit we haven't had a very open or helpful reception to our questions. Outside of that, I don't have any reason to be wary."

"That in itself is why you should be wary," Delta snapped. "There's no reason for anybody to not be completely open and helpful, unless you know something."

"I don't. Do you?"

"I understand there's the possibility of a merger or buy-out or something going on up there. The company is abuzz, and something is in motion."

"Really?" the deputy asked. "I hadn't heard anything."

"So, nobody in your family works there?"

"No, I don't have any family here," he replied, "but I do know a lot of people who do."

"Right. My guess is that most of them, or possibly all of them, are defending what goes on there."

"Of course," he stated. "They've all been working there for quite a while. They all seem relatively happy."

"It's the *relatively happy* part that confuses me," Delta stated, "because … I get it. When a single company provides the bulk of the employment in an area like this, providing paychecks, access to home mortgages, not to mention employing the people who support the rest of the commerce and the social service agencies, nobody wants to be bothered. So, at what point in time will people be bothered enough to stand up and to be heard?"

"The residents won't want to be bothered unless it's all about them," Deputy Halvorson admitted. He hesitated and then added, "Look. I did check out the kid's place, but I haven't been there recently."

"Well, I suggest you go again," Delta said, "and this time keep an open mind that maybe it's connected. It's highly possible that both Rebecca and Benjamin are in serious trouble."

"You really think so?"

"Two people and a dog are missing from the same company in a very short timeframe," he pointed out in exasperation. "How can that not be connected?"

"It's called a coincidence," the deputy replied.

At that, Delta groaned. "I'm not so sure such a thing even exists."

"Yeah, I know. I keep hearing people say that, but shit happens, and it doesn't always have an explanation. There just isn't always a neat and tidy ending."

"Oh, I'll give you that," Delta replied, "but there should be more than what we have."

"If you want, you can meet me there," Halvorson offered.

Delta stared down at his phone in surprise and then said, "Ten minutes?"

"Make it fifteen," the deputy growled, and then quickly hung up.

At that, Delta sent a text to Hannah, Benjamin's girlfriend, and explained what had just happened.

She phoned him and asked, "Should I meet you there?"

"Why not? Maybe he'll believe it if he hears it from you."

"I never talked to any of the deputies," she noted. "Nobody followed up with me at all."

Hearing that, Delta groaned. "Yes, you should definitely meet us there."

It didn't take very long to get over to the young man's apartment. Delta got out and waited for the deputy to show up, and, as soon as he did, he walked over to join him. "Did you ever talk to his girlfriend?"

"Not personally, no. Why?" Halvorson asked, as he walked toward the apartment.

"Because she would really like to talk to you about his disappearance."

He looked at him. "You've been talking to her?"

"Of course I have," he declared, with a smile. "She's pretty upset. Somebody she cares about a lot has gone missing, and nobody gives a shit." The deputy frowned at that. "Look. I know you're saying you do care. But what I'm telling you is that it doesn't appear that way for anybody who is in trouble and who is looking for help."

Just then Hannah showed up, and Delta introduced the two of them.

She crossed her arms over her chest, glared at Halvorson, and said, "Please tell me that you're finally taking it seriously now."

"I don't have a whole lot of choice," he grumbled, looking over at Delta. "This guy won't leave it alone."

She looked over at Delta and smiled. "Thank you."

Delta shrugged. "We have a mutual interest. Two people have gone missing, and, in both cases, there are suspicious circumstances."

She nodded. "Worse than that, nobody seems to believe us."

"Well, that's because they haven't bothered to look," Delta told her, with a nod. "But that's okay. Things are moving now." He gave a pointed look at Deputy Halvorson.

She smiled, misty-eyed, as she pulled out her keys and opened up the apartment.

The deputy frowned at her, as she looked over at him.

"We were supposed to move in together next month. He gave me his keys several weeks ago. It's quite normal to do that in a relationship," she added, glaring again at him.

"Of course it is," Delta agreed, nudging her forward. "Let's take a look and see if there's anything suspicious."

"I did look earlier," she admitted, as she wandered around, her arms still wrapped around her chest. "He doesn't have a whole lot here. That's one of the reasons we were moving in together was to save on money and to see if we could build up our life a little bit, saving for better times, you know?"

"What would you do then?" the deputy asked her.

"I wanted to go back to school, and he was looking at taking more training courses. I just hope he gets that chance."

"Let's not get ahead of ourselves," Delta stated, as he wandered the kitchen, looking around, opening drawers, taking a close look at everything. He headed to the living room and then to the stairs.

The deputy nodded at him and said, "I'm coming too."

"So you should," Delta agreed, "but that doesn't mean he was taken from here." He turned to Hannah. "Come on up too. Let's see if anything's missing."

They went through the entire place, and, just as they were heading downstairs, the front door opened, and somebody stumbled in and slammed the door behind them.

They raced down the stairs and saw a young man standing there, visibly trembling in front of them.

"Oh my God," Hannah cried out, throwing herself into his arms. "Benji, you're home. What the hell happened? Are you okay? You're bleeding."

He wrapped his arms around her, looked at the other two men, and stuttered, "I need help." He was half in tears. "Like … serious help."

"What's wrong?" Deputy Halvorson asked, staring at him.

"I was kidnapped, and they've still got Rebecca and Gracie." Benjamin scrubbed his face. He kept one arm wrapped around Hannah and held her close, rocking her back and forth. "Damn," he said, "I didn't even think it would work, but there was a momentary distraction, and I hopped over the fence. They'll be after me for sure now, and this is probably the first place they'll look. I did check in at the hospital and reported this mess but there's no way it's safe here."

He looked down at her and gave her a gentle shake. "We have to leave, Hannah. We have to leave *now*."

CHAPTER 6

REBECCA WAS LOCKED back up in her room, but that was a godsend, as all she could do was tremble. Even Gracie trembled beside her. The fury on the two men's faces when they realized she was alone was palpable. She stared at them in shock, just thankful the mean boss lady did not seem to be here now.

"What was I supposed to do?" she cried out. "He jumped the fence right in front of me. Was I supposed to call you guys and say, "Oh, gee, he's escaping. Look.""

She'd received a hard smack across the face for that—a bone-jarring blow that had her crying out and collapsing to the ground, setting Gracie off, ready to attack. And, for that, Gracie had been dealt a deathly kick to her ribs.

"Keep that damn dog away from me," Reggie raged, a mountain of fury behind it, "or next time I'll shoot her."

Rebecca had been yanked to her feet and dumped back into the bedroom, but thankfully Gracie was with her. The two of them were huddled together in the corner, her arms wrapped around the trembling dog. She kept trying to tell Gracie that it would okay, but Rebecca didn't have any idea if it truly would be.

She wanted to believe that Benjamin would get help and would come after her, but did he even know where they were? Did he have any clue what was going on? How was he to get them help? As she cuddled up with Gracie in her arms, a weird buzz went off, a buzz that she didn't understand.

Gracie shook her head, as if the buzz were bothering her.

Rebecca leaned closer and realized the noise came from her lower leg. She could faintly see the outline of some implant in her leg. She groaned. "Have they done something to you, girl?"

Gracie just whined and started licking the spot.

And then came a series of taps. Rebecca wasn't sure what the hell that was. *Morse code?* She stared at the spot and gently stroked it. If it was receiving signals, who would be sending them? Was it these assholes? Is this what they were doing, using the animals for some sort of testing?

But even if they were using Gracie for something like this, it surely wouldn't be so bad that they would need to kidnap people to hide it, much less threaten to kill them. What on earth was going on that was so horrific that they needed to silence people? That was the part she didn't get. Kidnapping was one thing, but they were threatening to kill her … and Gracie and Benjamin and Hannah too. Now Rebecca knew that many people wouldn't give a shit about a dog. It was *just a dog*, after all, just an animal. But, for Rebecca, Gracie was a whole lot more than that.

Still, her kidnappers wouldn't understand and neither would they care, and that just made Rebecca feel crappy all over again. She groaned as she sat here with Gracie, gently rubbing the spot where she was still getting a series of beeps. It was faint, and she doubted anybody who wasn't right beside them would hear it, but maybe that's what someone was trying to do. Could it be a detectable signal? She didn't know, and then she thought she heard a voice. She looked around in shock, but nobody was here. There may have been cameras or listening devices before, but now she wasn't even sure she was in the same room as earlier.

The beeps never stopped. Finally she responded in a faint whisper, "Hello? Is anyone there?" She wondered if her heart pounding so loud would drown out all other sounds, but then she heard someone say something, but it wasn't clear. Yet she felt a vague sense of familiarity, but she couldn't be sure.

Then a man clearly said, "Rebecca."

"Oh my God," she gasped, bolting upright. "Who is there?"

The man whispered, "*Shhh*. It's me, Delta."

She leaned closer to Gracie's leg and whispered, "Delta? Seriously? Help, help, please. I'm here with Gracie, and I need help."

"Calm down. Can anybody else hear you?"

"No, I don't think so. I'm alone."

"Thank God for that," Delta muttered. "Do you know where you are?"

"No, I don't, but a young man was here. Benjamin. He escaped, or he tried to anyway."

"Yes," Delta confirmed. "We've got him. He's been hurt, but he's getting treatment right now."

"How badly hurt?"

"Well, he was covered in blood when we found him, so we're not sure yet."

"Oh my God. The two men here were really upset, so they would have run him down, if they could have."

"And maybe that's what they did," Delta replied. "Just know that we are looking for you."

"Thank heavens for that."

"So obviously you have Gracie with you."

"I do," she cried out and then smiled in joy. "She's the only reason I'm staying sane."

"And Gracie is the only reason that we could find you, by using this mode of communication," he shared.

"What the hell is this communication?" she muttered, staring at the dog in shock.

"It's a transmitter device in Gracie. The company was testing certain modules. Gracie got one as a tracking beacon. But it's been disabled. We were trying to send a signal through it, and that's where we're at right now."

"Well, you did. You sent a signal, and we can converse, so it must be sending and receiving."

"Exactly," he stated, "but if you don't know where you are, and her tracker has been disabled, it's still not that helpful."

"Well, I can tell you we're in a house. There's a big high fence, and that's how Benjamin got out. He jumped the fence. Some sort of merger or a buyout is happening, and this other man and this scary woman came to threaten Benjamin and me, saying they didn't want us around to cause trouble and to screw up the deal."

First came silence, then Delta whispered, "We thought it could be something like that. I don't know if you're being watched, but try to not let anybody know that we are talking. We won't initiate conversation again until you do, so we know that you're safe and alone."

"Got it," she muttered, as she stared around the room. "I've seen the same guard since I've been here. However, this other man and woman come every once in a while, but I never see them for very long."

"They haven't shared what they want from you?"

"No, just basically silence, and, for some reason, they

think my little pet lovers channel is some huge social media risk. What worries me is that they've gone far enough that they can't just let me go now, at least in their minds. She even suggested that I might fall victim to one of my fans, *since you know how crazy animal lovers can be.* It sounded very much like a threat. She said to leave it with her."

"*Okay.* Well, try to avoid getting into trouble or making them angry, while we work on finding you. If we can send a signal and receive a signal, we should be able to figure out how to backtrack it, but I can't tell you how long that'll take. I'll back off for now, while we work on it." Then he stopped and asked, "Are you okay? Have they hurt you at all?"

"No, … no," she whispered. "I'm … I'm okay. No, I'm fine." Her hand instinctively went to her jaw, and Delta must have understood her hesitation.

He snapped, "But he did hurt you a little bit?"

"Just when Reggie found out Benjamin was gone. Reggie was very angry."

"Of course, because now he has to justify his own failure to the bosses. But Benjamin is safe, and he's in the hospital right now, and we are getting more info from him."

"Thank God for that," she muttered. "I kind of wish I'd tried to go over the fence with him."

"Probably best you didn't because you may not have made it, especially if you were carrying Gracie. At least now Benjamin's free, and he can help us get to you." With that, Delta whispered, "Over and out."

She sat here in the corner, her face buried in Gracie's neck and just cried. It was such a relief to not be alone anymore. The thought that it was Delta, the man who was coming to check up on Gracie, just blew her away, but it did make a weird kind of sense. Although nobody would agree with her, she was definitely seeing a sign here.

But the fact that he was here at all was a miracle, when really Delta was after Gracie. Still, he was military, and maybe that was something that all military could do. Rebecca shook her head at the idea. It would be wonderful if it were true, but chances were it wasn't.

Still, she was grateful that anybody was looking for her and Gracie. And she was also damn grateful that Benjamin had made it out. Nobody needed to go through this. Her conditions would only get worse, now that Benjamin had escaped, she realized, as she curled up in the corner, knowing that there certainly wouldn't be any pleasantries like tea, coffee, or even five minutes outside in the grass any longer.

She was in her designated room, and this is where she would likely stay. At least until her guard got over whatever punishment he was enduring himself for letting Benjamin escape. Pulling Gracie closer, Rebecca curled up into the corner, and the two of them fell into an uneasy sleep.

SHE WAS RUDELY awakened early in the morning, still groggy from sleep, eyes barely open, when she was hauled to her feet. "Come on. We're getting rid of you now."

"What do you mean?" she cried out fearfully.

"You heard me," Reggie snapped. "Piece of shit that you are, look at all the trouble you got me into."

And, with that, she was dragged roughly down to a vehicle and shoved into the back seat. Gracie was still with her and stayed close the whole time. She didn't want Gracie to be separated from her, and neither did she want anybody to have a chance to discover or to understand that Gracie was far more valuable than they could possibly realize. Very quickly they were racing down a highway.

"What will you do with us?" she whispered.

"Oh, shut up," Reggie snapped. "I should just pop you right here and leave you for dead."

"We didn't do anything."

"Don't worry. That stupid punk kid will get it too. He's in the hospital unprotected, and we'll make sure he's taken out for his little act of defiance. I will kill the little shit myself, if I have to."

She froze at that, hoping that maybe Delta was listening in on Gracie's transmitter. At least then they would know to provide protection for Benjamin. "I still don't understand what we could have done that would be so horrible that you needed to do all this," she muttered.

"Doesn't matter whether you understand or not," he snapped in a thunderous tone. "I do what I'm hired to do, and I don't ask questions."

"Right," she muttered bitterly. "What do you care? You just go around kidnapping and killing people and carry on with your little life, where you are the all-powerful."

Hearing that, he reached around and smacked her hard. "I didn't say anything about killing you, but don't worry. The elements will take care of that. Now shut up, or I'll shut you up. Another word out of you, and I'll drop you off the closest bridge."

And, with that, he turned back around and kept on driving.

"I'm getting a lot of interference," Delta noted, as he

talked to Stone on the phone. It seemed they lived on the phone now.

"So am I," he muttered. "Rebecca's on the move."

"Of course she is. After Benjamin escaped, the kidnappers had to get her out of there. We'll assume at this point that Rebecca and Gracie are together and on the move," Delta replied. "Obviously we don't know that for sure, but we can't operate with too many variables here. So, I'm happy to go on the assumption that they're still together."

Delta wanted Rebecca and Gracie to be together, but that sure as hell didn't mean they were. "The fact that we even got a message through is huge. I keep getting some background noise. Regardless, moving her definitely points to other players or some other orders right now."

"Probably because Benjamin escaped," Stone suggested.

"I heard something just now, but it was distant and choppy and hard to hear. Something about taking care of him too."

"Great. The kid escapes, and he's supposed to get popped because of it."

"We've seen worse."

"Unfortunately we have. Too much. These guys really don't want anybody to know what they're up to, so it has to be major."

"You would think so," Delta replied. "Yet you and I both know that we can't possibly think like these people do. We can only work off our past experiences with these types. Some of these criminals' reasons for doing this shit are insane. It could just be that they can't hold their head up in public, if we find out whatever this is about. People are devious for stupid reasons, but I can guarantee you that they did this for purely selfish reasons. If they told the truth, they would not get what they want, so they just lie and steal."

"You got that right," Stone agreed. "Any way to track where she is?"

"No, not yet," he admitted, with frustration in his tone. "I'm trying to backtrack the transmitter, but they seem to be out of range."

"Which means they're in a vehicle and probably driving."

"That would be my guess. Yet … I can't be sure."

CHAPTER 7

"I T'S ME," REBECCA muttered as she watched the vehicle she'd been in drive away like someone was after them. She couldn't believe he'd dumped her and taken off. "I'm alone now."

"Where are you?" Delta asked.

"I'm in the middle of nowhere," she wailed, frantic and obviously panicking. "Trees all around and nothing here. Reggie just dumped me and Gracie here and told me that Mother Nature would take care of us."

Delta disagreed. "Well, Mother Nature might have taken care of you if you were all alone, but you still have Gracie to help you fend for yourself out there."

"Yes, and she's fine. I can't believe you haven't figured out how to backtrack that signal yet."

He snorted. "Hey, no pressure though."

"I'm sorry. I'm so sorry," she whispered. "I'm just so scared."

"Is there a reason to be scared?"

"Well, Reggie drove off, so I don't think he's the reason I would be scared. But I don't know where I am, and, if you don't have a way to track me, I can't tell you how to get here."

"Was there a road? Did he drive up a road?"

"Yes, I'm sitting on it."

"Start walking," he ordered. "Stay on the road, but just because somebody is driving past you on that road doesn't mean that they'll be helpful."

She froze at that and asked, "Seriously?"

"Yes, seriously," Delta declared. "I'll keep the line open. We'll try to track you. ... As soon as we find out where you are, we can come get you."

"Yeah, well, do you want to speed up that process a bit?"

"How long were you driving for? Do you know?"

"About an hour, but since I don't know where we started, an hour from nowhere is still nowhere."

He laughed at that. "That's a good point," he muttered. "I, on the other hand, prefer to think we're a little further ahead than that. As long as Gracie is there with you ..."

"She's right here. I'm not walking at the moment. I'm just sitting on the side of the road right now, and she's here with me."

"Is she hurt?"

"Bruised ribs, kind of like my face."

"So, he did hit you?"

"Yeah, but, from his point of view, I deserved it because Benjamin got away."

"What? So you pay because Benjamin escaped?" Delta asked.

"Pretty much. I'm really surprised that you were looking for us."

"When you didn't show up to work for our scheduled meeting, what was I supposed to do?" Delta asked. "I can't meet with someone if I can't find them, and I don't like leaving anybody in harm's way."

"I appreciate that very much," she whispered. "I can't imagine how I would be feeling right now if you hadn't sounded an alarm."

"I did and you're fine. Obviously you're not *fine*-fine, but we'll get you. That's what you need to hang on to because we will find you. If I had a general direction to go in, I would already be in the vehicle and on the move."

"Somebody needs to keep Benjamin safe," she whispered.

"We got that part of the message, and don't worry. He's got a guard. We showed him some pictures of people related to the company, and we got lucky. Benjamin confirmed the woman threatening you both was a board member for the company. Even found a photo online of the man and the woman together, but the man was not ID'd there. Not this woman's husband, yet working in tandem. Not sure if the other board members are involved with any kidnapping plots. Since that female board member is not a local, the authorities here are suspect, protecting the company instead of looking for you and Benjamin. So Badger called in the FBI, and the woman has already been picked up and is being interrogated now. Either she'll give up her partner or we'll get a facial recognition hit on the guy. With any luck, somebody will try to hurt Benjamin at the hospital, and then they will pay for it."

"I'd like to see them all pay for it," Rebecca snapped, "for what they've done to Gracie. What the hell is this thing in her leg?"

"Some medical implant. And it's literally just to help people determine what's going on medically. It's like a monitoring device, for blood pressure, sugar levels, and that kind of thing. Who knows what all they could use it for. I don't know about all that medical and IT related business, but a guy named Stone is helping me, and he is better suited to find out more about that device. But that's what it was originally supposed to do. Now, whether it's been bastardized into something else by the company, I don't know."

"It's so stupid to kidnap me over a medical device I knew nothing about," she muttered. "I just want to go home."

"I get it," Delta said. "We did find a neighbor's home security video of your captor taking you from your apartment, all wrapped up in a sleeping bag."

"Yeah, that would be quite possible. I vaguely remember being carried, now that you mention it, but I don't know where I was taken to."

"You were carried to a pickup truck and dumped into the back."

"Into the truck bed?" she asked.

"Yes. It's obviously a lot easier to look after somebody if they're unconscious, where you can just drop them into the back like that."

"That's barbaric," she muttered.

Delta snorted. "Maybe so, but now you are free of that asshole, even if you are on your own, out in the middle of nowhere."

"Yeah. Did you hear what you just said?" she snapped, as she glared down at the device buried in Gracie's leg. "If anybody could see me right now, they would surely think I had a screw loose."

He chuckled. "Maybe. … Listen. I'll go silent right now, while we continue to work. Just know that I'm here, listening. So, if you see anything and want to keep up a running commentary of landmarks, do so. But, for now, stand up and get walking."

"It's dark out here," she grumbled, yet she stood up. She

shoved her hands in her pockets, and, with Gracie at her side, she started walking down the road where the tire tracks were.

"AT LEAST I can see the tire tracks," Rebecca murmured. "I don't know how far ahead of me that Reggie is, but I suspect he's long gone."

"He's either long gone or is waiting to see what you do."

At that, she froze. "Do you really think he's up ahead, waiting for us?"

Delta hesitated. "He could be up ahead, waiting for you, or he could have parked the vehicle, got out, and came back around, either watching you to see what you do or looking to pop you one."

"*Uh-oh*," she whispered, as she came up to a bend in the road. "I'm about to go around the bend in the road."

"Well, go carefully, just in case a vehicle is there."

She came around the bend and froze. "A vehicle is here," she whispered. "I think it might be the same one I was in because this is a four-door. I'm not sure though."

"Good. Go see if he's there, but be careful."

She walked cautiously to the car, yet felt better about this since Gracie wasn't growling or barking. As Rebecca peeked into the car, she found the car empty. She also saw the keys in the ignition, and, with Gracie settled in, Rebecca jumped in the driver's seat and started the engine and slowly drove forward. "Hey, Delta, you there? Can you hear me?"

"I can hear you. Did you check the vehicle?"

"Yeah, it was empty, but he left the keys. I wonder why. I'm driving it right now, hoping he's not running after me."

"Yeah, he's looking for you or taking a leak or somebody popped him."

"Oh my God," Rebecca muttered.

"Regardless, we'll search for him later. That's not your problem right now. Your problem is safely getting back into town, as soon as you can."

"I'm working on it," she said, still in a panic. "I don't know where I am yet, and I haven't put the lights on because I don't want anybody to know I'm driving."

"Smart, but pretty soon you'll need to. Just keep Gracie with you, until we can find you."

"You mean, you might find me?" she asked, feeling better for the first time, in control somehow, and definitely a whole lot happier. Looking in her rearview mirror, she asked, "How come Reggie's not here?"

"I don't know," he admitted. "There might have been two vehicles, and maybe they disposed of Reggie because he failed."

"I almost feel sorry for him, if that's the case."

"Don't. He would have popped you if he could have. And maybe that's why he isn't alive. Maybe they watched to see what he would do, but, when he balked at killing you, he took the bullet instead."

"Another thought I don't want to consider. That's just terrible."

"Terrible, yes, but it's also the way of the criminal world. They hired him to do a job, and, if he couldn't do it, he knew too much. So, being a liability, they couldn't count on him to do what they needed him to do."

"I'm not sure he would have balked at killing me," she shared. "Reggie had that kind of attitude that he didn't really give a shit about anything, especially me, so I don't think it's that."

"And that could very well be," Delta muttered. "Just keep going. Stay calm and stay safe. Another vehicle could be coming after you, and, if you see one parked on the side of the road, you ignore it, and you keep on driving. Do you hear me?"

"Yes, I hear you," she repeated. "I'm turning on my headlights now. It's getting darker and harder to see."

In a few minutes she spoke up again. "Oh, there's a turnoff up ahead." And feeling better about the whole thing, she took the turnoff, where all the tire tracks were, and headed back to what she assumed was closer to town. After driving for a good ten, maybe fifteen minutes, she saw another vehicle up ahead.

"Somebody is up ahead, so maybe I really am headed back to town," she reported excitedly, and then she frowned. "But it may not be the right person, could it?"

"Who knows? It could be anybody," Delta pointed out. "Don't try to pass them, just keep on driving."

"But if they know I've been left back there, probably nobody else has come this way."

"Right. So, either they know it's you or they're afraid that they didn't do a good-enough job killing off Reggie. Shut down your lights, and you keep driving. You really must keep going," he snapped. "Don't stop for any reason. Seriously, stop for nobody."

"What if they're hurt?"

"I don't care if they're lying down broken on the side of the road," he barked. "You keep going, no matter what. Do you hear me? People have all kinds of tricks to get someone to stop, and I don't want you falling for any of them."

"You're one scary dude."

"I'm not the scary one," he argued, "but I am very proud of you. Look at how far you've come."

"I haven't done anything," she muttered. "These assholes are all around the place."

"And, so far, you've managed to avoid them. You've kept your head, and now you have wheels. That is huge, particularly since you're out in the dark, and I'm not saying the wild animals would be dangerous. In my world it's the two-legged animals who are the worst."

"Oh, I agree with you there." She gave him a broken laugh. "I haven't even dated for a while because the last one, the last guy I dated, was definitely in that percentage of the crazies."

"What, an animal?" Delta teased, with gentle laughter.

"Yeah, you're not kidding. An animal in so many ways. Kind of like an octopus, with hands everywhere." He burst out laughing at that, and she found herself grinning. "Now, on the other hand, if I were to be asked out on a date by some guy who rescued me, that might be a whole different story." After a moment of silence, she flushed, wondering at her own temerity. "Don't worry about it," she added. "I'm just teasing."

"Oh, you might be teasing, but I'm not," he replied thoughtfully. "Although a lot of women don't like me because I've got a gnarly scar on my face, plus a prosthetic foot."

"I don't know what that scar or that prosthetic looks like," she shared, "but it really wouldn't matter to me."

"When you see me, you might change your mind."

"I highly doubt it," she muttered. "My father had a disfiguring scar, and he went through hell because of stupid, ignorant people. It used to make me so mad."

"Sometimes people can't … They can't stop their initial physical reaction," he explained, "so you can't blame them for it. It's something odd that you don't see too often."

"I don't care," she snapped. "Sometimes they were just absolutely shitty about it."

"Well, that's people, and I certainly wouldn't want you to be pitying me."

"I don't pity anybody," she declared, still in an angry tone. "My dad was made of steel, but I know, every once in a while, it would break him down too."

"Well, I think I would have liked your dad."

"You would have," she agreed. "It sounds to me like you would have been two peas in a pod."

He chuckled. "I don't know," he replied in a playful tone. "I've been through a lot, lots of, … well, two tours overseas. And look at me now. … Tracking down a War Dog."

"Sounds to me like a promotion."

At that, he burst out laughing. "You know that I'm not against Gracie being with you at all. It sounds like she's in a very good place, but I still have to check it out."

"I'm glad you guys are checking it out, but I still want to know what they've done to this poor dog. She's been through enough already. To think they might even be pulling shit like this on her? … It makes me so angry. I wonder what else is really going on."

"And it's probably that kind of thinking," he noted, "that you got into trouble."

"Well then, trouble will keep on finding me since I'm not likely to stop. People like this are just plain assholes."

He chuckled, then asked, "Can you still see the other vehicle?"

"I can, just lights continuously moving forward. Oh, wait. Looks like they're slowing down."

"Ah, I don't like the sound of that," he said in a worried tone.

"Why not?" she asked, stiffening in alarm. "What's wrong if they do slow down?"

"Well, they may want to have a talk with you."

"I'm not stopping to talk with them," she said, frantic.

"Correct, but, if you take a bullet through the windshield, you'll be stopped anyway."

As if understanding exactly what he was saying, she steeled herself. Just then, gunshots rained into the vehicle. She screamed, but instead of swerving off the road, she ducked low behind the wheel and hit the gas pedal, blasting past the shooter, even as bullets flew and the glass shattered all around her.

She kept going until she heard nothing but silence.

CHAPTER 8

"HOLY SHIT, HOLY crap." She kept screaming as she drove, her foot flat on the pedal, struggling to keep the car on the road. As she blasted past the shooter, she heard a *thump* and winced but didn't dare pull her foot off the gas.

"Keep driving," Delta yelled at her. "Just keep driving."

"Oh my God," she asked, "what if I've killed someone?"

"Let's not forget that they were shooting at you," he pointed out.

She shuddered. "I'm still not somebody who kills people," she cried out. "This is insane."

"Yes, it is insane. Remember that. It's insane. Somebody kidnapped you over something at work, and somebody else is pulling your strings now." he called out, loud enough that it enraged her, hearing it all over again. "This is all insane, and you need to do whatever it takes to stay alive."

"I'm trying," she replied, almost shouting. "The windshield is shattered, but I'm still driving."

"What about Gracie?"

"She's still beside me on the front seat, but we're both covered in shattered glass."

"That's okay. Just keep driving and don't stop. Check your gas. How much gas do you have?"

"It's just over half full."

"Good, you'll have hundreds of miles with that."

"Yeah, says you," she muttered, feeling her heart slam against her chest. Her palms were sweaty, and she was terrified to look in the rearview mirror. "Oh my God, Delta. I killed somebody. I know it."

"You don't know that," he pointed out. "You're assuming that because you hit him. Even if he is dead, it's not your fault."

"Who else is there?" she cried out, as that realization started to set in.

"Stop it now. You need to be calm about this. You cannot afford to freak out right now," he muttered. "This is as serious and as dangerous as life ever gets. You cannot be distracted. You cannot give up."

"I'm not giving up," she snapped, getting angry at him, and then realized that was what he was going for. "You're pretty tricky, aren't you?"

He chuckled. "No, I don't know about tricky, but I spent a lot of time in the military. I know that, when push comes to shove, things can blow up, and things can go wrong," he explained, "and right now this is not the time to panic."

"Yeah, well, let me know when it is time to panic, will you?" she quipped, glaring over at Gracie. "Now you've got me glaring at poor Gracie, and she didn't even do anything."

"Not only that, she is your salvation right now," he noted.

Rebecca heard the smile in Delta's tone. "We'll definitely go for coffee when I get out of this."

"Absolutely. I was looking forward to meeting you already."

"Yeah, I wondered when you called more than a few times."

"Oh? And what about you, who answered more than a few times?"

She flushed, feeling the color wash up her cheeks. "Well, there is that too," she muttered. "And all that phone tag."

"So, we're both interested in having coffee," he stated. "We will happily take that from this moment in time."

"I guess," she groaned. "I need something to take my mind off what just happened."

"I would like to take your mind off the whole mess," he stated. "Absolutely nothing is good about focusing on it. They kidnapped you and Gracie and Benjamin. I don't know what else they are involved in at that company of yours, but we have theories, and my team is looking into things. Just remember. You escaped. You're terrified, yet here you are. They dumped you out in the middle of nowhere, and you took their car, and they tried to ambush you. That's all there is to it."

"You make it sound so easy to explain," she noted, "but it isn't."

"Nothing in life is easy, but, in this case, it's pretty clear-cut."

She took several deep breaths.

"Good, now take a couple more."

"You can even hear me breathing?"

"Of course," he declared. "I can't hear it clearly, but I can certainly hear that you're trying to grab on to your shaky nerves, and I am definitely in favor of you doing that."

She smiled. "Are you always this nice?"

"Yes, I'm always this nice—well, nearly always. But, if you tell anybody, I'll deny it."

She smiled at that. "You're definitely being nice right now."

"Hey, I am trying to ensure you get out of this situation, safe and sound."

"Me too," she muttered. "I just … I still can't believe what a nightmare this has been."

"Did you ever get any confirmation as to what it's all about?"

"Something to do with a merger, or a buyout, something to do with us causing trouble, and they couldn't afford to take the chance on us screwing up the sale."

"Right. There was talk of a merger or buyout that I heard about myself," he muttered. "It's just such a pretty extreme response though. I can't quite wrap my head around it. It's gotta be about so much more."

"Yeah, ya think?" she muttered. "It's not as if anybody would care that I have a channel and talk about taking care of your dog."

"Well, that's what you think," he pointed out, with a knowing tone. "Obviously somebody cares, and in a big way."

"Right, I get that. I still think it sucks though. Oh, shit, I see more lights up ahead."

"Good, just keep driving. I don't want you to stop."

"What if it's the sheriff or something?"

"I don't care," he stated, his tone harsh and filled with warning.

She winced. "You can't really think they're involved, do you?"

"I don't know if anybody is involved, but, so far, the reaction I've gotten from around here—locals and deputies alike—doesn't give me any confidence."

"Right, okay. That's … That's not very clear, but I'll listen to you for the moment."

"Good. Remember. You're safe right now. I want you to keep driving, until you can find some signs that tell us where you are."

"You're not getting very far in tracking me, are you?"

"No, I'm not," he admitted. "I don't know if the sensors have been damaged or something else, or if it's just the fact that we don't have sophisticated-enough software on this yet. It's not what the device is intended for, so we're having difficulty. And we have to be careful so we don't screw up what connectivity that we have."

"Right. So, you have somebody hacking into Gracie's system? That's freaky, to put it mildly. You better not hurt her."

"We have no intention of hurting Gracie," he told her in a soothing tone. "Making sure she was okay is the whole reason I came up here. Remember?"

"Right. You gave me such anxiety because I was worried that you would take her away from me."

"I have no intention of taking her way from you. I'm just here to ensure that she's safe with you, that's all."

"Well, what do you think now?" she asked, with a half a laugh wondering if he truly had the power to make that decision and unable to let go of the niggling fear that someone above him could override his decision. "She would probably be just fine, as long as I am not being kidnapped and chased."

"Being chased is a concern, but more of a concern for you than for her. I don't know why these people are after you, but obviously Gracie is happy being right there with you."

"She is, and I would be absolutely lost without her." At that, Gracie whined beside her. "See? She can hear me."

"Of course she can hear you."

Rebecca laughed. "Hey, Gracie. Are you doing okay, girl?" Gracie turned to Rebecca, who smiled and shared with Delta, "Gracie is looking at me, with a very confused expression."

"Well, yeah, since technically I'm talking out of her body."

"Oh my gosh." Rebecca started to laugh. "Don't say that." Rebecca gasped for breath, but her laughter kept bubbling up. "That's terrible."

"It's not precisely true. She has the implant in her leg, so technically …"

"No, no, no, no. We're not going there either," she said, still giggling, "but I want that thing out of her."

"As soon as she's safe and sound, and this is over, it would probably be a good idea. Still, we'll need to take a closer look at her and confirm it's safe to remove."

Rebecca sucked in her breath at that. "Oh my God, I didn't even consider that."

"We need to consider everything because we don't know exactly what they're up to. Obviously you saw something that made them nervous."

"And yet I'm not even sure what I possibly could have seen. Obviously I wasn't happy with what I did see, as to the treatment of the animals, but I couldn't really figure out what the medical team was supposedly doing. Did I tell you how they banned me from the medical suite?"

"I think I remember that. So tell me about how they treated the animals."

"It just that the animals weren't … It seemed the animals weren't being treated as they should have been. It's as if they were doing experiments on them, and I saw more case numbers versus names. I thought they weren't being treated the way the contract specified they should be. Part of the reason I was really gung-ho on the contract for these animals was the fact that they would be helping them, … not hindering, and certainly not hurting them."

"Of course," he agreed. "I'm glad to know your heart's in the right place."

"I just don't understand how people can hurt animals." She groaned as she drove. "I also have no idea how far I've got to go before I see some landmark or road sign."

"It doesn't matter," Delta said. "I'm here with you. I'm not leaving, and we'll get you to safety. I just need a better idea of where you are. Then, as soon as we have some general direction, I can head some vehicles out to you."

"What about you?" she asked.

"Oh, I'm coming too," he declared. "Wouldn't miss it for the world."

After another few minutes of driving, she had a sudden realization. "I might have an idea where I am," she exclaimed suddenly.

"Great, let's hear it."

"Well, when you head out of town, a series of switch-backs lead up to a hiking road. It's on the north end of town," she explained, looking around at the landscape. "I think I recognize these switchbacks."

"Well, keep driving and be careful," he warned her, his tone sharpening. "I know you're tired, stressed, and in shock, but the last thing we want is an accident right now."

"Yeah, you and me both," she muttered, as she navigated past one set of sharp corners and then through to the next. "I'm pretty sure that's where I am."

"Good," he replied. "Keep driving."

She groaned. "Does that mean you're coming out now?"

"Sweetheart, I'm already on the road," he said, a hint of smile in his tone. "I have been for a while. We had a general idea of where you were, but we couldn't be sure. So right now, I'm heading in your direction. Therefore, if you see headlights coming toward you, don't panic. I'll flash them at you several times, and you'll know it's me."

"Okay," she muttered, still feeling the panic inside.

"Take a deep breath. We're almost there."

"*Sure*, but that doesn't mean those assholes aren't coming up behind me."

"If they are, then they'll have a whole lot more to deal with now, won't they?" he asked, his tone grim. "I'm not somebody they can just put down like a dog."

She winced as she looked over at Gracie. "I'm really hoping she's not been hit, but I haven't had a chance to see."

"Is she awake and conscious, maybe talking to you?"

"Not so much talking to me," she murmured, as she glanced at the dog, "but she's gone quiet."

"We'll check her over and get her right to the vet hospital," he stated. "We'll do everything we can for her. You know that, right?"

"Thank you," she whispered. "You don't even really know me, but you have become a big part of my world in a very short period of time."

"And that's fine too." He chuckled. "I kind of always wanted to be Sir Galahad."

She snorted at that. "Somehow I doubt it's all it's cracked up to be."

"Nothing ever is," he agreed cheerfully. "Still, the good news is that we're getting to you now, so let's keep our eye on what's most important."

"Please just tell me that I can get out of this nightmare fast. I want nothing more than to go home to a long hot shower and a good night's sleep."

"Any chance for a bath while you were being held?"

"Kind of." She cringed inwardly. "Most of the time I was kept in a bedroom with an en suite, so at least there was a bathroom. I had a mattress on the floor with just a blanket," she muttered. "Okay, I'm definitely at the hairpins."

"Good, so we're about ten minutes apart."

"Seriously?" she asked, straightening in her seat. She heard Gracie beside her and looked over and smiled because the dog was looking at her, although there appeared to be more pain in her eyes than anything. "I think Gracie's hurt," she said suddenly.

"With bullets flying around, I wouldn't be at all surprised," he stated calmly. "Remember. We're meeting up soon now. We'll take care of her."

"But what if we can't?" she asked. "What if she's too injured?"

"We won't know that until we get you both safe and assess her."

His tone was steady and true once again. She groaned. "God, you're so damn calm. How the hell are you so damn calm?"

"I'm calm because I need to be," he explained. "As soon as we have a better answer for you, we'll have a better idea of what we can do for Gracie."

"Right," she muttered. "I just feel … I guess I don't even know how I feel."

"That's because you're still in shock," he said gently. "Remember? We're coming up close now."

"Another hairpin is ahead of me," she told him, "and then there should be a big stretch, flat and straight, right through here."

"You hike a lot?"

"Not enough," she replied. "Certainly not enough. It's beautiful out here, and it's a place that Gracie and I have really enjoyed, just to get away for a bit."

"Was there ever any resistance from the company to your keeping Gracie?"

"Nobody said anything outright, but nobody was giving me approval of it either."

"Of course not," he quipped. "They don't have anything on paper saying they have the legal right to keep her, plus she went missing, so that puts us into a whole different ball game."

"Good." Suddenly she saw a vehicle up ahead, with its lights flashing immediately. "Is that you?"

"Yes, it's me."

Immediately she hit the brakes, pulled off on the side of the road, and shut off the engine. Bolting out of the vehicle, she raced toward him.

DELTA HEARD REBECCA'S feet on the gravel, and, at the last second, she appeared out of nowhere in the darkness, launching herself into his arms. He braced himself, hoping his ankle would hold, and didn't give it another thought as she crashed into him. He fell back against the car but held her tight.

"It's okay," he whispered gently, as he held the sobbing woman in his arms. "You did great." She just shook her head and clung to him. Finally he managed to calm her down. "Now let's check on Gracie." Together they walked over to Gracie, still in the front seat of the car. He went around to the side, closer to Gracie, and frowned.

Rebecca asked, "Oh my God, she's hurt, isn't she?"

"She's definitely hurt, the question is how bad," he muttered, as he opened up the door and talked to her.

Gracie thumped her partial tail at him.

He searched her gently. "She's got … glass everywhere," he said, using a light touch, so he didn't set her off. "I'm seeing what may be a bullet wound on her leg."

"Did it go through her leg?"

"It could have gone through any number of places," he noted, still looking over Gracie. "Bullets will bounce and careen off things too. It doesn't look to be too bad, but we better get her to a hospital right away."

"Yes. Absolutely. Let's get going and get her to a vet," she cried out, hovering at his side.

He looked around and suggested, "Let's put her in my car. By the way, this one was stolen and so was the truck used to kidnap you, just so you know."

And moving gently, he picked up Gracie and maneuvered her out of the passenger side, careful to keep the prosthetic in place. She whimpered several times but didn't fight him. "It's okay, girl," he whispered. "I know. It's been a tough day, hasn't it?"

She whimpered again, and he smiled, once again appreciating the beauty of these K9 dogs, the things made possible by their training, and Gracie's patient understanding that they would do everything they could for her.

"It's all right, girl. I promise we'll get you some help right away." He tucked her into the passenger side of his back seat and then helped Rebecca in beside her. "Now, let's get you both some care and attention."

"I don't care about me," Rebecca said immediately.

"I know. I hear you," he replied, "but you both need looking after. You need to be checked for any serious injuries yourself. And don't try to pick any glass out of your hair. When we get there, we'll try to deal with it without making it worse."

She reached up, felt the glass in her hair, and winced.

"Don't touch it," he repeated, gently touching her hand. "Not right now. We'll have to comb it out carefully to ensure you don't spread it everywhere. Otherwise it'll end up getting down to the skin."

"Right." She sighed, as she sagged against the seat of his car. "God, what a nightmare."

"Yes, but you should be really proud of yourself," he declared, with a smile in her direction. "You and Gracie have escaped, and you're alive, and you're relatively uninjured. That counts for a lot."

"Or"—she looked over at him—"it'll piss off the kidnappers all the more, and they'll be coming back after me, extra hard."

"And that is also a possibility," he admitted, nodding in understanding. "I won't lie to you. What you did was risky, but it's your life, and they had absolutely no business trying to keep you locked up."

"No, but I don't really think they give a shit."

He tossed her a smile, loving the valiant courage still showing through the obvious exhaustion she felt. "That's very true, and we'll do everything we can to put a stop to it," he muttered.

"It's not even your fight," she stated, looking at him.

"You came here because of Gracie." She shifted so she could look back at the dog. "Oh my God, I hope she's okay." Gracie gave a reassuring thump of her partial tail, and Rebecca smiled. "This dog has been so willing to do everything I've asked of her."

"Why did you apply to keep her?"

"I wanted her, like absolutely wanted her, right from the first moment she arrived, but the powers that be were against it. She would supposedly be a therapy dog, and, while I loved the idea, I didn't see why she couldn't be a therapy dog with a family of her own. I thought it was important for her to have a chance to know that she was loved too."

Delta smiled at her. "It is absolutely imperative that she knows that she's loved too," he agreed. "What kind of reaction did you get from them?"

"They stonewalled. Basically they just wouldn't give me an answer. It was as if they just halfway smiled but were patronizing. … *Of course you want to keep the dog. Everybody here wants to keep the dogs. That's the kind of place it is.* I didn't really understand that attitude because, sure, other people have dogs, but I don't know that any of them are War Dogs."

"Which could be a big difference."

"Right. The people at work are supposed to be healing the dogs that come through there."

He looked over at her as he drove. "Take some deep breaths."

She smiled and nodded, then complied. "I really am doing better. I just want to confirm Gracie is okay."

"I'm pretty sure she'll be fine. She'll need a little bit of love and care, but I'm sure we can give her that."

"Absolutely." Then Rebecca groaned and shook her

head. "I'm a wreck." She lifted her hand, and it still shook badly.

He nodded. "Just sit back, relax, let me do the driving, and we'll be at the hospital soon enough."

"I'm not going to a hospital," she declared, turning to frown at him. "No way, absolutely no way."

"Fine," he said. "I won't force you."

"Good, because it wouldn't work."

He smiled at her stubbornness, but he would have been the same way, so it made sense to him. "We're taking Gracie to a vet first because she definitely needs a doctor. So then find one for me."

"I don't have to. She's … We've got one that we work with all the time."

He hesitated, then asked, "Don't suppose you know of one you *don't* work with all the time, do you?"

She looked over at him, and awareness quickly fell into her gaze. "Oh, shit. I didn't even consider that."

"I don't want you to overthink it right now, but it would be nice if we had a place to go where we didn't have to worry about your safety … or Gracie's."

"Shit," she muttered again, then thought for a moment. "I don't have a phone." He tossed her his, and, looking at the screen, she said, "I need the PIN to unlock it."

When he quickly gave her the PIN, she looked over at him. "I could be a serial killer or something, and now I have access to your phone."

He chuckled. "You do, but you would have a hard time doing anything with that phone anyway. It's more of a burner phone for this op."

She shrugged. "I just want to find a place to take Gracie." It took her a few minutes to search, then she shared,

"Okay, there's one on the other side of town." She glanced back at Gracie, who was lying still, not moving. "Shit, I wish it was closer."

"Is there a faster route to get there?" he asked quietly, checking Gracie in the back as well. "She's holding."

"Yeah, holding, but she's not doing good."

He didn't say anything to that because honestly, Gracie didn't look like she was doing well at all. She was definitely out of sorts.

"I can get us there faster," she muttered nervously, "but I don't know that it will be any better for her."

"We just need somebody, … somebody we trust who can look after her."

"Oh, I have a friend who's a vet," she said, looking at him. "Jeez, my brain's not working yet."

"Well, make the call."

"But Robin won't know this number."

"It doesn't matter. Hopefully she'll answer anyway. Does she have an office?"

"Yeah, she does. She does." Rebecca dialed the number, grateful when Robin picked up. "Hey, it's me."

"Where the hell are you?" Robin cried out. "I'm hearing some really strange rumors."

"The rumors are probably lies, and I'll certainly fill you in at some point, but right now I need your vet skills really badly."

"What's up?" Robin asked in confusion. Rebecca quickly explained about the shooting. "Shooting? The dog's hurt?" Robin muttered. "What the hell are you doing in a shootout?"

"I was kidnapped, and so was Gracie. Remember how I told you about her going missing?"

"Sure, and you asked me to keep an eye out in case any-body brought in a dog like her."

"Exactly."

"Well, nobody brought a dog in like her."

"But then I was kidnapped and they kind of took me to her."

"Are you kidding me?" Robin cried out. "You know this all sounds a little bit strange. Are you sure you're okay?"

Sensing that her friend didn't believe her, Rebecca glanced helplessly over at Delta, who reached out a hand. She handed the phone over.

"Robin, this is Delta Granger. I was sent here from the War Department, checking the status of Gracie, a Malinois retired from the military K9 program, otherwise known as a War Dog. I can provide my ID when we arrive. It's true Gracie had been taken and that Rebecca was subsequently kidnapped. She's just come through quite a fight. After being dumped in the forest, she was able to steal a vehicle and run away. She drove through an ambush, was shot at, and the dog picked up some ricochet bullets. I don't know how badly, but Gracie is lying injured in the back seat. Will you help us or not?" He spouted it out with such an officious and snappy tone, he hoped that the other woman would jump in to pitch in and help.

"So this isn't a joke or some sort of prank?" Robin demanded.

"No, it's no joke," he snapped. "Yes or no? Otherwise we've got to find somebody else who can help. Why the hell would you refuse to help a woman who's supposedly your friend when she's now in desperate straits, and you have the skills she needs to help this dog?"

"I didn't say I wouldn't help, but you don't understand

the rumors we're hearing."

"Yes or no? Otherwise, we'll find another vet, and believe me. I'll be looking at why the hell you're a vet in the first place if you won't help when you're needed the most."

"Hey, hey, hey, calm down."

"No, I'm not calming down," he snapped once more. "For all I know, Rebecca is injured too, and she's refusing to go to the hospital and to get checked out herself, until Gracie is tended to."

"Oh, now I know you're telling the truth. That is so Rebecca."

"So, is that a yes?"

"Yes, I'll meet you at the clinic," Robin snapped right back at him and quickly hung up.

He looked over at Rebecca. "Is she always like that?"

"Yeah, Robin's kind of a cranky type." She laughed. "However, she's absolutely wonderful with animals."

"She would have to be because she doesn't seem to have any people skills." With that decided, Delta said, "Now, give me directions on how to get to her office." Rebecca did, but she was fading. He looked over at her and shook his head. "Don't you dare collapse on me."

She glared at him. "I wouldn't do that."

"No, maybe not now, but I don't want you dropping on me the minute we get there and get Gracie seen to," he said. "And I do want you to go to the hospital and get checked out."

"Well, that's not happening," she muttered.

But her tone was weakening, and he knew that she would fade very quickly. So he had to be ready before that happened. Swearing at this supposed friend who was great with animals, he followed Rebecca's directions until he parked in front of a small clinic.

Robin stood impatiently outside, arms crossed over her chest, glaring at the world.

He hopped out and said, "Wow. Nice to meet you too."

She shot him a look and then raced around to see Rebecca. "Hey, are you okay?"

"Now that I'm no longer a prisoner stuck in some godforsaken bedroom," she replied, as she slowly got out, "yes. I'm sore. I'm tired, and I really need a shower and some sleep."

Robin took one look, gave a painful squawk, and wrapped her up in a hug, barely even considering the glass on her. "I'm so sorry," she whispered, almost in a panic. "I'm sorry I didn't believe you. You look like shit."

At that, Delta snorted. "Yeah, that's a friend for you." Robin turned and glared at him, and he held up a hand. "I don't give a crap," he muttered. "But I do care about making sure Rebecca's okay. Once Gracie is looked after, I can get this one somewhere safe, before she keels over."

"Where will that be?" Robin asked, as she unlocked the clinic door, obviously not trusting him.

"I don't know yet," Delta responded, "and I'm not sure I would tell you anyway."

She stopped and turned to look at him in horror. "You can't think I'm a part of this."

"I don't know whether you're a part of this or you just don't have people skills," he admitted, as he headed to the back of the vehicle and gently picked up Gracie to bring her out and around to the front of the center. "But you sure as heck weren't a help when I needed you to immediately pitch in and do something. Now here you are all lovey-dovey with Rebecca, and I'm very suspicious."

Robin glared at him and snapped, "Look. You don't know me, and I don't know you."

"Yeah, and that's the way we'll keep it too," he stated, as he walked in and turned to look back at her, his gaze going to Rebecca. "Rebecca? Come on. Just a couple more steps, honey. We'll get you taken care of after this."

Rebecca gave him a wan smile. "I'm coming. I'm coming."

"Honey?" Robin asked in an odd tone.

Rebecca looked over at her friend and smiled. "Don't worry about it."

"Yeah, well, if he's taking advantage of you when you're at your weakest, he'll be on my shit list too."

"I thought I already was," he quipped, glaring at her. "Could we just get to the point?"

Robin led the way to the back. "Put Gracie down here."

He gently laid Gracie down on the gurney, and the vet stepped up to look at her. Gracie wagged her partial tail at her.

"Hello, sweetheart," Robin said, her voice dropping in tone. "You've had a rough couple days, haven't you?"

Not sure that he could trust Robin even now, Delta stayed close to ensure no harm would come to Gracie.

At one point in time, Robin looked over at him in exasperation. "This is my clinic. This is where I work and what I do," she snapped, "so just give me some space." He shrugged, but he didn't move. She glanced over at Rebecca. "Can you call off your watchdog so I can work?" she snapped at her friend.

At that, Rebecca half smiled and nodded. "She'll look after Gracie," she murmured to Delta. "It's all right."

"It's not all right," he argued, "not until I see how she

treats her."

"You think I'll hurt her?" Robin asked in astonishment.

He shrugged. "After what this dog's been through, I don't trust anybody."

"Good enough," Robin muttered. "I don't either."

"Yeah, that's obvious."

"Could you two just stop," Rebecca wailed in an exhausted voice. "I really don't have the energy to sit here and referee a fight between the two of you."

Immediately Delta felt bad. He walked to her, wrapped an arm around her, and tucked her up close, trying to be mindful of the glass all over her. "I'm sorry," he muttered. "I'm just worried about you."

She smiled and nodded. "I know." She looked back over at Robin. "How bad is it?"

"Gracie is exhausted. She's got this bullet wound, but it looks more like a deep scrape across her back, more like a burn versus an actual penetration," she muttered, as she quickly worked on Gracie.

Gracie whimpered a couple times, as she was poked and prodded and glass removed from her coat. "I know, sweetheart. I'm so sorry this happened to you." She looked over at Delta and asked, "Did you catch the asshole who did this?"

"Not yet."

Then Rebecca looked at Robin and whispered, "I think I ran over one of them, killing him," and she burst into tears.

The vet came running over and wrapped up Rebecca in a hug. "Oh my God, oh my God," Robin said, "I'm so sorry, sweetheart."

While the two women held each other close, Delta walked closer to Gracie to check out her wounds himself. "Hey, baby, how're you doing?" he whispered. "It's been a hell of a run so far, hasn't it, girl?"

He checked her over himself, and, when he straightened up with a clipped nod, he looked over to see the vet glaring at him. He shrugged. "Hey, you left her. I came to check on her."

"What's your prognosis, *Doctor*?" Robin sneered at him.

"She's got a bad laceration, but, with antibiotics to stop the infection, she should heal just fine."

Robin looked at him in surprise and then gave him a slow nod. "Yes. That's exactly right." She looked back at her friend. "Do you want me to keep her here?"

"No, I really want to keep her with us."

"Gracie stays with us," Delta declared, brooking no arguments. Robin narrowed her gaze at him. He just shrugged. "This is a missing War Dog, and that is my responsibility. The fact is, she was instrumental in helping rescue Rebecca, so I need the two of them to stay together."

"That's a different story, and I kind of get it," Robin replied, followed by a huff, "but the lack of faith and trust in me is really irritating."

"It's not because you give a great first impression." Just as she went to open her mouth and snap at him again, he held up his hand. "My apologies, Rebecca. I did say I would try."

Rebecca sighed. "Honest to God, you know what it is? You two are so damn much alike that, when confronted with each other, you can't stand yourselves. Welcome to my world."

They both stared at her, enough that he watched a smile crack her face. "Good," he said in satisfaction. "Now, maybe we can get this finished off, give Gracie some antibiotics, dress that wound a little bit, and get you someplace safe."

"Where will that be?" Robin asked, suspicion still in her tone.

He shrugged. "I don't know yet, and I wouldn't tell you anyway." She stopped and glared at him. "In this case, it's not a lack of trust as much as it would be to your benefit."

"Why?" Robin asked.

"Because Rebecca's the second person who was kidnapped," he shared, "and, unless you're really looking to be part of a fight that isn't yours, anything you don't know will be better for you."

Robin frowned, as she continued to work on Gracie. Finally she drew up an antibiotic shot and administered it to Gracie. Then she walked over with pills that she'd put in a small pill bottle and handed it to him. "Two a day for five days."

He nodded. "It's good to go open like that? Wouldn't—"

"It's better off open," Robin cut him off. "The wound is now clean. With any luck she should heal up pretty quickly. She has a few glass cuts, but those will be fine in no time." She turned to Rebecca. "Do you want to come to my place?"

She shook her head then stopped remembering the glass. "No. Honestly, I don't want you to get involved, any more than you already are."

"I'm not involved at all," Robin noted in exasperation.

"No, but you're helping us, so anybody who's pissed off could take that as a wrong sign."

"Well, they're likely to get the same reception as you got," she stated, as she glared at Delta sideways. "I don't like being manipulated."

Rebecca chuckled. "No, you sure don't, but I also don't want you hurt." She looked at Gracie and asked, "You ready to go, girl?" The dog perked up.

With that done, Delta walked over and carefully lifted the dog off the table and helped her down. "Let's keep her movements to a minimum," he whispered gently. He walked back out toward the front with both Robin and Rebecca in tow, Gracie following them.

He looked back at Robin and stated, "And, by the way, you didn't see us." She looked at him in confusion and then frowned. He nodded. "We may have gotten off the wrong foot, but, for your own safety, you did not see us."

"It can't be that bad," she said.

"How do you figure that?" Delta asked.

"The stories we've been hearing …" Then she stopped, as if not sure how to say it.

Delta nodded. "Yeah, the *stories* you've been hearing. Remember that. I don't know what they are, but I bet they are probably all kinds of crazy and make no sense. Your friend wouldn't do that, would she?"

"She wouldn't. She wouldn't go off half-cocked."

"Who do you think is putting out those rumors?" he asked. "I'm just trying to keep her safe."

"Yeah, well, as long as you don't try anything else with it."

He stared at her, shaking his head. "That's not an issue." But he didn't elaborate. It had made him mad to think that anybody would say such a thing, but considering this prickly pear woman and the relationship she already had with Rebecca, it didn't seem wise to antagonize Robin any further.

He walked out to the vehicle, opened up the backseat door, helped Gracie inside, then went back to Rebecca, who was hugging her friend as she said goodbye.

He waited for a moment, then said, "Come on. Let's

go."

Rebecca nodded and slowly stepped back away from her friend. "Now you stay safe," she whispered.

"I'm fine," Robin muttered. "You, on the other hand …"

"I'm fine too, or I will be. First, I need some sleep and a chance to regroup and to figure out what my next options are."

"What options?" Robin asked, throwing her arms out wide. "I don't understand any of this."

"No, and that's also why I'm trying not to tell you too much because then you can't know anything. If you deny we were ever here, then nobody will find any value in trying to torture it out of you."

Robin paled at the thought and shook her head. "Yeah, that's not cool. It's that bad, *huh?*"

"It's not cool, and it's also not a scare tactic," Delta reminded her. "Keep it close to heart because it is that bad. Your friend and this War Dog were both kidnapped, and now I'm trying to keep them safe."

And, with that, he helped Rebecca into the front seat and walked around to the driver's side. Feeling the urge to leave that he hadn't had before, he quickly fired up the vehicle and, without any other excuse, pulled away at top speed.

Rebecca looked over at him. "Is there a reason for the rush?"

"I don't know." He shook his head, uneasy at the feeling in his gut. "But I want to say yes, and I really don't know why. I don't know anything in particular. … I just feel that it's definitely past time to go."

"I won't argue with that," Rebecca added, as she settled

into the front seat.

"And your friend?"

"I don't know." Rebecca waved her hand. "Robin's always cranky and miserable, but I love her anyway. Her heart's in the right place, and it's always centered around animals."

"I don't have a problem with that," he muttered, "but if she'll contact anybody as soon as we leave …"

Rebecca nodded. "I'm a little afraid she might have done so before we even arrived."

"I wouldn't be surprised at that either," he muttered. "So, that's another reason to get moving fast."

"Get moving, yes," she agreed, "but, from the sounds of it, you are already panicked about it."

"Not *panicked*," he clarified, rolling his eyes at her. "My instincts are telling me to go—and to go now. I can't shake that feeling."

And, with that, he peeled off down the highway.

CHAPTER 9

REBECCA WAS SO tired, tired of fighting, tired of keeping the pace, just plain tired.

"Go to sleep," Delta muttered beside her.

She gave a strangled laugh. "How did you know I was two steps away from crashing?"

"I can see it," he said, with a gentle smile. "You don't have any reason to worry. Let's just get you some sleep, while I try to figure out where I'm taking you."

"Yeah, it would help if we had somebody on our side. You did contact law enforcement, didn't you?"

"I did," he admitted, with a hard tone slithering into his words. "The jury is still out on that one."

"Yeah. I was afraid you would say something like that." She yawned. "Can we just grab a room somewhere? Maybe downtown, so I can get some sleep, and Gracie can relax a bit?"

"That's the plan," he replied, checking the rearview mirror, "but I would like to find one that doesn't have people spying on us."

"One is farther down the road," she said, pointing in that direction. "Just as you come into town. He doesn't get a ton of business because, once you're in town, you always find something in town instead of farther out. We would be a little more anonymous there."

"Only if nobody feels like turning us in."

"Considering what we've already been through," she noted, "I agree that we can't take any more chances."

He nodded and smiled. "I'm glad to hear that," he said, with a chuckle.

"You really do like getting your own way, don't you?" she asked, with a knowing glance in his direction.

"In something like this? Yes," he declared, "and I don't make any excuses for it either. I have too much life experience telling me when things are about to go sideways, and I'm not willing to sit around and wait for that to happen. You've got a whole community siding with the company that had you kidnapped and wanted to kill you. This has to be something bigger than just some sale going on. Don't worry. We've got several people on that."

"Glad to hear it. Oh, there. Take that next turnoff," she pointed out.

He quickly swerved into a better position for the upcoming turn, also testing to see if anyone was following them, and soon they were parked in front of the motel. "Let me go in and take a look." He hopped out, walked into the reception area, and quickly booked a room with two beds. He had to pay extra for Gracie and figured that was money well spent. As soon as he got back into the vehicle, he said, "We're all set for the night."

Driving around to the back, Delta helped Rebecca out of the car, then scooped up Gracie, and they all moved upstairs to the room.

"Is there a reason why we're coming in through the back?" she asked with concern.

"Yeah, so my vehicle isn't so easily seen from the front."

"Right. We could go get my vehicle."

"No, not likely. The sheriff or the company bad guys are all over that one right now."

She nodded. "I guess that makes sense."

"I don't know whether it does or not," he admitted, with half a smile in her direction. "Not a whole lot about this town makes sense."

"I wasn't even thinking that until you brought it up," she noted bitterly, "but you're right. There's definitely some prejudice about the company."

"For the company or against it?"

"Oh, there are two factions. … Those who are with it and those who are against it," she declared forcefully. "They bring in jobs and money to the town, so you can bet the government officials and those kinds of entities are on their side. Still, some of the locals are less thrilled. The company kind of ran roughshod over everything and had plans all their own that don't necessarily get any vetting from anybody else, and so the company basically does what they want."

"Of course." Delta nodded in understanding. "So, in a place like this, with so many dependent on the company's salaries, the government is with them, and there's nobody to really go against them. At least no organized faction that could get anything done."

"Right, and that's always been the problem," she admitted sadly. "I was part of the problem too and hadn't even realized myself just how quickly things turn, when you can't buck the system."

"Sorry," he muttered, as he looked over at her. "You've had a few shocks lately, haven't you?"

"Yep, but I'm not a child," she said, "and I can see where there's been some problems that definitely need to be sorted."

"You can sort them … just not today," he noted, with a grin in her direction.

"You're quite right there," she muttered, as he unlocked the door and let them inside.

She walked over to the closest bed, and he suggested, "Before you lie down and crash, do you want a shower? Do you want some food? What do you want? I can see you're already about to dive under."

She groaned. "I would absolutely love a shower, but I don't think I have the energy for it."

He hesitated and then added, "Look. I can help you get the glass out of your hair, if you like. I really think you would sleep better."

She groaned. "You're about to make me get a shower, aren't you?"

"No, I'm not apt to make you do anything," he countered, giving her a searching look. "I just know how it is and that you would be better off in the end."

She sighed. "Okay, fine, shower it is. But we do need to get food … and dog food too. Gracie hasn't eaten either."

"I'll order in something that's got a protein base, so she can have it too."

"Oh, I'm sure she would love that," Rebecca said, with a smile. "Really a bad habit to start though."

"Not too worried about bad habits right now," he stated. She straightened and with obvious effort, made herself head for the bathroom, as he called behind her, "Don't lock the door." She stopped, startled, and looked at him. "I don't want you collapsing in there with the door locked, so I can't get in to help you."

She flushed. "I won't need your help," she replied stiffly.

"You might not. I'm not saying I'll come in there, but if you do have a problem …" He took a moment, as if searching for the words. "Look. You wouldn't let me take you to the hospital to get checked over, so please don't lock the door. If you do, and something happened, then I would have to break in the door, and I would rather not do that."

She shot him a look and headed into the bathroom, but, as requested, she didn't lock it, and that was a good thing.

He waited, listening to confirm she turned on the water and got in. The danger point would be when she was standing underneath the water, and, if she sat down, well, it was all over with. Only moments later he heard a crash, and he bolted, Gracie at his heels, into the bathroom.

He called out, "Are you okay?" When no answer came, he opened the door and stepped in. She was lying in the bathtub, with the water crashing down over her. He reached out a hand and shook her, but she was out cold. "Dammit," he muttered.

Shutting off the water, he quickly wrapped a towel around her and picked her up. She moaned as he did so, and then he saw the blood streaming from underneath her. He carried her out to the bedroom, where he grabbed a blanket and wrapped it around her to try and keep her warm, as he checked out the wound. Thankfully it was minor, but the hot water must have started the bleeding. There were also several small glass cuts.

He stared down at her wounds, wondering at the logic of not taking her to the hospital. But he didn't want anybody to know where she was, and this wasn't a major injury, although it could become major if it became infected. He quickly cleaned the wound, but he had no first aid medical supplies here.

He grabbed his phone and called Badger. "Hey, does anybody around this town deliver first aid, where we could get medical supplies without letting the cavalry know where we are? Rebecca passed out in the shower, and she's got a bullet burn and some smaller cuts and bruising from the broken glass. I'm cleaning her up, but she's out cold. I don't want to leave her or Gracie, yet I don't want anybody to know where we are."

"Hang on," Badger said. Delta heard rustling and then keys clicking. "I'll get back to you in a minute." When Badger called back a few minutes later, Delta had Rebecca completely bundled up. "A package will be at your door in a few minutes."

"I didn't even give you the motel name and room number," Delta noted.

Badger laughed. "Don't need it." And, with that, he rang off.

Sure enough, a few minutes later came a tiny rap on the door, and, when Delta went to open it, nobody was there but a package wrapped in a paper bag. He quickly brought it in and opened it up. He bandaged up Rebecca as best he could, realizing it really wasn't as bad as it first appeared, and a good night's sleep would go a long way to making her more comfortable.

He should have asked for more than just first aid. He could use some food too. But, hey, that was life. When another knock came a few minutes later, he got up and checked through the window, and all he saw was somebody walking away again. He waited and watched until the vehicle drove off, and then Delta opened the door and grinned. "I don't know if you're listening in, Badger, because of course that is a possibility, but, yeah, the food is definitely welcome, so thanks."

He picked it up and took it inside. He found burgers, fries, and to-go sandwiches, plus milk and coffee. This motel room had no microwave, coffeepot, or teakettle, so he figured he might as well drink the coffee while it was hot.

He ate some of the burgers and fries himself, digging the hamburger meat out of two more, which he gave to Gracie. Then he ate a sandwich, while he waited for Rebecca to wake up. He figured she would probably have a long sleep at this point.

But when she rolled over not much later and groaned, he got up and walked to her bedside and said, "Hey, I'm right here. It's me, Delta. You're not alone, and you're no longer a captive."

Her eyes opened, then fluttered ever-so-slightly, and closed again. "Am I safe?"

"You're safe," he whispered. "You can go back to sleep, or you can eat some food and then go back to sleep."

Her eyes opened again. "You left me alone to get food?"

He chuckled. "Nope, I sure didn't, but we did get a delivery. No need for alarm but you need to move carefully because you do have some wounds on your side, and there's still glass in your hair. I did get some of it out but not all of it."

She frowned, then looked around and asked, "What happened?"

"You collapsed in the shower," he replied, with a wry look. "So, thank you for not locking the door."

She groaned. "I just wanted to sleep, but the shower sounded good too and …"

"You didn't want to be stubborn."

"Actually I did, but being stubborn doesn't always go my

way."

"Not this time either," he noted. "You crashed, and I had to go in, collect you, clean up all your wounds, and let you sleep."

She just stared at him. "Where did you get the first aid stuff?" she asked, as she patted her side, trying to locate the wound.

"I got a delivery."

"I thought we were trying *not* to let anybody know where we are.'

"We are, but the first aid supplies and the food were delivered by a secret duo."

She shook her head at that. "I don't know what that even means," she said, "but I don't care. As long as we're safe, none of the rest of it matters."

"Exactly," he agreed, with a smile. "Now, how about some food first, and then you can go back to sleep."

She sat up experimentally, wincing at the pain in her side. "Did I really get shot?"

"It's much like Gracie's wound. It mostly missed you but burned you along the side. Plus, you had some glass cuts on your side that weren't doing you any favors either. That's probably what was hurting as much as the bullet burn, but I got the glass out of it, at least all I could find. Your head was covered with more glass, but I think I combed most of them out."

"So much glass was everywhere," she said. "I remember standing in the shower, trying to get it out of my hair, and that's the last thing I remember."

"I know, and we'll have another go at that later, just to ensure we got all the slivers out of your hair," he suggested, "once you're a little more rested. Your head will probably ache like hell too. There may be some more trouble along the way, but this time they'll have to deal with the two of us."

She sighed, nodded, and muttered, "Fine. Doing it my way didn't get me very far, so we'll do it your way after this."

"Glad to hear it," he teased, with a gentle smile. He asked her to sit up and then handed her a burger.

She looked at it, then quickly unwrapped it and scarfed it down. She was looking at the bag, even as she did so. He smiled and handed her another burger. She beamed and nodded. "I must really need this. I didn't even think I would eat the first one, much less cold fries, but, right from the first bite, there's just something magical about it."

"There absolutely is." Delta smiled. "Eat up."

CHAPTER 10

As SOON AS Rebecca was done eating, she got up and slowly made her way to the bathroom, and, when she returned, she smiled at him. "I can see you're worried, but that went just fine."

"Good," he replied, with a nod. "I do want to make sure you stay safe."

She chuckled. "It's nice to know somebody cares," she muttered. "It seems like a very long time …"

"That bad?"

"In some ways. You don't really think about it until your life changes, and then you realize, yeah, it *was* that bad. But it's all good now. We have progress. I'm safe, and our lovely little girl here is safe." Rebecca smiled, patting Gracie. "That's all that really matters to me."

"Exactly." He too smiled, as he looked down at Gracie.

"The question is, how do I get my life back now?"

Delta hesitated, and her gaze narrowed, as she asked, "What is it that you're not telling me?"

"It's not that I'm *not* telling you anything," he began. "I wouldn't try to keep anything from you. It's too important that you understand just what a mess you're in."

"Oh, I think I understand just fine now, after being kidnapped, left to die, then shot at," she stated simply. "I just don't want it to be any worse than it has to be, you know?

Will anybody even care about my kidnappers? Will they take any actions against the company?"

"That is my concern too," he shared. "I haven't told anybody local that I have you yet."

She nodded. "Why? What is your reason for that?"

"Well, first, I didn't really have the time to inform Deputy Halvorson. Besides that, I don't know whom to trust."

She winced. "I was afraid of that."

"Just think about it." Delta raised a hand. "Think of all the people we have come across so far and how lackadaisical it seems to be for all of them."

"Lackadaisical," she reiterated. "Surely that's not what it is."

He shrugged. "Nobody seems to care. Your friend Robin took a lot of convincing to even believe that you had really been kidnapped and not just what? Off your rocker, off your meds, just *off*? I don't know." He stopped and looked at Rebecca and asked her, "Are you normally on medication?"

"No, I'm not," she said in apprehension. "I think that's because Robin doesn't trust anybody."

"Maybe, but I would have thought if you were friends …"

"Well, that's one of those questions, isn't it? Are we friends? Aren't we friends? How is one to know? I can't answer that."

He nodded. "I'm not trying to make you feel pressured or anything. I understand how distressing this is."

She shot him a look. "So, what do you believe?"

"Honestly, I don't know. I don't have any answers for you. I'm just trying to help you find them."

She groaned. "I'm sorry. … I shouldn't be angry at you."

He chuckled. "Well, if you can't get angry at me, who

can you get angry at?" he asked, with a smirk on his face. "I'm an easy target."

"That's the problem. You are an easy target, … and that's not fair."

"Ah, well, it's nice to know you care."

She smiled. "I didn't even know what you looked like until we met."

"I saw a picture of you on the company website, plus, I watched a few of your YouTube videos."

"Well, good for you, but I had no idea what you looked like. I could have been throwing myself into the arms of a serial killer on a dark country road." She had a laugh at her own expense. "Regardless, I like a good surprise, so there's that at least. Also, now I know …" She hesitated.

"What?" he asked, looking at her curiously.

She shrugged. "You walk with a limp."

"Yes, I sure do," he confirmed. "That prosthetic I mentioned earlier."

He kicked out his leg and pulled up his pant leg, so she could see it. She looked at it and nodded. "That explains it," she said, unabashed. "Sometimes you have more of a limp than at other times."

He rolled his eyes at that. "Yeah." He chuckled. "Sometimes the leg works better than others. There's a problem with this joint. A friend of mine does these prosthetics, and she's working on it. But, so far, we haven't got a solid fix for this one, and so a new prosthetic is in the works."

"There can be so many mechanical issues," she admitted, staring at his leg in fascination.

He shrugged. "It's just a joint, a mechanical joint like anything else."

She nodded. "And, if that's supposed to make me think

I understand better, you're wrong. So tell me how it doesn't work for you?"

He laughed. "The leg is only an issue when it becomes more of a hindrance than anything. It's as if I have a kink in my ankle that could drop me without notice."

Rebecca nodded. "Sorry about that," she replied, with a sad smile. "How did you lose it?"

"I was doing my second tour, just finishing. We were driving into our home base, and we hit an IED," he explained. "I was on the passenger side in the front, when it went up." He took a moment and then added, "It caught my side more than the others, and, for the most part, they all seemed to have fared better than I did. That's how it goes. It just is what it is."

She wondered how he could be as nonchalant as he was or if it was more of an act, a sort of complacency for somebody who'd already been through it all? "It still can't be easy."

"No, it sure isn't easy," he admitted, "not at all. However, having people like Kat, who handles all these mechanical issues for me, is making life a whole lot easier."

"So, she builds them?" she asked curiously, wondering at a woman who specialized in such a thing. "For humans?"

Delta frowned at her wording but ended up laughing. "Yep, she sure does. She and her husband are also missing limbs and have a few other issues," he shared, staring off into the distance. "She is quite resourceful. We work with a whole crew of men in the same boat as I am. She can be a little eccentric, but she's a specialist. She builds and designs individual prosthetics for people like me."

"And that must be hugely important, to have them individually made."

He laughed again. "She's working hard on creating a whole new joint for me, so I have to be nice to her."

"I think you're probably nice to her all the time regardless."

He looked at Rebecca and nodded. "Believe me. Anyone would be nice to her if they ever came face-to-face with her. She is kind of a scary force in her own right."

"You are the same in a way, but maybe a nicer one." She burst out laughing. "And just so you know, I meant that in a good way. It's not an insult. You know that, right?"

"Sure." Yet he shook his head. "Doesn't matter whether I'm a nice guy or not. We need to deal with the issue at hand."

"Sounds good." She searched his face as to where he was going with this. "You got any suggestions?"

"Not yet," he shared, with half a smile, "but while we're still working on solutions for that, how about we make sure all the glass is out of your hair, then you can finish that shower you started. And I'll get you some clothes."

"God, I would love to go home and get some clothes," she noted, with feeling.

He shook his head. "Not sure about going home. They picked you up at your house, so it's not safe right now."

"Okay, so how am I getting clothes?" she asked, staring at him.

"We'll buy them."

"And there's still a chance that we'll run into somebody who knows me."

He nodded. "I think we can get around that problem," he replied. "We can go to the next town over. I would have asked Robin to pick up some clothing for you, but that's not necessarily a good idea, based on how she behaved earlier."

Rebecca shook her head. "You shouldn't judge her for it."

"I'm not judging anybody just yet, but, man, she's one cranky lady. I really don't have it in me to trust her right now."

"You also don't know it, but you might have disturbed her too."

"Doesn't matter. I'm still saying it. That's one cranky gal."

Rebecca burst out laughing at that. "Honestly, you two would love each other if you got a chance to get to know each other under better circumstances."

He shook his head. "Not so sure about that. If we end up with some unwanted persons at our motel room door, then she's the first person I'm gonna blame."

Rebecca's eyes widened.

Delta showed both palms. "Just saying. So, what do you want to do?" he asked. "Try and get back into your place? I can go in there with your keys and grab you some clothes, but that would mean leaving you here alone."

She winced.

"That's what I thought. I can leave Gracie with you," he added, lost in thought for a moment, then he shook his head. "I just don't like the idea of leaving you two alone."

"No, I don't either," she agreed. "So, I'm not sure that we have an answer or a solution to this."

"Well, let's deal with the glass first," he suggested, "and you get some more sleep. Then maybe in the morning, we'll have a better idea."

"Sure. But if nobody will do anything about the kidnappers," Rebecca noted, "I can never go home or back to my job."

"*If* you still have a job," he stated, glancing at her sideways.

She looked at him in astonishment. "Why wouldn't I?"

"Well, because nobody seemed to think that you'd really been kidnapped. Word on the street was that you'd just walked."

She stared and then slowly shook her head. "Why would they even begin to think that? I never handed in my notice."

"Yep, I hear you. But then I don't think Benjamin did what he was credited with either. The only reason I knew Benjamin was missing was because of his girlfriend. The cops were passing that off as him wanting to get away from her, after a really ugly breakup."

"You did say he was safe, right?"

"I did, but I don't know how safe and for how long though. He's got the same problem as you, having escaped from them. And no doubt they'll be after him as well."

"Reggie said something about taking out Benjamin, while he was unprotected in the hospital."

Delta winced, pulled out his phone, and contacted Badger. "Hey, do we have a phone number for Benjamin?"

"I've got it and sending it to you now. I spoke to him right after he first got settled at the hospital, and we arranged for security, after that threat was made."

"I just want to confirm he's safe. We need to come up with a solution for Rebecca as well. She can't go back to her place, not while she's still in danger."

"Right. We were contemplating that here," Badger noted. "I'm still not getting a ton of cooperation from the sheriff or his deputies. Still, Deputy Halvorson appears to be more on board though."

"Yes, I think he saw a little bit more than what the sheriff was willing to see. The sheriff seems to be highly invested in the company."

"How so?"

"I heard his wife works there."

"Yeah, she does," Rebecca confirmed at his side. When no one spoke from the other end of the call, she introduced herself. "Hi, Badger. My name is Rebecca. Thank you very much for the help."

His tone warm, he replied, "Absolutely. That's not an issue. We kind of specialize in damsels in distress at times."

She burst out laughing. "I would hate to think so many damsels in distress were in the world that we needed a whole team."

"You would be surprised," Badger declared in all seriousness.

At that, a woman came on the line. "Hey, Rebecca, are you injured? Have you found anything more than a few cuts and bruises, now that you're up and moving around?"

"No, I think I'm fine," she said, not recognizing the voice, but thinking that she must be Kat. "I don't know how we got the first aid supplies, but I appreciate that too."

"Yeah, I arranged that," Kat noted.

"Did you arrange a new ankle joint for me too?" Delta popped in.

She snorted. "No, I would think you might have stayed put and just waited until this one was done."

"I could have," he countered, "but then who would have rescued Rebecca?"

"*Right*. Back to that damsel-in-distress thing." Kat chuckled.

"Not sure that's how I want to be regarded," Rebecca protested.

"No, I'm sure you don't," Kat agreed. "And that's all right. It's just an easy bit of fun for the guys. Something to help on the long days when they don't get quite the same results."

Rebecca winced at that. "That's not anything I want to think about."

"So don't," Kat suggested cheerfully. "Just work on healing, while we come up with a plan."

"How is it that we need a plan?" she asked. "I was kidnapped, and yet it seems that nobody's doing anything about it."

"That's not true," Badger countered. "I can't have you thinking that, not when my people are doing stuff. Locally it's a matter of who in the sheriff's department will cooperate, who won't, and why is there any kind of discord between the two in the first place? And more nationally, why does this solo company in a little town worry so much about what you might have seen?" He took a moment to add, "Therefore, first off, you two need to stay put. Stay as far as possible from that town and that company. You are to stay in that motel today, and that's final. Got that, Delta?"

"Yeah, I hear you, but we'll need more angel trips. She'll need clothes, and we'll need food throughout the day."

"Right," Badger agreed. "I'll leave that up to my sweet wife and her angel network."

"How is it that you even have an angel network?" Rebecca asked, when Kat came back on the phone.

"I don't. It's just what my husband likes to call it," she explained. "We are fairly capable at getting deliveries, when need be."

"Oh, some clothes would be nice. I've been wearing these since I was kidnapped from my house," she muttered.

"I also need to get back into that shower and get the glass out of my hair."

"You didn't do that already?" Kat asked.

"Not all of it apparently. I collapsed. Delta tried to comb it out, but I think I still feel some."

"Ah, yes. That explains the first aid kit I had delivered. Now, go take care of yourself, and we'll get you some clothes." And, with that, Kat hung up.

Rebecca looked over at Delta. "You really do have nice friends."

"I do have nice friends," he agreed, with a smile. "Hard-working, caring people."

"I need a few more like that," she muttered.

"Well, if all your friends are as *charming* as Robin," he noted, scrunching his nose, "you could use an upgrade."

At that, her lips twitched. "Honest to God, she's got a heart of gold."

"Maybe," he conceded, with a sigh, looking over at her. "I'll have to be nice to her, won't I?"

She slowly nodded her head. "No, not necessarily."

"Good," he muttered but then flashed her a grin. "However, if that means I can still keep spending time with you, then it might just be worth it."

She flushed and then laughed. "Yes, that would be okay."

"*Okaye.*" He chuckled. "How to damn with faint praise."

She flushed again and stood up. "Now you're embarrassing me. I'll go have that shower now."

"I'm not sure you can do the job without help," he shared gently. "The glass removal part."

She winced. "Fine. You can come in first, but, after my

hair is free of glass, I really want to scrub, from top to bottom."

He froze in the act of getting up, then turned and looked at her. "Did they touch you?" he asked, his tone sharp.

Surprised, it took a moment for her to realize what he was asking, and she shook her head. "No, he didn't."

"Good, because otherwise I would go back to confirm the one you maybe killed was the one who did that to you."

"No," she said bitterly, with an exasperated sigh. "And thank you for the reminder that I may have killed somebody."

He winced. "Not sure you did. Badger sent somebody out for a look."

"God," she muttered. "How messed up is your life when somebody has to be sent out to see if you killed your kidnapper?"

"Well, just because you hit them and maybe ran them over doesn't necessarily mean that they died. Given the fact that these guys are probably as tough as nails, it's quite likely that he did survive."

"And if that's the case," she muttered, staring at Delta in horror, "somebody out there will be really pissed at me."

"Reggie doesn't know where we are. And it's already two in the morning. So grab a quick shower and then let's rest up and even sleep in late and figure out the rest after we're rested and awake."

DELTA SIGHED. HE didn't sleep well, as he was keyed up, worrying someone *might* know where they were. However, he would catch up on his sleep another day. He snuck Gracie outside as needed for bathroom breaks too, but Delta didn't go very far. Meanwhile Rebecca had slept straight through for like eight hours. She really needed that. Then Badger delivered them a late breakfast, which they gobbled up.

Even now, just eight hours later, Rebecca wanted another shower, yet had to dress in her dirty clothes from days ago. Delta planned to have a shower himself but he at least had his bag with him. While he waited for her to finish in the bathroom, he phoned Badger. "Any update on bodies?" he asked in a low whisper.

"No, the men were out there looking earlier today again, once the sun came up, but, so far, nothing." He hesitated. "You're sure she hit someone?"

"It sounded like she hit someone," he replied, uncertain. "I only had the communication through Gracie, but it sure sounded like it."

"Interesting." Badger hesitated, then added, "Unless they got rid of the body."

"That is always a possibility too. ... Rebecca's finishing off in the bathroom, but new clothes would make a huge difference."

"I think you're probably okay to go to her townhome," Badger suggested. "I told the sheriff that she's alive and that you have her. He wants to talk to you, and it might be best if you meet there. Just to be safe, ensure he doesn't know where you're staying."

Delta didn't like the idea but could understand the need to do something about it. "I'll tell her when she comes out. I can't imagine it'll make her terribly happy, though."

"No, I don't imagine it will, but you can at least reassure her that we haven't found any dead body. That will be a relief for her."

"She'll just assume that somebody's injured and lying on the road with no help," he replied in a casual tone. "You and I are both okay with that, but she won't be."

Badger, his tone hard, replied, "Yeah, okay. We've still got people out there searching."

As Delta hung up, he turned to see Rebecca standing there at the bathroom doorway, brushing her hair.

"They didn't find anybody?" she asked.

He shook his head. "No, they didn't. Not yet anyway."

She nodded. "I don't know if that's better or worse."

"It's hard to say," he admitted. "Obviously we want to find Reggie, if he's out there. We don't want anybody lying in pain in a ditch." Although personally he wouldn't mind seeing Reggie dead. People like that don't deserve a second chance.

"It's more likely that, if he was in the way, they would have deep-sixed him," she noted.

"And yet they stopped short of killing you," he pointed out, deep in thought. "So, it's definitely a concern. I'm not sure they're quite ready to take that step themselves. They just expect the hired help to do it."

"Right. So they don't want to kill me outright, yet killing their hired help who failed to carry out his orders is okay? Wow. Isn't that what you mentioned earlier?" she asked.

He smiled. "Do you really think these people *won't* be an issue?"

"Good point," she muttered, staring around the room. "What about my place?"

"Badger suggested that we meet the sheriff there. He knows you're alive and that you're safe but scared."

"Yeah. Ya think?" she muttered, as she sank down onto the bed. "I go between wanting to get clothes and not wanting anything to do with the place because people will know that's where I am. And, since that's where I was kidnapped from to begin with, there's that too."

He nodded. "Do you remember me telling you that we have video of somebody carrying a sleeping bag out to a pickup, where they just dumped the package into the back of the truck?"

"*Great*," she muttered. "That goes along with the way I feel, too."

He smiled at her. "You are safe now, though."

"And I want to stay safe," she declared, chewing on her words. "I'm just not sure that staying safe is a possibility if we go to my townhouse."

"We still have the option of another town and getting you clothes that way," he reminded her, "and that is totally up to you. I'm okay either way."

She frowned. "I can't keep hiding, which is the main problem," she noted, as she slumped in place.

"But neither do you have to face everything all at once," Delta pointed out. "There is likely to be a fair bit of turmoil over the next little while as it is, until we get more of this figured out."

"But that's only if anybody continued to do something, as far as scaring me," she shared, "and I'm not sure I believe that somebody will."

He walked over to her on the side of the bed, wrapped an arm around her, and replied, "Look. Why don't we go to the next town over, and we will grab some coffee, then lunch, and get you some clothes. You'll feel a whole lot better once you're not in those same clothes."

She nodded at that. "And then we go back to my place?" She winced at the thought.

"I think we need to meet the sheriff or the deputy, who-ever you feel comfortable to meet. Deputy Halvorson is somebody I did talk with earlier," Delta explained. "I don't know that he's completely on the up-and-up, but I would like to think so."

"Yeah," she grumbled, "that's the problem. Thinking so is not the same thing as being sure."

"No, it isn't. We can't count on anybody right now," he admitted, "except for ourselves." He looked over at Gracie. "I don't want to leave Gracie alone either."

"No way, she's definitely coming with us," Rebecca stat-ed. "Otherwise I'm not going anywhere."

He smiled as he gazed at Gracie, stretched out on the floor. "We need dog food for her too."

"Right." She groaned. "So, we really need to go out."

"I'm not leaving you alone, so yes," he said, with a nod. "We have to go out, so we will. You won't be alone."

"I'm kind of glad to hear that," she admitted. "I don't really want to deal with the world on my own just yet."

"You don't have to," he agreed, looking at her intently. "I'm not leaving you alone, and we'll sort all this out."

"If I mentioned how you were a nice man again, you would probably roll your eyes at me."

He rolled his eyes at her, making her laugh. "Let's go. The sooner we do, the sooner we can get back."

"Did you book the motel for two nights?"

"I'll change the booking right now, so we're here for a day or two. I did leave it open though."

"In that case, then maybe don't tell him," she replied. "The fewer people who see us, the better."

With that decision made, he got her and Gracie out to his vehicle, hopefully without being seen.

CHAPTER 11

A S THEY DROVE to the next town over, she was perking up. "I guess it's probably time for me to move, isn't it?" she asked him.

He shrugged. "Depends on what we find out about the company. Do you want to move? Do you like living there?"

She stared out the passenger side window, then sighed. "I don't want to stay now," she said, "so that doesn't leave me much choice."

As they came up to the city limits, he pointed at the sign. "How about moving another town over?" he asked.

She shook her head. "Even if you find out what the company's up to and arrest them all, what will stop them from hiring another Reggie to kidnap me or worse? No. ... When I move, I need to make a real one."

"Okay. Where would you like to move to?" he asked, as they drove by more and more buildings and houses.

"I don't know," she admitted, with a shrug. "I've been tossing the idea around for a bit, but I haven't really come up with a location I like better than where I am."

"Which is why people tend to stay," he stated, with a smile, looking over at her. "Not that I'm telling you to stay, just that I'm saying, maybe don't make any hasty decisions, especially after what you've just been through."

"Hardly hasty," she noted. "This just reinforces how I've

been feeling for a while."

"I won't argue with that," he replied in a serious tone. "You've been to hell and back, so you have the right to choose where you want to go next." He went quiet, just giving her time to think and to reflect. The town was coming up soon.

She finally spoke. "And that's the thing. … Everybody around here seems to have been here forever, and nobody wants to move. They don't want to go anywhere."

"Lots of people are like that," he added, with a smile. "That was my family. They moved into one house and never moved again."

"I think that would kill me," she muttered. "I want to go and do things, to see places, and I'm just realizing how much of a rut I've gotten into here."

"In that case, maybe it is time for a change," he acknowledged. "Pick another spot, try something else. Nobody said you're locked into this town or the next."

She nodded. "But now I have Gracie."

"Which is not a problem," he stated firmly. "Gracie adds to your world. She doesn't take away from it. You'll always have her. So it doesn't matter where you go because she will be there with you."

She smiled at him wishing she could believe it would be that easy. "I like the way you think."

He shrugged. "To me, animals are part of the family. Therefore, they don't get dumped just because somebody moves, which I've never understood, but it happens all the time. If you care about them, they're not a hindrance. Plus, considering what Gracie has been through already, I would say she deserves a chance at a new life too, away from all this madness."

"Yeah, but where?" she pondered.

At that, he smiled. "There's no pressure, no time frame." He grinned, as he hit a traffic light and looked her way. "You can do you, all on your own time."

"Maybe," she muttered, as she frowned at him. "Where are you from?"

"I've been in New Mexico for the last few years," he shared. "That's where Badger and Kat are too."

"New Mexico," she muttered. "What's it like there?"

"It's decent," he replied, "but it's not for everybody. It all depends on what you want for yourself."

"I want good people," she declared. "I want to know that, if I get kidnapped again, somebody will care enough to give a damn."

"Let's hope that won't be an ongoing issue," he stated, looking at her in alarm. "I really would like to think that, once we get this settled, it won't happen anymore."

"Me too. … I don't really have a ton of friends here. I want people around me who can see me for who I really am."

"I understand where you're coming from. You do need good friends. And the ones you do have are definitely suspect, if you ask me," he declared, with a groan. The speed limit dropped here, as they were nearing their destination.

"Robin's not that bad." He didn't say anything, just shot her a look. She chuckled. "Honestly, she's good people."

"I didn't say she's not. I'm not saying that at all," he clarified. "However, she's definitely not the easiest person to deal with."

"Okay, but she hasn't had it all that easy in life either."

He nodded. "That's how it works, isn't it? You end up with some things that are good and some things not so good. Then you make the best of what you've got."

"Unless you don't like what you got, and then you need to change it," she pointed out.

"Oh, I'm not arguing that. Anytime you want to make a change, and your heart's in it, you need to make a change. Whether the people around you understand it or not, change is good for the soul."

She laughed. "I don't think a lot of people would agree with you."

"No, maybe not." They came to a railroad crossing, just in time for a train. He put the car in Park and waited for the train to pass. Delta continued. "I joined the military against my family's wishes. My brother joined the military at the same time. Unfortunately he didn't come home, and I came home battered. So my family isn't at all happy with our choices. And then they didn't so much write us off but more a case of *This is the bed you made, so you get to lie in it.*"

She stared at him in shock. "That's not very supportive," she muttered faintly. "How can they do that to you?"

"Not everybody wants to be bothered with a cripple."

"But you're not a cripple," she countered, staring at him, astonished. "Good God. You fought for our country. You fought for those who didn't enlist. And now you're the one who's been here for me through this whole mess."

"Yeah, but not everybody wants to see things like that," he shared, with a smile in her direction. "Sometimes people are not very good about handling my situation, which is so odd to me in that they don't have to deal with it every day, day in and day out. Plus, I don't see myself as disabled. So if *I* don't see me in that way, I don't see why it should bother anybody else. Yet somehow it does."

"That's just stupid bullshit," she snapped, glaring at him.

He laughed. "You don't have to tell me that. I'm the one

who lives it."

The crossing arms came up and allowed them to drive on.

She snorted. "It sounds like you need better family and friends."

"Yep, you got a point." He nodded. "I probably do, except Kat and Badger. They are great friends," he said, with a big smile. "They're just good people."

"You're right," she agreed. "Kat sounds like a lovely person."

"She is. She's also good people, but … that doesn't mean that the people you know aren't also good people."

"True. I know plenty are good people, but that doesn't mean they're *my* people."

He looked over at her, seeing the pensive look on her face. "Nothing wrong with making a change," he repeated, looking at her intently. "Nothing wrong with wanting more. Nothing wrong with needing more. It doesn't make you greedy. It doesn't make you weak. It's just life. Some people need to go out and to do things, and other people are just content to stay at home. You have to do what's good for you."

"Have you done much traveling?" she asked, looking over at him.

"Sure, with my tours and other assignments in the military, you could say that. Of course that's not the kind of traveling I would choose to do."

"No, and I'm not sure we can even call that traveling," she muttered. "Would you want to do more?"

"Absolutely." He grinned. "Why? Where do you want to go?"

She laughed. "Just like that?"

"Absolutely just like that." He smirked. "It's a big world out there, and, by and large, it's a good world. Just be prepared and be open to whatever comes."

"Maybe," she muttered, as she stared around at her surroundings. She pointed up ahead. "Let's check out that strip mall over there for clothing."

"Sounds good to me." And, with that, he pulled into the mall. "All the better, look, restaurants are here too."

She looked over where he pointed and laughed. "You hungry already?"

"Absolutely I'm hungry. "It's not as if we've really eaten."

She thought about the fast-food breakfast they had shared and nodded.

"Yeah, and that was just refueling from what we missed yesterday, not to mention the adrenaline burn we went through. So, if we need a little more, let's eat while we can."

"I want a lot more," she agreed, "like an actual meal. We didn't get much breakfast."

"Nope, so let's go. Clothing first or food first?"

"Clothing first," she said, frowning, thinking about it. "It's never good to try on clothing just after you ate."

He grinned at that. "I can't imagine it would be an issue either way." She shot him a suspicious look, but he smiled back at her. "You're perfect the way you are. Don't even begin to think otherwise."

She laughed. "I'm not fishing for compliments."

"Don't have to fish," he replied, with that same grin on his face. "You're perfect."

Much later, as they exited the restaurant, feeling happy and flushed, calm and relaxed, Delta suddenly stopped and tucked her behind him.

"What's going on?" she asked.

He shrugged. "I don't know, but something feels off."

She stared at him. Slipping his hand into hers, they quickly headed back to the vehicle. Letting Gracie out of the vehicle, he walked her around a little bit, as he checked out the neighborhood. "You still feel like something is wrong?" she asked him.

"Yes." As soon as Gracie peed and was back with them, Delta was all business. "Let's get her in the car now."

Not wasting time, Rebecca quickly hopped into the vehicle with Gracie, and they took off. As they left town, she looked around. "This isn't the way we came in."

He nodded. "I don't want to use the same route twice."

She sucked in her breath. "You really think it's bad."

"I don't know what it is," he admitted, looking over at her. "I don't want to make a mistake. That could have implications that we can't deal with."

"Right," she whispered. "God, how did we get into such a mess?"

He smiled. "I would like to say we got into it by simply *being*, but this isn't the time." He drove quietly, without either of them saying a word.

However, she kept twisting to look behind to see if they were being followed. Finally, after a few minutes, she asked him, "Are we good now?"

"I'm not sure yet," he admitted. "I just want to ensure we won't run into any trouble that we aren't expecting."

"Are we expecting any trouble?" she asked.

He chuckled. "I guess I'm always expecting some," he murmured. "Let's go straight to your house and meet the deputy there." He tossed her his phone. "His number is two or three back. Maybe I saved it."

She brought up his recent calls on his phone and showed him the screen. He quickly pointed out which one it was. As she went to dial it, she looked over at him. "Are you sure?"

He nodded. "Yeah, we really do need to see whether local law enforcement's on our side or not."

"How can they not be?" she muttered in wonder. "That's just wrong."

When a man answered on the other end, she asked, "Deputy Halvorson?"

"Yes, who is this?" he barked.

She took a deep breath and replied, "Rebecca. Rebecca Postal."

First came silence, then he exploded. "Good God, are you okay?"

"I am, but no thanks to you guys," she replied waspishly. "But definitely all right, thanks to Delta."

"Is Delta there with you?"

"Yes," she asked. "Why?"

"Put him on the phone."

"He's driving."

"Of course he's driving. Put it on Speaker then, dammit."

She quickly put it on Speaker, and Delta leaned over ever-so-slightly. "I'm here, Deputy."

"We got a phone call from a couple people interested in your welfare," he shared. "You really know how to stir up trouble, don't you?"

"I guess that's your perspective," Delta noted, his tone calm. "I know how to make shit happen, and, in this case, it needed to. Did you talk to Benjamin?"

"I did. However, now he's gone underground, and he doesn't want anything to do with any of us."

"I can't say that I blame him there," Delta admitted. "I will still be talking to him."

"What makes you think he'll talk to you and not to me?"

"Maybe because he knows I would listen to him, and I'm not out to kidnap him or worse," Delta explained, with a groan. "How do you expect people to trust you guys if you won't help them, especially with the sheriff being pro-company?"

"It's not that we won't help," Halvorson snapped. "Where are you?"

"Coming back into town. We had to get her some clothes."

"You didn't go back to her place?"

"No, we didn't go back to her place, but we'll do that now."

"Why?"

"I thought you wanted to meet."

"Why there though?" the deputy asked.

Something was off in the deputy's tone. "Deputy, what are you not telling me?"

He hesitated and then relented, "Her townhome was broken into a few hours ago."

She sucked in a breath and let out half a cry.

"That's interesting," Delta stated calmly, "and it goes along with why we didn't take that chance by ourselves."

"That may be, but you do realize that some people will say you're the one who did it."

"Really?" Delta asked in astonishment. "Why would I do that when she's right here with me?"

"Because nobody knows she's right there with you. And you've been known to be a little bit … enthusiastic about your premise that she was kidnapped."

"You mean, the truth that she was kidnapped and that nobody would listen to me?" he stated, hardening his tone.

"I *was* kidnapped," she snapped into the phone. "What the hell is wrong with you people?"

"It's just that the people involved, or the people anybody has spoken to, don't see any reason why you would have been kidnapped. However once news that the FBI is involved goes out in the rumor mill that will change."

"Because you don't know what's on the kidnapper's mind, it means I didn't get kidnapped? Is that it?" she asked in exasperation. "Good God," she muttered, "no wonder you guys have such a bad reputation in this town."

"What do you mean, a bad reputation? We're doing the best we can, with the manpower we have. We are trying, despite budget cuts and whatnot," he argued.

Rebecca leaned closer to Delta and whispered, "New Mexico sounds better and better by the second."

"What are you talking about?" Deputy Halvorson asked in confusion.

"Never mind. It's above your pay grade," Rebecca spat.

Silence came, and then he spoke. "Look. I get it. You're not happy with us. However, we still have minimal resources, and we have an entire town to look after."

"You seem to be looking after the company, all right. Yet, if nobody believes I was kidnapped, you won't even double-check? So people aren't important to you, just that damn company? What about Benjamin? Do you think he wasn't kidnapped, as well?" Rebecca was desperately trying to hold back the sarcasm but not managing to. "You have no idea who kidnapped me. Yet Delta and his team are working on it. Not only that, … you don't really care."

"I didn't say that," he grumbled, and she heard his own

frustration and impatience. "I'm glad that you're safe."

"I'm glad I'm safe too." She looked over at Delta. "I think we should go talk to Benjamin first."

Delta nodded. "I think you're right. I'm not feeling very comfortable about the fact that he won't talk to anybody. It sounds to me that maybe he's getting pressured."

"Yeah," Rebecca agreed, "sounds to me that the kidnappers are already looking for him, particularly if they've already broken into my place again."

"Hey, hey, hey, you don't need to be bothering him," the deputy replied, perking up. "I've already spoken to him. He's fine."

"Pardon me, *Deputy*," Rebecca interrupted, trying hard but failing to keep her tone neutral. "That is not anything that gives me confidence. He was kidnapped before me, was held in the same house with me, and he escaped by going over the fence. Since I had Gracie and didn't have that same window of opportunity, I stayed behind. So excuse me for not believing you when you *say* you've already spoken to him. Obviously, if you have, you don't believe him any more than you believe me. However, we don't need to speak to him ourselves, as we already believe him. I want to see for myself that he's safe."

"What do you think I did?" Deputy Halvorson snarled. "Do you think I kidnapped him?"

She thought about it and replied, "Maybe you did." And, with that, she hung up. She glared down at the phone. "That man just …"

Delta smiled and squeezed her hand gently, as he took the phone from her fingers. "He's the only guy I trust even a little to work with, so I need him for official purposes. He's not a bad guy or at least not as bad as the other deputies or the sheriff himself. I don't think Halvorson's involved, but he's also dealing with a sheriff who's not terribly proactive."

"*Not terribly proactive?* Sounds to me like this sheriff doesn't give a crap."

"And that's what it'll sound like for a while, until we can get through this," he muttered. "Nothing quite like having Halvorson's methods questioned. Did you hear him say it had something to do with budgets and man-hours and all that stuff?"

"So, I don't count?" she asked in a fit. "I pay taxes, like everybody else, but I didn't count enough to have precious man-hours put into searching for me or even verifying I was gone?"

"That is because, honestly, I don't think they believed you'd been kidnapped."

She shook her head. "Good God. The whole time I was out there, I kept thinking that somebody would be coming to the rescue since I didn't show up for work, but, in reality, *nobody* was coming to my rescue at all. What would have happened if you didn't …"

He winced, hearing the sadness and the disbelief in her tone. "I'm sorry. I'm sure it's a shock to realize that the authorities weren't coming for you, when that very thought kept you going."

"If you hadn't come, what would I have done?"

"But I did come, and, for all you know, you would have been just fine without me. Look how you took that car without fear."

"No," she countered bitterly. "I don't think I could have gone through that roadblock. I … I probably would have hit the brakes rather than hitting him."

"Well, I'm glad you didn't," he said, "because right now

you're here, and you're safe, and Gracie is safe. That's what counts. And Gracie is here because of you, so you should be proud of yourself."

At that, she turned to Gracie, lying on the back seat. "Gracie, you okay, girl?" Gracie gave her a *woof.* Rebecca released her seat belt and climbed over to the back seat, where she wrapped her arms around the dog. "I am so glad you made it," she whispered. As the two of them cuddled in the back seat, she asked Delta, "What did you decide about where we're going?"

"I think we need to see Benjamin first, and then we'll see what your townhome looks like and go from there."

"I'm not sure I even want to go to my house. *Ever,*" she murmured. "Sounds to me like bad news the whole way. The kidnappers are still after me and probably Benjamin too. What a mess."

"I think you're right, but we still should meet the deputy there, as planned. Plus, do you *not* want to collect any of your stuff, even things you could probably use, like your laptop, phone, clothes, important papers, and things like that? Can you afford to replace all that?"

"No, I can't," she muttered. "Damn it."

"It's okay. We'll go in, and we'll get what you need, and we'll get out."

She shook her head. "And with the kidnappers still on the loose, obviously?" she pointed out, looking over at him. "That doesn't sound like the easiest of things to do."

"It's not easy, but it's doable," he replied. "Then, while we think about where you'll go from here, we can stay at the motel, until you have a chance to make a plan."

"Well, according to you, I probably don't have a job."

"I'm not sure about that," he clarified. "I'm just saying

that you didn't show up and that's how I found out that you weren't there."

"It's funny how we talked so much about Gracie, and I knew you were coming. While I was being held, I kept hoping that you would at least sound the alarm when I didn't, … when I wasn't there for the meeting."

"I did sound the alarm," he confirmed. "It just happened to fall on deaf ears."

She winced. "That's the problem. That's the part I don't get," she muttered. "How is it that it's okay for the *complete sheriff's office* to just ignore the fact that I didn't show up for work?"

"I think they did the bare minimum—knocking on your door but not going inside. Checking on your car and glad it was still there. Waiting twenty-four hours to do basically nothing else. The party line that I got was that nobody was worried because, as far as they're concerned, you're an adult, and you can go and do whatever you want."

"Exactly how women end up in trouble, even after all these years," she muttered. "My heart goes out to anybody who's involved in domestic violence or abuse, where they *want* to get away. Yet it seems like nobody can get away when they want to. Then there's the opposite end of the spectrum, where women are abducted and trafficked for years. How do they survive that? They end up in constant trouble."

Delta nodded. "Everybody deserves to have somebody looking out for them," Delta noted. She seemed to have talked herself out for the moment. "So, how do you feel about seeing Benjamin?"

"Benjamin, it is," she declared. "I want to see for myself that he's really okay."

"Good." Delta nodded. "His apartment is only a few minutes away."

She looked at him. "I didn't even know he lived in this corner of town."

Delta pulled up in front of the small apartment building, and, with her at his side, they headed to the front door.

"Are we sure he's at home?" she asked. "He told me that he was taken from his home too. I doubt he's here."

"True. Yet we can't guarantee that until we look."

"Of course not," she muttered, as she walked along the crosswalk. "I don't …" Then she stopped.

The door was ajar.

Delta nodded. "I don't either."

She frowned at him, "Not again, right? They didn't kidnap him again? Did they?"

"I don't know," he whispered, as he stared at the door in front of him, "but I don't like anything about this. Go back to my car and get Gracie."

She stared at him for a moment and then asked, "What will you do?"

He just smiled and repeated, "Go get Gracie, honey."

"Okay, but, if you get shot, I'm not big enough to carry you anywhere."

He snorted. "I don't need to be carried, but Gracie would come in handy."

"As long as she doesn't get hurt," Rebecca added, as she turned to look back at him.

"It's her nose that I need."

She stared at him, and her face flushed in fear. "Oh God," She raced back to the car, while he stood here and watched.

DELTA WATCHED HER every step as Rebecca returned with Gracie. Then he took the leash from her hand and whispered, "I want you to stay out here." When she shook her head, he gave her a hard look. "Fine, but I want you to stay behind me, as we go inside."

She bit her bottom lip but nodded.

He pushed open the door and headed inside. No immediate sign of anybody. No sounds of life. Delta knew the place was empty, but all he could hope was that it was literally empty, not just empty of life. He called out, "Benjamin, you here?"

When no answer came, Delta called out again, as he moved through the bottom floor of the house. When he got to the staircase, he called out, "I'm going up."

She winced and nodded. "Do you really think he's injured?"

"I just want make sure he's not dead," Delta shared.

She sucked in her breath and nodded. "I'm coming with you."

He didn't try to dissuade her. At this point in time, he would just as soon they not get separated either. They made their way upstairs, and, with great relief, the bedroom was also empty.

"So, where is he then?" she asked.

"With his girlfriend, I would think. The problem would be *where* they both are at this moment." He pulled out his phone and quickly placed a call to Hannah. When he got no answer, he frowned again. "I really don't like this," he muttered. "I much prefer when people answer their damn phones."

She smiled. "Yeah, I get it, but not everybody is on your schedule."

"Isn't that the truth," he admitted, flinching. When he called Hannah again and still got no answer, he muttered, "Don't suppose you happen to know where the girlfriend lives?"

"I didn't even know where Benjamin lived," Rebecca noted, as she looked at Delta in frustration. "We might have worked together, but we certainly weren't close. He'd been gone for a week, and I wasn't even aware that he'd left."

"Okay." Delta sighed. "I need to find out where Hannah is. She works at the café."

Rebecca nodded and mentioned the name of the café. "Yeah, I knew that, but I didn't know that you did. However, I didn't know they were together, but she's always seemed nice. Benjamin told me all about her one day, before he escaped."

"Yes, she seems like a nice girl," Delta agreed. "I met her at the café, and she told me about Benjamin's disappearance."

"So, what do we do now?"

"Let's see if he has a set of wheels here. Plus I need to get Badger involved." He sent off a text to Badger immediately, and Badger called right back. Delta told him, "Nobody is here at Benjamin's place, but his door was ajar. I don't have a number for him, and I doubt Halverson will share that with me, not now that I've insulted him and the sheriff's office. I do have Benjamin's girlfriend's phone number, but she's not answering either. And I don't know where she lives. If you could get me Benjamin's cell number and Hannah's address, we'll check out both. Oh, and if you don't already know, Rebecca's place was broken into a few hours ago this morning." Delta checked Benjamin's garage and found it empty. "Don't know what Benjamin's driving, but his parking space is empty."

"Right," Badger said absentmindedly. "We are still following some leads on the company," he muttered. "Let me just see what I've got on Benjamin and his girlfriend. Okay, yeah, I've got a phone number for Benjamin and an address for Hannah. I'll send both to you. Let me know what you find."

"Nothing feels right here."

"Well, you keep that instinct going strong," Badger said, "because nobody gets shot on my watch."

"How about *shot at*?" Rebecca asked, with a note of humor.

"Yeah, that's not allowed either," Badger noted, still with a smile in his tone. "But after you've been hurt once, the last thing I want is to see you get hurt again. The body does not like repeated offenses." With that, he hung up.

She smiled. "He's quite a character, isn't he?"

"That he is." Delta led them to the front door, and he carefully opened it a bit, as he glanced around outside. "Let's go. We can try Hannah's apartment."

"Do you think he's there?'

"Well, if I were in this situation and had a girlfriend whom I hadn't seen and had come close to losing, I would be with her," he muttered. "Wouldn't you?"

She thought about it and nodded. "That's exactly what I would do, but why wouldn't they answer their phone?"

"They wouldn't answer if they thought they were still in danger," he replied, "so let's go find out. I just hope they are there, or else I have no idea where to find them."

CHAPTER 12

REBECCA KNOCKED ON the door to Hannah's place. When no answer came, she frowned and looked around again.

Delta nudged her toward the door once more. "Knock again." She shrugged and knocked a second time. This time, he smiled and nodded. "I hear noises inside."

"Sure, but you don't know who it is or what is going on."

"No, I don't. But this time, maybe identify yourself."

In surprise, she nodded and called out, "Benjamin, this is Rebecca. I need to know that you're okay. Remember? I promised to get help if anybody got out of there. I just ... I don't want to go running off, trying to rescue you, if you're already rescued."

At that, the door opened, and there was Benjamin. He took one look at her, opened his arms, and wrapped her into a big hug. "Oh my God, oh my God." He pulled her inside the house, then saw Delta and frowned.

He's with me," Rebecca noted quickly.

"Come in. Get in quick, both of you."

They stepped inside, and Delta saw Hannah and smiled at her. "Hannah, I'm glad to find you here. Are you doing okay?"

She nodded. "Yes, but so many vehicles are slowly driving by, as if they're looking for him. His phone's been going off steadily, and so has mine," she muttered. "So, naturally …" Hannah hesitated.

Rebecca filled in the rest. "So, naturally you're terrified."

Hannah nodded. "Yes. So you're the Rebecca who was kidnapped with him?"

"I was held hostage with him. I wasn't kidnapped at the same time, but I was with him."

"I am so glad you got out safe. He's been sick with worry that he couldn't get back there to help you."

She looked over at Benjamin and smiled. "I'm fine. How did you shake them? Delta said you were a bloody mess when you stumbled into your apartment."

"I ran and ran, cross-country. It felt like every vehicle I saw was after me. Someone shouted at me, probably just to help me, but I jumped and fell over something and got all scraped up. Finally I hid under a tarp in the back of a delivery truck that I hoped was going somewhere and caught a ride that eventually ended up back in town, really close to the hospital too. So I checked myself in. I was such a wreck, beside myself, and feeling pretty low. I reported the kidnapping—of you and me—to the hospital staff, who called the sheriff's office, while giving me an IV of fluids. That helped a lot because I was dehydrated too. Still, I was too scared to stay there because I felt like a sitting duck. Then I phoned the deputy myself and told him that, but … he didn't really seem to be too bothered.

"After I made it home and met up with Hannah and Delta, we got my car and tried to find the house where I was held to get you some real help, Rebecca, but it was dark at this time, and I was that hidden hitchhiker for a big portion of my escape, so I couldn't find the damn place," he admitted, his voice strained. "And when I called back and told the deputy that, he said they would handle it, how I shouldn't go back there or the kidnappers might recapture me. I am so sorry, Rebecca. I knew that you were still there." He threw up his hands. "Thank God, you made it out of there." Then Benjamin snatched Rebecca in his arms and gave her a big hug again.

She smiled and gently disentangled herself. "Thankfully we both got out. Now maybe you two can relax."

"But can we?" Hannah asked nervously. "He was kidnapped from his apartment, and they probably know his car too."

"That's a very good point," Delta pointed out. "If they took him once, what's to stop them from taking him again?"

Benjamin looked over at him in horror. "Surely the kidnappers don't really want to do that, now that the authorities are finally involved. Although that evil boss lady has already been picked up…"

"My concern is," Delta explained, "that we still don't understand exactly why they took you and Rebecca captive in the first place. Also, now why does the company need you to be silent surrounding some upcoming sale, yet they didn't silence you? We have some ideas but no proof yet. From what Rebecca says about Reggie, your captor was trigger-happy and kept threatening to shoot her and Gracie."

Benjamin swallowed. "I know. I was kind of worried about that myself. None of it makes any sense."

Delta nodded. "I don't trust the sheriff's department either, other than maybe Deputy Halvorson. And, so far, we don't know exactly what the kidnappers and the company are up to, although we have some doozies of theories we are bouncing around. Still, until we figure out what is driving the company to kidnap you and to even threaten to kill you, we'll be in trouble ourselves. However, I have a team of people looking deeper into the company and even into the sheriff's office. Still, we need intel fast to fend off these people, who still seem intent on getting to you and Rebecca."

Benjamin nodded solemnly. "I don't plan to go back to my apartment. I could stay here at Hannah's place, but, if the sheriff's office or any of the bad guys know that we're an item, then she'll be in danger, and I don't want that either."

Hannah walked over and wrapped her arms around Benjamin. The two of them just cuddled close, clearly exchanging support and conversing quietly.

For Rebecca, it was a poignant moment, and she worried that she didn't have any such long-term support in her life. Except that thought had no sooner crossed her mind, when a hand slid across her shoulders, and she was tucked up against Delta's chest. She smiled at that. "Always there to give comfort," she teased.

He nodded. "At times like this, that's exactly what you need."

She sighed happily and snuggled in closer. "I can't say I ever expected you to be like this."

"Ha, you probably didn't have the time to consider this, not while kidnapped, or now on the run. So, you just weren't really thinking about it."

"I don't know that I was mulling over much of anything," she muttered. "I … I was mostly worried that you would take Gracie away from me."

Delta looked at her in astonishment. "I wasn't trying to take her away. I was trying to confirm that she was safe and in a good home."

"Yes, but who's to say whether it's a good home or not?" she asked, with a wry look in his direction. "For somebody who absolutely loves that dog, any threat that I might not be good enough to keep Gracie was paralyzing."

Delta smiled, held her close, and whispered, "I don't see any issues, so you need to rest easy. My boss has okayed it as well so it's all good."

"Well, I'm glad to hear that," Rebecca replied, feeling a certain amount of relaxation hitting her shoulders at those simple words. "I was afraid you didn't have the power to make that decision and your bosses would see this case differently. You could have told me that earlier."

He burst out laughing. "If I had any idea that was on your mind, with all this other stuff going on," he noted, "I might have. However, I figured we had a lot bigger issues to deal with, and it was already obvious you take wonderful care of Gracie."

"Sure," she muttered. "Except the part about Gracie disappearing. Here's another thing though. The company never gave me a release to take ownership for Gracie, so I think technically she belongs to the company."

Delta frowned. "I'm not sure how that works though, considering they lost her, they abused her, they put some experimental device in her leg."

"Did they lose her or was she kidnapped, like me?" Rebecca asked.

At the word "kidnapped," Benjamin and Hannah joined Delta and Rebecca.

"Well, if the company owns her, and the company moved her to a different department," Benjamin suggested, "then technically it's not a kidnapping."

"But why did Gracie end up in that room with me

then?" Rebecca asked.

"Good point," Benjamin replied in confusion, as he looked over at Delta. "That doesn't make any sense either."

"None of it makes any sense yet," Delta admitted, "but it will later. It always does. It's just that we may not be privy to the information yet, which is kind of scary. Plus, I don't suggest the four of us stay together, making it easier for the bad guys to find us all in one location."

Everyone nodded to that.

Benjamin looked at Hannah and announced, "We have someplace where we can hide out together, hoping for your team to get ahead of the kidnappers. You have our phone numbers, so text us if something turns up. With so much crap going on, and now that Rebecca and I have both escaped, we would like to think that it was all over with."

"And it will be. It will be, just not quite yet. Rebecca's townhome was broken into earlier today, and your apartment door was ajar. I don't know how long it's been like that. Still, give my team some more time," Delta declared. "We can't have something like this just hang on indefinitely. We need the FBI to get answers that we can't and get this over and done with."

"Yeah, good luck with that," Benjamin muttered. "The deputy I talked to when I first arrived at the hospital seemed reasonably cooperative, but I'm not sure I have that same feeling now."

Then came a knock on the door. Hannah gave a startled yelp and jumped into Benjamin's arms. Benjamin stared at the door.

"Hang on. Let's not get freaked out." Delta raised a hand. "Let me answer it."

"Why would you do that?" Benjamin asked hoarsely.

"They'll know I'm here."

"They probably already know you're here," Delta suggested, raising an eyebrow. "Chances are, it's Deputy Halvorson."

"Well, that's not helping either," Benjamin muttered. "We already saw how little he cared."

And Deputy Halvorson was at the door. Delta let him in. As soon as he saw both Benjamin and Rebecca, he pushed his hat back and muttered, "Well, now look at that."

"Yeah, *well now*, but don't go thinking that they were just making up all this about the kidnapping and the threats or some other BS," Delta snapped, glaring at him.

Halvorson looked at him. "Never crossed my mind."

"Oh, don't give me that crap," Delta muttered, as he waved Halvorson farther into the living room. "We've been to hell and back already, so I'm not in the mood for anything that isn't helpful."

"Yeah, well, you've also got some very persuasive friends," Halvorson shared, "and they sure as heck are trying to stir things up."

"They're only *stirring things up*, as you say, because issues need to be dealt with, and you are supposedly the law enforcement around here."

"I'm a deputy, yes," he confirmed. "However, the sheriff is quite connected to the company, and the company has reassured him that all this has nothing to do with the company, and that Ms. Postal's psych evaluation done recently revealed that she was getting too attached to the animals. … Hence, she was no longer capable of doing her job."

Rebecca stared at him in shock. "What psych eval? I never had one."

He looked at her in surprise and then shrugged. "Well, it's in your file."

"Of *course* it is," she muttered, her gaze going from one to the other. "Benjamin, did you have a psych eval?"

"Nope, I sure didn't," he replied, "but they control the files, so they can put in whatever they want, can't they?"

"And that's what they are doing, apparently," Rebecca said, still in shock. "Hell, I definitely need a new job now."

"You won't get a reference," Benjamin pointed out, "because *obviously* you're unstable, per the company."

She rolled her eyes at that. "*Obviously I'm unstable*," she repeated. "Much more of this shit and I'm about to be. Unbelievable."

"Unfortunately, with everything else that's gone on surrounding that company," Delta offered, "I absolutely do believe the company is putting out this false narrative on purpose, hiding their true intent in all this."

"The problem is," Deputy Halvorson pointed out, "without any proof, we have no way of determining whether the company is involved or not. It makes no sense that a big company with a good reputation would be involved in something so murky and underhanded as this."

"The other thing we have here is," Delta noted, staring at Halvorson, "no way to determine that they *aren't* so pristine and worthy of consideration, all due to the lack of an investigation by the sheriff's office."

"Yeah," Benjamin snapped. "How can you clear the company without even doing an investigation?"

"We can't do an investigation if there's nothing to investigate," the deputy restated.

Delta grumbled, "And yet two employees of the same company, plus Gracie, disappeared and then found themselves held against their will at the same location."

"Sure," Halvorson replied. "That in itself is something we need to take a look at, but it doesn't mean that anybody from the company is involved."

Benjamin snorted. "Even though I identified the two people who arranged to have us kidnapped and then threatened to kill us if we didn't keep our mouths shut?"

Halvorson frowned, sent a look to Delta.

"So," Benjamin concluded, "my fake psych eval negates my witness statement now? Oh, my God."

Delta added, with a sharp look at Halvorson, "But everyone remember this. The war department has a vested interest in this abuse of War Dogs and the unlicensed testing on them by this local vendor, the company in question. Plus our federal authorities have hauled off the lady board member so Halvorson here should be worried about an investigation into the local sheriff's department and all the dirt that will be dug up and all the inaction that the sheriff promoted, while lining his pockets."

Halvorson went silent and seemed to be contemplating this further.

Rebecca wondered about that, even as they all talked further. The deputy may have been right in some ways, but in others, it just didn't fit. She also understood that maybe Halvorson's hands were tied. She wanted to blame him. She wanted to lash out and to make somebody pay, but that didn't mean she had the right person in front of her to place the blame on.

"So, what do we do from here then?" Hannah asked, staring at each one in turn. "We can't presume that we're safe. Whether it was the company or not, somebody kidnapped Benji and Rebecca," Hannah declared. "So, staying here means we're in danger of their coming back for us. We only came to pack our bags, and Benji was feeling so bad about not being able to find Rebecca and to help her get out, that we haven't had a chance to get out of here ourselves. But we need to," she stated, turning and looking at Benjamin. "We really need to go. Let's go, Benji. I don't even care where we go. Let's just pack up and get out of here."

He looked at her, a wry look on his face. "Between us, we probably have enough money for what? A couple weeks."

"I don't care." She raised both hands. "I'm in a dead-end job here, and I can get another dead-end job somewhere else," she muttered. "Also, if I'm working at a restaurant, I can get free lunches and cash tips and employee discounts on your food, which can help us tide over until you are employed too. We can sleep in the car, shower at truck stops. I can do all that. What I can't do is risk my own life or yours. I don't ever want to go through losing you again."

"No, I really don't want to either." Benjamin rubbed his temples. "My brother's down south."

"Good," she replied, with a somber face. "Time for a visit, I guess."

He burst out laughing. "You're really ready to just pack up and go?"

"Sure." She smiled at him. "Our rent is month-to-month, and tomorrow's the end of the month, so we hand in our notice, and we … just go."

"Don't hand in a notice," Delta interjected. "Not right away."

"But we can't afford to maintain rent at both places."

He pondered that and asked, "Can you afford to maintain the rent at one place for another month?"

"Why do that?" Hannah asked, looking at him puzzled.

"Because otherwise it will tell people you're on the run."

"Don't we want them to know we are on the run?"

"Not yet. Not for a while, especially if they have some idea where you would run to," he pointed out.

She winced. "God, I hate this. What will you do?" she asked, turning to look at Rebecca.

Rebecca winced. "Honestly, I haven't had two seconds to even get enough sleep to think about it."

"I'm taking her back to New Mexico with me," Delta butted in.

She looked over at him. "What if I don't want to go to New Mexico?"

"You'll love it there," he replied, flashing her a grin. "It's just for a visit, and you can come back, when this is all over."

"Well, *thank you*," she mocked, "but it's not for you to make my decisions."

"Nope, it's not. But neither do you want to go back into that kidnapping scenario you just got out of. Apparently you don't have a job, so that is not an issue either."

"That just pisses me off even more."

Delta smiled. "Get angry. Please, get angry over this. Don't be a victim. Don't let them dictate everything in your life, not when you need to be safe."

"And New Mexico will be safe?"

"It will clear your head and it gets you out of whatever nightmare we're currently in, yes," he clarified, giving her a hard look. "Will it be the final answer? No. Considering we have a deputy here that we haven't vetted and who's listening to us, if anything does happen to us in all these relocation trips, we'll know who knew about the move."

Deputy Halvorson's jaw dropped for a moment and then he bellowed, "What? You're accusing me?"

"It's not a case of accusing you," Hannah pointed out, quietly looking at him. "It's a case of realizing that you have done nothing proactive to help us."

"That's not true," he blustered. "I've done everything I could."

"Which apparently isn't very much," Rebecca declared, with a headshake, "and that is concerning."

"What is it you think I should do?"

"Are you investigating the company?" she asked him bluntly.

"Again, I can't if there isn't any proof. We can't just go around causing trouble for upstanding citizens."

"Unless, of course, they're *not* upstanding citizens."

"And, if that were the case, then give me some proof," he said, flailing under the weight of staring eyes all around him. "I don't like standing here, with my hands tied, listening to you guys talk as if your worlds have just collapsed, and you're running for your lives."

"But we are," Rebecca snapped, "and we are very much in a position of knowing that, having lived for days as prisoners of our captor, even though you fail to recognize these facts."

"Then show me where you were held. Give me something."

Delta looked at him. "Have you talked to Badger yet?"

He frowned. "You know, that's kind of a weird name, but there is a message on my phone here."

"I suggest you listen to it," Delta said, with a nod. "Badger might have a weird name, but there's nothing weird about the man. You'll find him to be very helpful when it comes to bringing clarity to the situation. He has impeccable credentials with very significant levels of security clearance. I would expect that he can help you realize that I have been very thoroughly vetted and that these people have been as well. He has dealings and contacts with military operations going all over the globe."

At that, Deputy Halvorson's eyes widened. "So why do I need to talk to him?"

"I think you'll find out he has much information that you need to have. Call him." Delta motioned at the door. "Then you come back inside and talk to us."

Halvorson shook his head. "I don't take orders from you."

"No, you sure don't, but I bet you'll take orders from Badger."

"I do not. He's not my boss."

"Well, *your* boss is a piece of shit," Rebecca snapped. "It's not as if you were out there looking for us, when we were kidnapped, or even now helping us at all as we run for our lives."

He pushed back his hat and glared at her.

"Oh, *right*, I got it," Rebecca quipped. "Once again, *you* have no proof we were kidnapped. Like we'll lie about something like that."

"Right?" Benjamin said, shaking his head. "Good Lord. I'm still pissed about those fake psych evals."

"Yeah, you and me both. They manufactured them just today, I'm sure."

"Any way to prove that?" Halvorson asked.

"Depends how careless they were with the documentation," Rebecca muttered. "If we had the computer they were written on, we would see some timestamp information. No guarantee that it would give us what we need though, as they probably wiped the computer immediately afterward."

Delta nodded. "Listen, Halvorson. You asked for proof, So if you want it, you need to talk to Badger."

DELTA STEPPED OUTSIDE on the front deck, listening as Halvorson fought with whoever was on the phone.

Finally the deputy hung up his phone and swore, then turned to catch sight of Delta staring at him, "You knew, didn't you?"

"Knew what?" Delta asked, with a smirk. "Knew that you needed to talk to him? Yes," he replied. "Hell yes, I knew that, but you wouldn't listen to me."

"No, of course I wouldn't. You're not part of this."

"Apparently I am now," Delta declared, sending a knowing smile in Halvorson's direction.

"What I want to know is how the hell you pulled that off?"

"It's all about having connections, and realizing that, at some point in time, somebody has to step up and do something."

"I was trying to," Halvorson wailed, "but I also didn't want to lose my job."

"And in my case," Delta added, looking over at him, "I don't have a job to lose, so it's really not anything I have a problem with. Granted, I know that you're in a tough spot here, and I understand that somebody in your world, like maybe your wife and your brother, also work at the company."

The deputy flushed, and then he shrugged. "It's my *ex*-wife and *her* brother," he clarified, "so you're not getting any grief from me over ending their employment with the company."

Delta chuckled. "Well, that's good to know, but it's really not an answer I can work with."

"Well, you could if you wanted to," he muttered. Halvorson swore, scratching his head and shifting his hat off his head. "So now, what the hell do you want to do?"

"I want to catch this Reggie asshole, if he is still alive—their captor, their guard, maybe the actual kidnappers—and confirm he worked for the company. Or maybe Reggie worked directly for and was hired by the female board member, who threatened Benjamin and Rebecca. Regardless, the feds have the woman ID'd by Benjamin, if you will remember, Halvorson, from our earlier discussion today. I'm sure Rebecca can confirm these two as well. So Badger and his people can connect two of these three to the company already. That means they and that company are all going down."

The deputy shook his head. "Nobody here will thank you for that."

"Sure they will, once people here realize a takeover was happening, which means they have no more jobs at the company. So the company won't be the savior for them anyway."

Halvorson looked at him in surprise and whistled softly. "You've got a point there. They could possibly shut it down, couldn't they?"

"They could do all kinds of stuff, and nobody will stop them. Big companies come in, reorganize, take the assets, and shut things down all the time."

Halvorson winced. "I wouldn't want to see that. This is a small town, and the company has roots here, has enticed many people here to work for them, even some people to move here specifically to work for them."

"You might not want to see that, but you won't have any say in the matter, not when it's all about the company and its owners and shareholders and the bottom line," Delta explained. "Just so you understand."

"If that company shuts down, laying off everyone who works there, it would really suck because it's the biggest employer here."

"That's one way it could happen. Another way is, and you and I both know, or at least you *should* know, that these companies can be legally shut down for various crimes."

Halvorson slowly nodded. "I really don't want that to happen. I was hoping, if we just kept the company out of all of this and didn't have to stir anything up," he shared, giving Delta a side look, "then it would be fine."

"Sure, if you want a takeover." Delta snorted.

"Well, I'm not against a takeover or a sale, depending on what it is, as long as the company remains here, keeps it employees."

"If it's a hostile takeover, that's a different story. If hostile, then these company guys—the one board member, her partner, Reggie, the sheriff, and whoever else is on the company payroll—are looking to cause trouble," Delta noted. "I personally think the theft of intellectual property was going on, with these devices and the patents and maybe even cloning of whatever to sell on the black market. These company guys were stealing from the company, in my opinion. The sale of the company would bring that to light. I think Reggie kidnapped Rebecca and her key card, then entered the building that night and wiped out the inventory of devices and implants and whatnot, which is why everyone was so rude and tight-lipped when I arrived and asked to speak to Rebecca, who had been kidnapped at that point. Granted, Badger and the feds will get proof of my theories, one way or the other. And that may take more time. However, just the mention of the kidnapping of Rebecca and Benjamin would impact the financial proposal in the wings, so the sale would not go through."

Deputy Halvorson pondered that. "Well, if it can make the company look bad, it could drop the price at least."

Delta added, "The company's reputation is already sullied with even the rumors of the kidnapping, before we find out the real reason for the death threats against these two. While they may not have seen anything incriminating or heard anything revealing, they were calling attention to the company at the worst time possible—before they got this huge sales price paid by some poor schmuck."

Halvorson seemed to be more worried now, hearing all these behind-the-scenes details.

"Still, we definitely need more intel." Delta stared at Halvorson. "By *we*, I mean Badger, his team, and I on behalf of the victims here. Now let's compare that, shall we? And what is your sheriff ordering you to do?"

Halvorson grimaced, not saying a word.

"Exactly," Delta pointed out. "The bottom line is, I am here to stay, and I want to ensure that whatever we do is right for Rebecca and for Gracie and Benjamin and keeps all of us here safe."

The deputy snorted. "I can't believe you came here for a damn dog."

"Yeah, that's because some of us care about *damn dogs*," Delta muttered. "Especially damn dogs that have served and sacrificed for their country."

The deputy shook his head, then sighed. "If that don't

beat all. Well, *apparently*, whether we like it or not, per Badger and the War Department, you are now part of the investigation, Delta. Therefore, if there's something you want to get done, apparently we have to get it done." He shook his head. "I can't believe the sheriff okayed that."

"I do believe it was above the sheriff's pay grade," Delta shared, with a bright smile in Halvorson's direction. "So, you might want to avoid the office for a little bit."

The deputy snorted at that. "You're not kidding. I'm not going anywhere close to him, not when he is fuming like this." Just then his phone rang. He looked down at it and glared. "Except for the fact that he's still my boss."

"Yep, but a minor boss. Still, he is your direct boss—under me, I might add—and now he's a really pissed-off immediate superior of yours, until he's arrested of course," Delta said, with a cheery smile. "You better take that one. You can explain that you had absolutely nothing to do with this and that you're not happy either."

For a brief moment, the deputy looked hopeful, and then he shook his head. "It won't make a bit of difference," he muttered. "The next few days are sure to be complete shit."

"Well, you could help solve this situation," Delta suggested, "and we would get out of your hair faster. Meanwhile, my presence and the War Department keeping an eye on things here will help keep Benjamin and Rebecca and Gracie and even Hannah safer now."

"You'll really take Rebecca with you?" he asked, as he turned to look back, where Benjamin, Hannah, and Rebecca were staring out the window, all having a separate conversation.

"If she'll come with me, absolutely," Delta confirmed.

"Pretty sure she's done with this town."

"Yeah, they won't be real popular if things go bad."

"*They* didn't do anything. All the events point back to the company," Delta declared.

"If they were kidnapped by the company, then I agree with you," Halvorson agreed, staring back to the gathering behind them. "However, if these kidnappings were conjured up to hurt the company, which leads to the company going under or the town's jobs all being lost, then believe me. The memories here will be very long and very strong for everyone. And they will all hold Benjamin and Rebecca liable."

"Which is complete bullshit," Delta replied.

The deputy shrugged. "Call it what you want, but those paychecks inure a lot of loyalty around here. These unsubstantiated charges won't change anything."

Delta chuckled. "Until they are duly substantiated, by the feds and the US government, no less.

Halvorson groaned, as he walked over to his cruiser. "You better be coming into the office soon. They're all expecting you to do a debrief."

"I'll be there," Delta said, with a wolfish smile.

"Make sure you aren't too friendly to me," Halvorson demanded. "I want to keep my job when you're done and when the fault has fallen wherever it may."

"Yeah, that depends on your being honest and true with me though," Delta noted, "because if anybody's crooked in that office, I want to know about it, and I want to know now."

Deputy Halvorson frowned at him in surprise. "Crooked? No. … Loyalties? Yes."

"You say that, but, when I see it like it is, not one of you in the sheriff's department was willing to go out and to help find Rebecca—not until I pressed you and pressed you hard."

At that, Halvorson winced. "The company did say that she … that her shrink eval wasn't very good and that she was probably off her medication."

"And that was an easy answer for you guys, right?"

"I'm not saying it was an easy answer," he protested, "but maybe we should have taken a little bit more notice."

"Ya think?" Delta asked in astonishment. "I'm **pretty damn** certain not a one of you wanted to do anything. And, for the record, if somebody was having a mental health crisis and was off their meds and was missing, shouldn't that make them an even higher priority for your attention?"

The deputy glared at him. "You'll be a pain in the ass, won't you?"

Delta gave him another wolfish grin. "I sure hope so."

CHAPTER 13

"**W**HERE ARE WE going?" Rebecca asked, as she got into the vehicle with Delta.

"To a motel, for the night," he said. "We'll stop in at your place and get a few items for you, your electronics and many more clothes, so that you don't have to live in just the clothing we got from the store. I'm sure there are things you'll want."

"Yeah, there sure are," she agreed, as she blew tendrils of hair off her face. "What was that conversation with the deputy? It looked pretty intense."

Delta gave her a rundown, short, sweet, and succinct but shocking enough that she could only look at him in wonder. "You managed to get yourself on the sheriff's staff?"

"Not on staff, per se," he corrected, smiling at her, "but definitely as a consultant, checking in on behalf of the War Department."

"Wow," she muttered. "I didn't think that kind of power came with your job."

"I contacted Badger and got him to get me in. He's got all kinds of connections," Delta shared. "The one thing everybody agrees on is that something is not very normal about this place."

"I'm glad at least that much got through in the conversation," she snorted, "because I highly agree. Something is so very strange when people won't help you, especially when that's the industry they're in."

"That's the industry they are *supposed* to be in, but I'm not really seeing that the sheriff's office is doing it to any recognizable law enforcement standard."

She nodded. "I am very happy that you showed up though. Does that mean you'll be going to the station now?"

"I will be. Just not right now," he told her, looking out the windshield. "Are you okay with that?"

"Sure. You're working to keep me safe and to keep Gracie in a good place, and I am totally okay with that." And then she stopped suddenly and asked, "Or is Gracie not part of the equation?"

"You can bet that not a one of these men gives a rat's ass about Gracie," he declared. "However, I do, and, yes, Gracie is a part of the equation, as far as I'm concerned. And certainly as far as Badger's concerned. Remember. I have official connections to the War Department when it comes to safeguarding retired War Dogs."

"War Dogs. … What a concept," she murmured. "Poor Gracie, what she went through, it's hard to even imagine."

"And yet they make up quite a lot of the patients you guys have at the company."

"I know that a lot of surgery is experimental limb stuff, prosthetics for animals, and the like," she murmured. "It's always been so fascinating to work there. I'll really miss it."

"Ha," he muttered, thinking about that.

"What?"

"What exactly is it that were you doing there?"

She gave him rundown of how she was helping with the electronic modules for the prosthetics. He nodded, yet frowned. She shrugged. "I know. Nobody ever really expects that, but I'm … I'm not a dumb bunny."

He chuckled. "You should contact Kat. She does kind of a similar thing but for people. You could ask her if she needs a hand."

She stared at him. "Well, it would be fascinating to do something like that," she replied cautiously. "Yet I can't imagine she would hire me with my limited skill set."

"I don't know about any *limited skill set*, but Kat could definitely use somebody to help her so I can get my damn leg fixed," he shared, with a note of humor.

She cracked a smile at that. "I see that's become almost a running joke between the two of you now."

"Except it's no joke at all, just a joke in the sense that she knows I need things. … I need improved prosthetics, but I'm also here now, so it's not as if she can do anything from a distance. Although hopefully the parts she ordered have arrived in the meantime."

CHAPTER 14

A T HER HOUSE, Rebecca slipped inside and quickly packed a to-go bag. She looked around, wondering at the sense of complete apathy she felt about this place. It had been broken into but there didn't appear to be anything stolen – except her phone was smashed on the floor. So then what were they looking for? Particularly when the kidnappers already had her and Gracie. Her laptop was still behind her nightstand where she usually tucked it if she was using it in the evening. Inside was an old phone so she snatched that one up along with the rest of the few belongings she was packing.

As Delta walked in to see what was keeping her, she smiled and explained, "It feels odd, but a part of me ... This was my safe place, before it wasn't anymore, so I'm just saying goodbye. Yet it seems that I should care more somehow, but I don't."

He nodded. "I'm not surprised. When you think about it, all the things that have happened, it's still associated with this place." He shook his head. "If it's not where you want to be, then there's no reason to stay."

"Yet it feels weird to just be so detached from it all."

"As long as you're not trying to run away from it, you're good," he pointed out, "because that's never a good thing and is destined for failure anyway."

"No, I don't think that's what it is." She smiled, as she walked toward him, her bag in hand. "It's really not that hard to say goodbye though."

"Are you saying goodbye?" he asked her curiously.

She shrugged. "I think in a way I am. I'm just not quite sure what's coming next. As long as I've got Gracie," she chuckled, as she glanced down at the dog, who even now was waiting at the front door, anxious to ensure she wasn't left behind, "I don't have a problem with it. Of course there are logistics to be solved. I have a place to sell for one."

Delta opened her front door, and, just as it opened wide, a shot rang out, slamming into the wood just beside his face. He quickly nudged Gracie inside, slammed the door shut, and threw Rebecca gently to the floor, even as she muffled her scream. "Stay here."

She groaned at that, as he rolled up and raced to the window, shutting off all the lights and peeking out from the side. When she joined him, he glared at her. She shrugged. "I would like to know who the hell just shot at us. Did they want to shoot us or just me?" she whispered.

"It doesn't matter," Delta said. "At this point in time, it's one and the same." With that, he stepped out the front door and disappeared.

She loved that, absolutely loved how he just jumped into the fight full on, not caring about any side but the side of right. You could really get attached to a man like that. Even the thought of it felt comforting. It was no longer a surprise to see the attraction between them or to hear her own thoughts on the matter because something had grown, probably starting from the first moment she had spoken to him on the phone, about a mutual love of dogs.

They'd gotten along so well, and there'd been such a

sense of satisfaction and happiness that he was even coming, even with the worry about Gracie. And yet here, with everything going on, she barely had a chance to even get to know him. She was hoping they would get that chance later, but now some asshole out there was determined that she wouldn't get a chance at all.

When he finally came back to her, after having done a full sweep around the townhouse complex, she looked at him expectantly. "Anything?"

He shook his head. "No, I'm pretty sure they've taken off."

"*Great*," she muttered. "Yet I didn't hear the vehicle."

He nodded. "If I were them, I would have parked a long way from here."

She winced. "It does bring it home, what your life has been like, when you say things like that."

"This all looks and sounds too familiar. This kind of work doesn't look like an amateur at all," Delta shared, turning to look back at her. She had a confused look in her eyes. He studied her carefully for a moment. "Remember. The only time I ever had to deal with something like that was in a war."

She replied sadly, "War sucks."

His grin flashed, warming her heart again, and he nodded. "I'll never argue that point. It does suck. It sucks for the people on both sides because there's never just one story in a war, and people on both sides are having their lives destroyed too."

"You would think that, with all the things we can do, there would be an opportunity to stop these wars, instead of letting them get as crazy as they are all over the world."

"Until people are ready, there isn't anything any of us

can do except keep trying to bring peace."

"What can we do about peace here and now in our own lives?" she asked in exasperation. "Is there any point in contacting Deputy Halvorson?"

Delta held up a little baggie in his hand that she didn't even see him get from the kitchen. "I'll pop the bullet out of the door, and we'll take it in and get it analyzed."

"Do we trust anybody there to analyze it?"

"Good point. If nothing else, I will take it to Badger."

"How? … Badger will get it analyzed?" she asked in astonishment.

"He'll know somebody who can do it," he replied, with a nod. "The one thing about Badger is, there's never any case of *can't*. He's always a can-do kind of guy. And Kat? She's even worse than that," he teased, with a chuckle.

And with the bullet popped out of the wood it had slammed into, he motioned her toward his car. "Let's go."

"You really think they're gone?"

"I do," he said in a certain tone. "They don't dare stick around on something like this."

"And yet," she muttered, "somehow it feels that they did."

He stopped and stared at her. "Is that what you're feeling?"

She shrugged. "Maybe I'm just too scared to go out there."

"And that would make total sense, but standing here and waiting for them to come back and shoot us isn't a good idea either."

On that note, Delta scooped up Gracie and held Rebecca's hand and raced out to his SUV. Once inside, he noted, "We still have the reservation at the one motel."

"But you don't seem happy about that."

"I think we'll at least change rooms for sure. I'm of two minds as to whether we should change motels."

"You think the shooter knows where we are?"

"I'm not sure that they do. … Send Benjamin a text, telling them to get out of there."

"I already did," she confirmed. "It's one of the first thoughts I had, … just in case." Her phone buzzed, and she looked down to see it was a text from Benjamin. She laughed. "They already left town, just after we left Hannah's apartment."

"Good. Tell him to drive like hell and to keep on going."

After she sent that message, she looked back at Delta. "It feels like running, and yet you just want to put an end to it and go."

He nodded. "In your case, … I don't know if running will do the job."

"Why do they care about me or Benjamin or Gracie?"

"I think they'll probably just write off Benjamin as being a scared kid, who's already long gone and not worth following. In your case, I don't know."

"What you really mean is because you showed up, their perception of me has changed."

He looked over at her and nodded. "Very perceptive, and we have to deal with the fact that I may have put you in danger."

"You didn't put me in danger," she snapped, glaring at him. "These assholes are doing the whole danger thing."

He smiled at her.

"It doesn't mean that I wouldn't have still been in danger anyway."

"Maybe not," he acknowledged, "but I would like to keep you safe."

"I don't want you injured because you came to check on a dog and wound up in a gunfight."

He burst out laughing. "That's a good way to look at it."

They pulled up in front of the motel. "We didn't even pick up food again."

"No, but I ordered a delivery to the motel," he shared. "It should be here, or, if not, it should be coming in few minutes."

She looked at him in wonder. "Do you think of everything?"

"God, no." He quickly glanced at her. "I wish I did. It would make life a whole lot easier. But like you, I'm reacting as we go and trying not to overreact just because I don't like the scenario."

"I don't like the scenario either," she muttered. "So, feel free to overreact."

He and Rebecca walked into the reception area, and, sure enough, packages awaited him. He nodded his thanks to the woman at the front desk and then asked her, "Is there another room available?"

She stared wordlessly at him.

"I would like to change rooms." She still hesitated, and then he shrugged. "Unless of course you're full up or you have a problem with that."

"No, I don't have a problem with it," she replied quickly.

"Preferably if it's on the backside. Even better if it's near any exit but still near our current room."

She glanced up at him but didn't say anything and continued clicking away on her keypad. She nodded and said,

"How about four doors over?"

"That would be fine," He looked at her and asked, "Has anybody been here, asking about us?"

Surprised, she shook her head. "No, I haven't had anybody asking about anyone."

"Good." then leaned over and whispered, "If they do, … we aren't here." And, with a smile in her direction, he wrapped an arm around Rebecca, as he led the way back out.

As they climbed up to their new motel room, Rebecca looked up at him. "Was that deliberate?"

"Deliberate what?"

"The arm around the shoulder, the insinuation that we're together."

"We're sharing a room," he noted, "so I don't think the arm around the shoulder was a statement in itself. But I did want to reinforce the idea that you are not alone."

"Ah," she said, with a happy sigh. "It makes a lot of difference, doesn't it?"

"Well, they might think twice about taking on a woman who has somebody with her versus going after a single woman they think they can take out fairly quickly."

"The fact that they even think that is irritating."

"It might be irritating, but, having done it once, they won't be expecting resistance."

"Ouch," she muttered. "I wasn't expecting them either."

"Even if you were, it wouldn't make a whole lot of difference." He looked over at her. "So, stop feeling guilty and just accept that this is where we're staying."

"Fine, but I want it over with."

"I know you do." Just then his phone rang. He glanced down at the number and frowned. He answered it, only to have a man identifying himself as the sheriff blasting away at him. Delta just hung up on him.

She looked at him and raised her eyebrows. "Did you just hang up on the sheriff?"

"I sure did. If he wants to pick a fight, I'm happy to have it, but I won't do it over the phone, and I sure as heck won't do it without being prepared." At the door, he led her inside.

She looked back at him, as she flung herself on the nearest bed. "You need to leave and deal with that, don't you?" When he hesitated, she nodded. "Go. I'll keep Gracie with me and stay out of sight. Nobody will even know I'm here."

"Except the fact that the receptionist knows."

She nodded. "But we've also changed rooms, and, if you want, we can change again."

"Again, that's not out of sight either. She'll still know."

Rebecca grinned suddenly. "What are the chances that you could get into one of the other vacant rooms without telling her?"

"I could certainly get into another room, if you would like to stay here until I get back. I can just pick the lock."

"Why don't we do that? Then it won't matter who comes visiting because they won't find me."

He laughed. "I like that idea. Good thinking. You stay close to your phone though."

"You too," she said, with a smile. "You know you'll get ambushed at the sheriff's office, right?"

"I might," he agreed, his tone turning cool, "but they haven't seen anything yet."

And, with that, he gave her a hard kiss, completely out of the blue, and added, "Watch your back."

As he headed out the door, she asked, "Don't you want to eat first?"

"No. I would rather eat after I deal with these assholes.

Save me some." And he closed the door, waited, and she quickly locked it. He came back minutes later, ushering her to a room two doors over, and left again, this time for the sheriff's office.

DELTA WALKED INTO the sheriff's office, as if he owned it. Only one way to handle this, and that was with power because these people wouldn't respond to anything less.

The sheriff stormed out of his small office and snapped, "Who the hell are you?"

"You already know who I am," Delta replied, glancing around the office and completely ignoring Deputy Halvorson. He pulled the bullet from his pocket and put it on the nearby desk with force. "One of you shot at Rebecca's house today, while we were in it." The deputy beside him stiffened, but he continued to ignore him. "When I find out who that is, believe me, there will be charges."

The sheriff started blustering. "You can't know it was one of my men. How dare you come in here …"

Delta waved him off with his hand, and he could see the man turning almost apoplectic when Delta then showed his back to him. "I'm done," he declared authoritatively. "I'm done with this office. I'm done with the lack of cooperation. I'm done with everybody protecting that blasted company, yet having absolutely nothing to do with two employees who were kidnapped, Rebecca and Benjamin."

"Just because you're getting a piece of tail," said one of the younger deputies snidely.

Delta didn't hesitate even a moment, as he turned around, and the deputy took a swing, which Delta avoided, but his uppercut hit his target. Delta literally picked the kid up off the ground and shook him. "What did you say?" he asked, his voice deadly quiet. He noted his name tag. "*Clark.*"

"Whoa, whoa, whoa," the sheriff jumped up and joined them. "None of that here. And none of what you just said either," he stated, with a warning look at his deputy, as Delta dropped him.

Delta addressed Clark. "Listen. I understand that the sheriff is your daddy, but I don't give a shit. You will not disrespect the victim of a crime, regardless of whatever schoolyard chatter or rumors you and your pals may partake in."

The deputy got to his feet, stepped back and away, his bluster now gone.

"And furthermore, if you think that your daddy here will protect you if you were the one who shot at us today, you're wrong."

"I didn't do anything wrong," Clark argued, glaring. "You got no business coming in here and causing all kinds of trouble."

"The trouble was well underway before I arrived," Delta pointed out. "If you're too stupid to get the facts straight before you come out swinging, you deserve just what you got."

Clark obviously didn't like that either, but stood there sputtering, at a loss for words.

"Now, in case any of you think my presence is optional, it's not. I'm here on orders from Commander Cross of the US Defense Department, and I'll keep a close eye on what happens from here on out for a whole lot of reasons. If you don't like it, tell somebody who cares, but it's not me." With that, he looked around and declared, "I'll need a desk. So either you guys find me one that I can use, or I'll just commandeer one."

The sheriff glared at him. "I've already protested and put in a formal complaint."

"Buddy, you can put in as many formal complaints as you want, and, if you stay with it, it'll probably match up to the number I've put in about you. We'll just see how many of these politicians who have been supporting you feel about your making no effort to investigate the disappearance and kidnapping of two of their taxpaying constituents."

The sheriff paled. "Now hang on a minute ..."

"Oh no, there's no hanging on about anything. You've had plenty of time to investigate these cases and to help these people. Instead you've done absolutely nothing," Delta announced. "In fact, you've done less than nothing by participating in the smear campaign against the characters of the two kidnap victims, supporting your inaction. I happen to know some of the supporters who have helped put you in place here, and I can assure you there will be some interesting conversations coming up about how only certain people warrant the legitimate time and effort from this department, and how a single woman, and a kid just starting out in the world, both of whom went missing, and were in fact kidnapped, didn't make the cut for the help of the sheriff's office."

The sheriff swallowed hard. "Now, there's no need to get nasty."

"*Nasty?*" Delta repeated, glaring at him. "You're lucky you're still standing in this building and still have your badge. Now, about that desk?"

The other men looked at each other and then over at the

sheriff, who barked, "You can have the one in the corner."

"Who was there before?"

He hesitated, then said, "Somebody who quit."

"When?"

"A while ago."

"Well, I want his file, and I want to know why he quit."

"You don't have the right to pull personnel files," bellowed Clark, the sheriff's son, standing a little taller again as he spoke.

Delta looked over at the kid again and smirked. "I have the right and the authority to do anything I need to do," he shared in a commanding tone. "And again, if you're the one who shot at me and Rebecca, you and I will be having a talk soon about the attempted assault of a government officer."

The kid jutted his chin out, but his father interrupted. "Clark, go back and sit down."

At that, the kid just glared at his dad. "I'm not a damn dog. I have this job fair and square."

"I wonder about that," Delta noted, still smiling in amusement. "You do know that nepotism can be a problem, particularly when we have crooked sheriffs around."

"Whoa, whoa, whoa," the sheriff mumbled, staring at him in shock. "You got no cause to say that."

"Really? So, you can give me the full report right now, verbally will do, and then a written report within the next oh, say thirty minutes, of exactly what you have done on the cases of the two missing persons, meaning the two kidnapping victims. In the meantime, I'll be right here at my desk."

The sheriff paled and slammed his jaw shut. For the next twenty minutes, Delta received a verbal rundown from each of the deputies as to what each had done, which, in Delta's book, was damn little, and all of it was after Delta had initiated his complaints with Halvorson.

With that, he looked over at Deputy Halvorson, using the same tone he had used with the sheriff. "Now, do you want to tell me what you've been doing?"

"You already know what I've been doing. You've been on my heels the entire time."

"Did you write it up, and does the sheriff know everything you know?"

"Probably not," he admitted, unabashed. "I haven't had a chance. I've been out looking for the victims."

"You've been out looking for the woman because I've been on your ass," Delta stated bluntly. "So, let's not sugarcoat it. I'm the only reason you were out there, and you know it."

"Now that's not true."

"Okay, maybe not, but you sure weren't looking for Benjamin, were you?"

Halvorson flushed at that. "I didn't realize that he was kidnapped, and that is a bad deal."

"It's a bad deal for all of you. It's one thing to take certain reports with a grain of salt, so to speak," Delta pointed out, "but it's another thing entirely to ignore reports when your own townsfolk are or could be in peril."

"We didn't realize it was a kidnapping," Halvorson stated. "I already told you that."

"You did. But nobody here even bothered to check up on Benjamin. It was easier to make up or to pass on a scenario about a messy breakup instead of simply doing your jobs."

Halvorson nodded. "You could be right, … and for that I'm not very happy with myself, and I'm sorry for all that both of them went through."

"How do we even know that she was kidnapped?" Clark snarled from the side in a loud voice. "It's not as if there's any proof."

Deputy Halvorson flushed, as the sheriff jerked his head over and glared at his son. "Just stop it, will you?"

"Well, he can't just come in here like that, like he owns the place," Clark wailed.

Delta smiled. "Maybe you just don't understand how the law works, and the fact that your father is in a position where he's supposed to uphold the law and to look after his citizens, not just a select few who put money in his bank account."

"That's a damn lie. I'm not on the take," the sheriff bellowed, glaring at him.

"It depends on whether there is any correlation between your choice of action or inaction and the interests of the men putting money into your election fund. It will be interesting to get that sorted first."

The sheriff shook his head. "You're just determined to cause trouble, aren't you, boy?"

Delta could see that the sheriff was getting angry again. Delta may have shaken the man's confidence, but he could see it rebounding. "That's good, Sheriff. Get angry. Let's see, right here and right now, what you're really made of. Let's see whether you're the one out there shooting up the townhouse of an innocent crime victim in your jurisdiction."

He glared at him. "I can't tell where the bullet came from. It's not as if you've documented it," he sneered.

Just then a courier showed up. "I'm here to pick up a package."

"Yep, this is what you want," Delta replied, as he walked over and handed the bullet to the courier. "Have you got the special packaging?"

"Yes, sir, I've got it right here."

And, moments later, with it all properly signed off and sealed, Delta let the courier take off.

The sheriff was dumbfounded, and, as if he suddenly woke from a stupor, he yelled. "Hey, where … what the hell are you doing with that bullet?"

"It's gone to processing." Delta smiled back at him. "Isn't that what you wanted me to do? It's not as if I trust the labs here, right? Not after all the irregularities so far. We'll know soon enough whose gun it came from."

Silence filled the room, as the sheriff slowly looked at his son, the color draining from the sheriff's face by the second. Clark, on the other hand, had turned multiple shades of red. "I … I was just … trying to scare them away."

"You fucking did what?" the sheriff roared.

Delta shook his head. "Yeah, that's what I thought," he stated, with a death glare at the kid. "So, Sheriff, what is it that you will do next?"

He turned and glared at him. "You don't need to be here. You can just get the hell away."

"I *could*, but I have no intention of doing so, not until my job is done," he shared. "I'm still on the hunt for a kidnapper, and we already know that's not your prime concern. You are probably more focused on keeping your ass out of jail."

"I'm not going to jail," the sheriff yelled immediately.

"Oh, that depends on what all we find out about what you've done wrong, and when I find it? Believe me. … I've got no problem passing it on for prosecution." He looked around the room at the stunned faces and the hanging heads. "You might be the sheriff, but, when you're crooked or bent in one direction, you can go to the slammer, just like everybody else."

Now Delta started getting *ping*s on his phone, all the reports he'd asked Badger for. Reports that made his eyes water, as he watched the numbers come across the screen. Swearing, he got up. A blank whiteboard sat off to the side. He brought it over in front of his desk and started writing down the names of all the staff in the building.

In the sheriff's office were four full-time deputies, one full-time receptionist, and the sheriff himself. So, a total full-time staff of six. As Delta started writing down the names, a couple people stopped and looked at it, then one raced over to the sheriff. Delta just continued to post the numbers and the names as they came in.

"What the hell are you doing now?" the sheriff asked, as he came around to look at the whiteboard.

"I'm looking for connections. Seeing as you guys aren't being very open about it, I had to get the information myself."

Then he wrote down who had connections to someone working at the company. As the list grew longer and longer, Delta stepped back and whistled. "You're all really heavily invested in the company, aren't you?"

"Not all of us," argued Sal, one of the deputies. "I don't have anybody working there."

"Neither do I," said Deputy Halvorson.

Clark looked at Halvorson and nodded. "But you did."

"I did, yes." Halvorson shrugged. "That was my ex-wife."

"Hell, I don't know about that. ... An ex-wife? Maybe you're still all over her." Clark glared at Halvorson, as he glared back.

"What the hell do you know?" Halvorson asked.

"I know that, if you wanted to get on the good side of your wife again, you would be all over it."

"Hey, that's not fair."

For Delta, it was interesting to listen to them wrangle among themselves.

Finally the sheriff interrupted. "Would you guys just stop it? We don't need to be giving Delta any more fodder for his asinine little investigation. I've already got phone calls in to have this guy's ass kicked out of here, so I'm sure he'll be gone in no time."

"Yeah?" Delta chuckled. "Let me know how that works out for you."

The sheriff just glared, as Delta went back to adding more info on the board. "So, Sheriff, I see your daughter works there, as does your mother. Even your sister and your brother-in-law. They all work there."

The sheriff nodded. "So what?"

"So, you are heavily invested in the well-being of the company. If we factor in the money poured into your campaign accounts, and this is just the official ones, added to get you elected, it's huge. You've received over forty thousand dollars from the company alone."

He glared, as one of the deputies whistled and muttered, "Holy shit."

"It's only forty grand," the sheriff repeated.

Delta cleared his throat. "Yeah, this is only a two-bit town. So now we have you taking bribes."

"Hey, it's not illegal to accept funds for election."

"No, it sure isn't, but these aren't election related. These bribes are to get you to turn a blind eye to all the shenanigans going on at the big company in town, right? We have proof of monthly bribes showing up in your bank accounts," Delta said, as he brought up that info on his phone and showed the screen to the sheriff.

The sheriff turned white. "What the fuck?" His tone turned low and deadly.

"Oh, did you think I wouldn't access all that? Shall I bring it up for everybody to see? Like the regular payments that have been made into your account on the first of every month? … That would be fun to share with the class. Can't wait until we get *that* investigation going."

Several of the deputies shifted uneasily.

"You aren't … You aren't taking bribes, right, Dad?" Clark eyed him nervously.

"It's not bribes. Of course it's not bribes. You know I do extra security for people, that's all. It's a second paycheck."

Delta laughed. "Right. A second paycheck. That's not how that works. And I'm sure you've been claiming taxes on all this too. Correct? Maybe not? Oh boy, the tax man will have a field day with you."

At that, the sheriff got belligerent. "You get the fuck out of this office right now." He ran over to the laptop and slammed it shut, then grabbed it and took it away.

Delta waved a hand. "I've already forwarded all that information to the War Department and to the IRS too," he shared, without moving an inch. "People from both departments are on the way here. So taking the laptop doesn't stop the forward momentum already initiated and won't make a bit of difference."

The sheriff pulled back his jacket, revealing his weapon.

Delta stood up. "You sure you want to play that game, Sheriff?" he asked, his gaze deadly soft. "Because, if you want to, I'm all for it."

"Whoa, whoa, whoa, whoa." Deputy Halvorson jumped in. "That's enough of that. Man, when you come in, you sure know how to cause trouble."

"I didn't cause this," Delta declared. "This shit's been happening here for way too long, and you've all turned a blind eye to it. You're just as guilty as the rest of them."

"No. I'm not," the sheriff replied angrily. "I haven't taken any bribes, and I don't know anything about this other shit, and I would be extremely disappointed if that has been happening. It's not taking bribes. I do extra security work, that's all."

At that, Sal, one of the deputies, shook his head. "No, Delta's right, Sheriff. That's not how it's done. We are the security for this town. You're not a security guard, and you don't go up there and look after that politician's place," he stated in a shrewd tone. "So, if you've been taking extra money on the side, you and I both know exactly what that is."

"You need to stay out of this, Sal," the sheriff snapped. "There's shit going on here that you don't know about. It's why you never got promoted."

"There *is* shit going on here that I don't know about, and I never got promoted because you're trying to keep it that way. I can see that now. You've got this inner circle of people you think you can trust because you're crooked, and I'm not in it," Sal snapped, glaring at him. "I may have been silent, but that's not okay in my book."

"Oh, what the hell," the sheriff snapped, "as if anybody cares if it's okay in your book."

At that, Clark stepped up. "Dad, seriously though, you're not taking bribes, right?"

At that, the sheriff turned and looked at his son.

"There's a time for you to be quiet, and there's a time for you to talk. This is not the time for you to talk, so just shut up."

"Ooh, ouch," Delta quipped, looking over at the younger man. "That had to sting."

Clark shrugged. "I should be used to it."

Delta shook his head. "I know you want to be part of the team, but, in this case, that's a bad move. I don't know who will still be standing when the investigation comes down, but it won't be anyone involved in bribery in any form or fashion."

"I don't have money to bribe anybody with," the sheriff snapped. "I get a paycheck, that's it. I don't get handouts from any companies."

"Oh, so if that is the case, and it's all on the up-and-up, then maybe you should have been a little more transparent. Then it wouldn't have come as such a surprise, and I wouldn't be able to air this extra monthly income, … like dirty laundry." Delta laughed.

"I've had enough of you," the sheriff growled. Turning to the others, he ordered, "Put him in a goddamn cell."

One of the men got up and took a step forward, but none of the others did.

"Smart move," Delta told the others, before he turned toward the sheriff. "You might get them all on your side, and five to one, or even four to one, they might succeed. However, if you think that will be the end of it, you're wrong. I'm more than happy to sit in a jail cell for a bit, while you try to cover your tracks. Just remember. The data has been sent already, including the log-ins to your … Let's just say a few other things that you've been hiding."

The sheriff swore heavily. "You—"

"You ought to calm down before you pop a vein or something. What I don't get is that you had to know that one day you would get caught." The sheriff glared at him, but Delta continued to smile. "You knew perfectly well that day would come, and you were trying hard to figure out how to get out of it. Yet most of the time you just convinced yourself that you would be completely fine."

"You won't ruin my repu—"

"No, you did that all on your own. It makes no sense to me, but maybe you really thought nobody would ever know, and you could just carry on raking in all this money and *keeping the peace*. Now, what I would like to know is which one of you was involved in the kidnappings?"

"None of us," the sheriff snapped. "Absolutely none of us." Then he turned and looked at his kid. "Isn't that right?"

"I sure as hell didn't have anything to do with it," Clark replied, staring at his father in a new light. "I ain't got no use for that shit."

"Good to hear, Clark," Delta noted. "So, who's been off for a few days or notably absent around the times of the recent kidnappings?" Delta kept his eye on one of the men, sidling anxiously toward the door. He turned to him, then smiled. "Trying to make an escape, by any chance, Sal?"

Sal shook his head. "I don't know what the hell's going on here, but this is starting to sound like some comic book caper."

"Oh, it's definitely a bad story, especially considering the huge holes in the plot," Delta agreed, with a nod. "Now, the next question is whether the people who were kidnapped can identify you."

Sal shook his head. "I didn't have anything to do with that shit. Right now, I just want to be off shift and go home to my family."

"That's too bad, particularly considering the fact that your family also works for the company."

Sal swore. "What did you do? How many laws did you break getting all this information?"

"No laws broken. Turns out there is a public registry for all kinds of information," Delta shared, with a smile. "Not to mention the fact that people happily post their information on social media these days. Too bad you guys just aren't smart enough to understand what the hell is really going on."

"You don't have to be so insulting," Sal snapped. "I didn't have anything to do with the kidnappings."

"No, maybe not deliberately or personally, but one of you is connected to the kidnappers," Delta stated, "and that's another story altogether. It's one thing to be involved in a hands-on way yourself, and yet it's another thing to know what somebody else is doing and not do anything about it." Delta turned to face the sheriff again. "You know all about that, don't you?" Delta asked, with a knowing smile.

The sheriff, his hands opening and closing, as if struggling to keep himself from pulling out his weapon, sputtered, "You don't know what you're talking about."

"Unfortunately I *do*, because we see it all the time. Power goes to your head, and you think nobody is watching over you, so you can do whatever the hell you want, and it's all yours. Then you get other people to believe that you can make things happen and that it's all within your power. But the truth of the matter is that you're still required to follow the law in action and in deed. That doesn't include allowing someone to kidnap other people," Delta explained.

"Circumstantial evidence at best."

"For now. It is all circumstantial evidence for now. But

give it less than twenty-four hours, and we'll see if any of you still have jobs."

"I want to keep my job," Clark stated, looking from Delta to his dad, the sheriff. "What the hell? What have you done, Dad?"

"I haven't done anything, son," the sheriff replied in a calm and soothing tone that didn't fool Delta one bit, considering the sheriff was sweating profusely.

"Yeah, he won't talk to you about what he's done," Delta pointed out. "And the truth of the matter is, it'll take more time to dig up all his criminal activities that your dad's worked so hard at hiding, all designed to line his pocketbook."

"It wasn't harming anybody," the sheriff declared. "It's not as if the company had any troubles up there. So it was just like a thank you in appreciation for doing my job."

At that, Silva, another one of the deputies, groaned. "If that's not the definition of a bribe, I don't know what is, Sheriff."

"No, a thank you is not a bribe."

Delta chuckled. "Right. So first off, it was money for a job, and now it's a thank you. See a pattern here, deputies?"

Two of the deputies nodded, Halvorson and Clark.

"It didn't have anything to do with me," Clark said, with a groan. "I really need my job, so I would like to be left out of this."

"You and me both, except you shot at Rebecca," Deputy Halvorson agreed, turning to look at Delta. "What the hell kind of investigation are you running here? It's all been in the background."

"That's the easiest way to catch people, isn't it?" Delta asked. "But just because you've got a crooked boss doesn't mean I know who was involved in the kidnapping, and believe me, I'm not going anywhere until I find that out."

"Are you sure about that?" the sheriff asked, a smirk on his face. "Maybe if that piece of ass wasn't available, you would be ready to turn around and leave."

"Is that a threat?" Delta asked. Meanwhile his stomach sank. "Is that what you've done? Did you send somebody out to pick up Rebecca again? What will you do to her this time?" Delta snapped, glaring at the sheriff. "What a piece of shit. Capturing girls, is that what you're into? This is what you guys are proud of?" He turned to face the deputies. "This is the man you want to work with? Are you nuts? Where is your pride? Where's your sense of honor and duty? Did you hear what he just said?"

"We heard," Deputy Silva confirmed, his tone turning faint, as he shook his head. "I just … I never thought I'd hear any of this stuff from one of us."

Delta nodded. "Well, you've heard it now and from the sheriff's own mouth."

Halvorson eyed Delta and then the sheriff, with disgust on his face. Halvorson asked, "Now, Sheriff, you tell me. Have you sent somebody after Rebecca?"

"I'm not talking to you. Delta needs to be reminded who is in charge in this town. … I am the law."

Delta replied, "I don't know about these guys, but I don't mind knocking you into tomorrow. Let's see if that'll loosen up your words." Delta was screaming on the inside, but his tone was deadly calm. He turned and asked the deputies, "Is anyone missing right now from the office who works here, even part-time?"

Clark looked up at Delta and paled. "Yeah. We call him the Hulk. He's not here."

"Why isn't he here?"

"He doesn't work all the time, and he's pretty ... He's kind of rough when he does work."

"Meaning, he beats up your prisoners?"

"Sort of." Clark winced. "He's kind of an animal." Realization dawned, and he turned and looked at his father, wide-eyed. "Did you send Hulk after that woman?"

The sheriff shrugged. "I ... don't ... know ... anything." He pivoted and stared down Delta. "But maybe Mr. Special Investigator should go find out."

"Oh, I'll find out," he declared. "Believe me. If I find out you had anything to do with it, I'll be back."

"I'm just standing here, doing nothing but yapping at you."

"Meaning, you just turned a blind eye, and that's what the payments were really for, isn't it?"

Deputy Silva was yelling at the sheriff now. "Are you serious? My God—"

"Stay out of it, Silva."

Silva turned to Delta. "Where is she? We've got to go get her."

"Yeah, but I'm not sure I can trust any of you," Delta replied, as he bolted out the door and headed for the motel. The entire time, all he could think was, *Hang on, sweetheart. I'm coming.*

CHAPTER 15

REBECCA AND GRACIE dozed on the bed, waiting for Delta to return. He had been gone way longer than she had expected, but she also knew that this could get ugly at his end. It was remarkably freeing to be in a different room than the one they had been in before, but that didn't mean she was safe from someone finding out where she was.

She still couldn't figure out why anybody would care though. Outside of the fact that the company people believed she could somehow stop a merger from happening. But it's not as if she knew anything, or seen anything. As she pondered that, she wondered about the things she had seen. Was something happening there which, if found out about, would scare them, making them afraid of what she might have seen? She couldn't put a finger on anything that would raise that level of concern. Just as she was dozing off again, relieved to have peace and quiet in her life, she heard a sound next door.

She opened her eyes and hazily looked around. Someone wasn't at the next door over. They were still one more from that. Thankfully Delta had set this up as one of those little things to give Rebecca and Gracie an extra measure of protection in his absence. When she heard a pounding on that door, she winced, wondering who was getting into trouble now. When she heard somebody yelling, she strained to hear, getting up and going to the door, pressing her ear against her door to hear better.

"Get out of there, you stupid bitch," yelled the guy.

She recognized the voice, or at least she thought she did. Not her captor, who may be dead now. She didn't know yet. This voice matched the second man she had seen while in captivity. She frowned, her heart slamming against her chest, as she realized how smart Delta had been to move her to another room.

She was safe. But for how long?

How long before this guy went back to the lobby and further intimidated the woman at the front desk, who would have her jumping at the chance to give him the room number they were supposed to be in.

He had apparently busted into the other room, and he surely didn't have keys for it. She frowned as she slowly walked back to her bed, wondering just how safe she was. When her phone buzzed, she looked down to see it was Delta.

"Are you okay?" he asked, when she answered.

"I don't know," she whispered. "Somebody's yelling at the door to the room we were supposed to be in."

"Listen," Delta replied in a calm tone. "I'm on the way to you right now. I ruffled some feathers, and you are in danger, so stay put."

"Damn it," she muttered, as she looked over to Gracie, snoozing. Hearing her voice, Gracie got up, walked over, and placed her muzzle in her face. "Gracie is here."

"And that's a good thing. Has she ever gone defensive on you or helped to protect you?"

"When the kidnapper kicked her for interfering," she whispered.

"Asshole," he muttered.

"Yeah, that's what I thought," she agreed, smiling through teary eyes, as she realized that, once again, she was likely to be in trouble. "How far away are you?" she asked worriedly.

"About ten minutes," Delta said. "No matter what, do not answer that door. Don't let anybody know you're in there, okay?"

"Oh, I wasn't planning on it. That's why I'm whispering."

"Good. Stay safe. I'll be there quickly."

"Do you know who it is?"

"Could be a part-time deputy I have not seen yet. But believe me. I want to find out," Delta stated. "The sheriff has been taking kickbacks from the company to look the other way."

"What?" she whispered in horror. "So, the company can do whatever and never worry about the sheriff getting in their way? What a crock."

"Right."

"We still don't even know all of what's at the bottom of this. What is the company doing that has them so worried about me and Benjamin and Gracie? What a mess," she muttered.

"My team is still digging into the company. I expect to hear something, even if it is early days. As for the sheriff, maybe the company's arrangement with him is why the company didn't go as far as killing us, with that shot at your door or while kidnapping you and even threatening you. Maybe the sheriff wouldn't condone that. It's also possible that he didn't know that the female board member had taken it that far. Either way, the sheriff's in trouble himself right now."

"Can you really get him kicked out?"

"I can certainly make it public and cause all kinds of chaos in his life, until he retires or resigns or is charged with something," Delta noted. "I threw around a lot of threats, and it might not take the sheriff all that long to figure out they were just threats."

"Oh, crap," Rebecca muttered. "If you don't have the power behind it, how will they react? It's only a matter of time until they figure it out."

"Who's to say," Delta said. "I don't really give a shit. My point was to stall a bit, as Badger and his team and those of us here on the ground try and figure out what was going on here with the company because something sure smells bad, and believe me. The sheriff is part of it, even if only to look the other way."

"That's just wrong. He's supposed to uphold the law, not give in to anybody who wants to manipulate it."

She heard the smile in his tone as he replied. "Absolutely, and that's why I like you," he shared. "We're on the same wavelength."

She snorted. "We might like each other, but that's a long way away from your suggestion."

"I haven't suggested anything," he teased in mock horror. "I'm just telling you the invitation is open."

She sighed. "I've got to say that, after all this, I'll be pretty happy to get the hell out of Dodge."

"That's what I thought," he confirmed. "And I'm not kidding. I think New Mexico would be a great place for you to come and visit."

"But visiting is one thing," she pointed out. "That doesn't mean I'll like it enough to stay."

"If you ever connect with Kat, and she figures out what you can do, I suspect she may want to hire you instantly."

Rebecca laughed. "I wouldn't mind a change of pace and location, but I'm not at all sure I have the skills that she needs."

"I've already texted her, so you should be prepared for a call."

"What?" she asked in horror. "Would it be like a job interview?"

"Yeah," he said. "That's the whole point." With a laugh, he added, "I'm coming in hot, and I'll be there in just a few minutes." And, with that, he hung up.

She sat at the edge of the bed, staring at the door. She heard no more pounding outside, but that didn't make her feel any better. If anything, it just made her worry what this guy would do when Delta came roaring in.

If this yelling guy was armed, chances were good he would open fire on Delta. She frowned at that. How the hell had she become so accepting of the idea that people would be walking around with guns that they were ready to use? Well, it was the US, and that generally meant gun-toting people were probably all over the place. She didn't want anything to do with that. She just wanted to live a peaceful life someplace with Gracie at her side.

Getting up again, Gracie walked over to the door and barked. Immediately Rebecca gasped and ran over, putting a hand on her muzzle.

"Don't. Don't do that. *Shhh.* Gracie, be quiet."

On the other side of the door, she heard a chuckle.

"Well, well, well …"

Her heart froze, as she stared at the door to her room in horror.

"Look who we have here."

The yelling man knew she was in here because of Gracie. She looked down at Gracie and whispered, "Why did you do that?"

"Hello, Gracie. How are you, girl?" the man asked through the door.

Gracie growled in the back of her throat.

That was all the man needed to know. He started pounding on the door. "Open up, you bitch, and let me in."

Gracie growled again and again.

Rebecca didn't know what to do to stop this madness suddenly spinning out of control. Delta had warned her, but Gracie had already given them away. Rebecca opened her mouth to reply but snapped it shut again, not sure if she should say anything or not.

Then the man spoke again. "You better say something. Otherwise I'll just start shooting into the damn door, and I don't care who I hit."

She stared in shock at the door. Then she heard the ratcheting sound of a gun on the other side.

"Stop," she yelled.

The gunman burst out laughing. "Well, there you are. Finally. Do you know how much trouble you've caused me?"

That voice *was* familiar. She was pretty sure this was the man who had partnered with that scary woman who came to visit Rebecca in captivity, specifically to threaten her and Benjamin.

"You even got Reggie killed. Do you know that?" the man yelled.

She winced at that but remained silent.

"Reggie was your guard. Remember him? You sure as hell tried to run him over, didn't you? I owe you for that one. The thing is, you didn't finish the job. His boss, … our boss, one and the same, she finished him off. Apparently that's what's waiting for me too, if I screw this up. Do you know how much money the buyers are paying for that company? Hundreds of millions, and everybody wants that payout. But not you, no. You had to go and cause trouble."

"I didn't do anything," she replied in confusion.

"That's not what they say. According to them, you saw something you weren't supposed to, and, as soon as that is exposed, it's all over."

"But I didn't see anything," she cried out. "I don't even know what you're talking about."

"It doesn't matter if you did or you didn't because you're still marked for death. As far as I'm concerned, the sooner I can get this over with, the better."

"I didn't do anything," she repeated.

"Maybe not, but they think you did. Besides, you've got Gracie, and they want her back. She's got technology in her that's worth a lot of money, and they need it to show the buyers."

"Oh no. No, no, no," she said in a panic, backing away from the door. "That's not happening. No way in hell you're getting Gracie," she cried out. "Gracie stays with me." At least she hoped she could convince the War Department of that.

"Only as long as you worked for the company, but now you don't work for the company, do you?" he asked, with a sneer, a scary playfulness in his tone. "I could happily shoot the damn dog myself, but I can't. I'm not allowed to."

Such sadness filled his tone that Rebecca shook her head. "What is wrong with you?" she cried out through the door. "You're a monster."

His tone turned ugly. "A monster, am I?" He growled low. "I may be a monster to you, but nobody else thinks so. We know exactly what side our bread is buttered on."

"That doesn't matter when what you're doing is just wrong."

"Oh, don't give me that bleeding-heart BS," he sneered. "There is no right and wrong when it comes to this stuff. Too much money is at stake. You got caught up in it and that damn dog too. So now that you've got her, they want her back. It's as simple as that."

"So, it's never been about what I supposedly saw?"

"Sure. It's been about you and the damn dog the whole time. Even after she went 'missing,' you wouldn't shut up about it. You even brought in the War Department. Who the hell does that?" he cried out in astonishment. "That's just too much trouble, and you brought it on yourself."

"Then why didn't they kill me when they had the opportunity?"

"Oh, trust me. They've been kicking themselves ever since. But don't worry, sweetheart," he sneered, "I'll make sure to put you down for good."

"You don't have a clue what you're talking about," she snapped. "I'm not a dog you can put down. I'm a human being. I have friends and people of influence ready to help."

"No, you don't. You are just another damned interfering piece of shit. And your savior sounds like he caused quite a ruckus at the sheriff's office today too. Although I haven't heard from anybody recently," he muttered, "so, who knows? Maybe they're taking him out too."

She didn't say anything, knowing perfectly well that Delta was on the way and must be very close by now. "You're just jealous," she said. "He's got more heart than you'll ever have."

"I don't want heart," he snapped. "I'll have my money, and that's all I need."

"That's pretty sad," she whispered. "Money does not buy you everything."

"No, it sure doesn't, but it will buy me a ticket out of here and a start in a new location," he explained, with half a laugh. "It will buy anything and everything I desire, and I don't really give a shit about anything else. I'll get my payout, and then I'm gone."

"Did you kill anybody yet?"

"Nope, I haven't had to," he replied. "You'll be the first."

"*Great*," she muttered. "What will you do with Gracie then?"

"Give her back to the company, and soon. They have a meeting with the new buyers tomorrow."

"I'm surprised Gracie was left with me."

"They were measuring certain things, and something was going wrong on the transceiver side."

Then she started to laugh. "Or something went very *right*," she corrected, with a chuckle. "You have no idea how far other people have gotten with that technology already."

After a shocked moment, he asked, "What are you talking about? This is proprietary information, patented and all. Nobody knows how to do the shit that they did."

"Oh, I think you'll find that, when all that supposedly weird stuff was going on, that stuff they needed to check was other people hacking into the chip they'd installed."

He growled, his tone turning uglier. "Get the fuck away from that door," he said in a deadly tone. "You better be wrong. We're all counting on that payout."

"You might be counting on it," she snapped, then shrieked as he busted through the door. She glared at him, frozen in fear, yet recognizing him as the second man who'd been with that woman, threatening them, even while in captivity.

"Ain't no way you're getting anything from me. And I'm not taking any shit from you," he declared, as he lined up the handgun. "This is just a run-of-the-mill breaking-and-entering. Happens all the time. It's so sad. You were just in the wrong place at the wrong time."

Gracie growled at him, looking from Rebecca and then back at the gunman. She kept growling.

He turned his gun to Gracie and yelled, "Shut the fuck up."

Rebecca shook her head. "Gracie won't, and you can't shoot her because then you'll really be in trouble. You might as well put a bullet right between your own eyes," she suggested, searching, digging deep for the bravado she could barely feel. Surely Delta was here. He had to be here by now.

"That's all right. I could shoot her in the leg, and that'll shut her up."

"No, no, it won't," she whispered, stepping up in front of the dog. "All you'll do is hurt her, and I'm sure that will mess up the electronics there."

He looked uncertain for a moment and then shrugged. "Then you better behave yourself," he added, "because you're coming with me."

He grabbed her arm and dragged her roughly out to the door and to the steps. She fought hard. "Stop it," he yelled, as he shook her hard. "If you scream or resist, I'll shoot the damn dog."

Not sure whether she could believe him or not, Rebecca

shut up, and he laughed. "See? That's the stupid thing about you. All you want to do is to save and protect everything." He laughed in her face. "There isn't any protecting anybody in this world, you stupid bitch. It's everybody for themselves."

"You're wrong. Everybody is not for themselves. Hell, Delta is not like you at all."

"Oh, was he the guy who raised so much trouble with the sheriff? That's a hoot. They got kickbacks for years for keeping trouble away from us. And now look? At the first sign of trouble, they're caving all over the place." He laughed. "They won't be getting any more kickbacks after this. Matter of fact, they're moving the entire company somewhere else."

She winced at that.

The gunman nodded. "That's what happens with takeovers. They shut down and take what they want. The owners are selling, and the buyers can do whatever the hell they want with the company, after the property changes hands. We take the money and run."

"There's no *we* about it." Rebecca chuckled. "If you're no longer alive, it just means fewer people to split the money with. You said yourself that your life was on the line over this job. I bet your life is on the line no matter what because you know too much. Just like Reggie."

"I don't need to listen to any more of your shit."

"Maybe not. But that's what you are, that's who you are," she added, seeing a shadow of doubt on his face. "Your friends are thieves, and they're greedy. You know yourself they won't want to split the money with anyone."

At this point, he was shoving her down the stairs to the parking area. She kept looking around to see where Delta was. He had to be here. Unless something had happened to him too. Just the thought of that was enough to make her heart ache. She really, really loved the idea of New Mexico.

As she had started to really consider it, understanding that it might be a real possibility for a new start, here was somebody trying to take it away from her. She hated that. She hated that she was being pushed around by these people, who had such little regard for animals or humans.

"Why are you such an asshole?" she asked, staring at him. "Where do you get off playing with other people's lives? That gun doesn't give you the ability to just do whatever you want."

"No, it sure doesn't," he agreed, "but it sure helps. You're one of those diehard bleeding hearts who wants to save all the animals, but you don't even know what's happening right under your nose. Do you have any idea what kind of testing they're doing on the animals in there? Everything from poisons to shooting them up with drugs and trying new medicines." He laughed.

"That is aside from the devices, like the one buried in that damn dog. You've got no idea that the boss lady, who's in the know as a board member, was stealing all those devices from the company, stealing the patent info, then selling them off. The Chinese company that holds the patent has seen some of these clones and has figured out it is our location with this side business. So they are coming for a visit—one day after the sale." He laughed again.

"Perfect timing. That's why we had to hold you and the other guy and the damn dog. Reggie stole the devices still at the company, right after he kidnapped you. He stashed them somewhere, and now he's dead, and we don't have that inventory. The last of the Chinese prototypes is in that damn dog. Boss lady needs that one to clone some more. All this was going on right beneath your nose, and you've worked there all this time, and yet you were clueless."

"But now that you've told me, I do know," she declared, hating to hear all this. "You're supposed to be helping those animals. You're supposed to be helping update and rebuild this research center into a modern state-of-the-art facility. An ethical facility that does its work without harming animals."

"Sure, but in order to rebuild, they also have to test on animals. And that entails pain, which is exactly what they're doing." He smirked. "I don't even understand all of what they're doing, but you can bet it ain't all aboveboard."

She was sick to her stomach at the thought of it. "Then it's a good thing it'll get shut down now anyway."

"First it's being sold. And we split the money. Then the buyers will find out they have no prototypes, and the Chinese company won't give them anymore. So, the boss lady's clones will be sold for high-dollar price tags. She'll hold the new buyer hostage. That's a whole different story."

"No, it's not really." She stared at him. "It's just the same old BS every time. It's all about money and power."

"Exactly." He smiled with satisfaction. "Now you are getting it, yet you still don't get the whole picture. Now shut the fuck up and get in the car." He pointed the gun at her. "Move it."

She stopped, looked at him, and saw Delta pull up behind him. "And what will happen if I don't?"

He turned the gun toward Gracie, who started to growl in the back of her throat, almost as if she saw her other team member coming up behind the gunman. If so, Gracie was prepping herself to join in the fray.

"You leave Gracie alone," Rebecca cried out, stepping

forward. "She's already been hurt enough."

"I ain't stopping nothing," the gunman snapped, waving the gun at her. "You jump in on this, and believe me. I'll pop her." Then he raised his gun arm to fire.

Gracie took off at a lunge but unfortunately not away. She was lunging right for him.

He just laughed and asked, "Which leg should I take out?"

Just then, Delta grabbed him from behind, raising the firearm and pulling the trigger so it fired aimlessly into the air, as he kicked the gunman's legs out from under him and brought the handgun down against his own temple.

As he lay here, dazed, Delta rolled him onto his stomach, clipping his hands against his back. "How about neither. Just in case you have any ideas racing in that mind of yours, know this. I'm okay shooting your legs out from under you. So go ahead and move, and we'll see which one of us wins this battle." He looked over at her, smiled and asked, "Are you okay?"

Shaking, with tears in her eyes, she wrapped her arms around Gracie and nodded. "It's Gracie they wanted," she whispered, "Not me. They want Gracie."

"I thought you told me that Gracie was the first to be kidnapped?"

"She went missing, but this gunman told me that it was because I was spending too much time with her. They were afraid I would get too close and find out she had additional technology in her beyond a standard chip."

"That's why Stone had a chance to do what he did, allowing us to get that transmission to you," he pointed out. "Believe me. He's already been talking to the government about it."

"What the company did to these animals is just sick," she shared, her arms wrapped around the dog. "How can they abuse animals that way?"

He looked over at her with a sad smile. "Animal testing has been going on since forever and a lot of times to the benefit of humanity. It's just that most people don't know the cost to the animals involved."

Tears in her eyes, she nodded. Then she stood and walked over and kicked the gunman once in the leg. "You're an asshole."

He snorted and yelled, "You can't go far enough to hide from me."

"Oh, give it a rest," Delta snapped at him. "You aren't getting paid, and that's the only thing you care about."

He lifted his head. "What do you mean, I'm not getting paid?"

"We already picked up everybody involved in this kidnapping from the company, and all the assets have been frozen. This operation has been going on in the background for a few days now," he muttered. "We know about the buyers coming tomorrow. They got a visit from some officials too. And now we also know about the Chinese, who were coming the following day. However, we updated them, so expect the Chinese on your doorstep tomorrow instead."

"Who the hell are you?" the gunman asked.

"Hello, Hulk. I'm Delta," he replied. "I work for the War Department and came here a few days ago to check on a retired War Dog named Gracie. Things were not kosher long before I got here, and I sure as hell wouldn't let this atrocity continue," he snapped. "The sheriff's been picked up. All I needed was you. You're the one who was in the wind. If you'd stayed in the wind, you would be free for a while

251

longer, but, no, you had to come around and get Rebecca and Gracie."

"They needed Gracie," he snapped, "and *her* out of the way."

"That's not happening. You're not taking Rebecca or Gracie anywhere. Rebecca won't be out of the way. She'll never be out of the way, so I would forget about her."

"That's just bullshit," Hulk snapped.

"It doesn't matter whether it is or not." Then he watched as Gracie squatted over Hulk's shoe and pissed on him. Delta laughed and pointed it out to Rebecca.

She looked over to see what Gracie was doing and giggled. "Oh my gosh, that's just too funny."

"What's she doing?" Then Hulk shook his leg. "Oh my God, that's gross." And he started swearing and complaining, as he realized Gracie had just peed all over him.

Gracie got up and raced around as Delta stood, now that the gunman was secured on the ground.

Rebecca threw herself into Delta's arms, and he wrapped her up tight. "Are you okay?" he asked.

"I am now," she whispered. "Gracie growled and then barked, letting Hulk know where we were. I think she recognized his voice."

"Yeah, she would," Delta confirmed. "This guy's a part-time deputy, and also works around the company, and has for quite a while. Doesn't mean he liked any of the dogs, but Gracie would have known him."

Rebecca burrowed her head against Delta's chest. "Can we go home now?"

"Depends on where home is," he quipped, with a laugh, as he pulled her up close, leaned down, and kissed her gently.

She grabbed him by the ears and pulled him down for a

deep, soul-searching kiss that had him gasping for breath, when he finally raised his head. "Home is wherever we are. I really don't care where, but not here, not this town, not this place, not these people," she muttered. "I just want to get the hell out and away from here."

"Good enough," he replied, keeping the gunman in sight. "Home for me is New Mexico. How about that?"

"I can find you in New Mexico," the gunman growled, from his prone position on the parking lot.

"You could," Delta agreed cheerfully, "but I don't see you getting paid. The sale will not go through as planned. Plus Reggie, one of your partners, is dead, and you helped make him that way. Then the sheriff, another one of your partners in crime, has been arrested. Then the female board member, who was stealing from the company and its special Chinese vendor, has also been arrested. Now you've been caught. So I don't think you're going anywhere for a while. We're just getting started in sorting out who did what, so I have no doubt more intel will come."

Hulk took a moment to digest all the news and then muttered, "Hell."

"Yeah, that's how life will be going for you, I think," Delta stated, laughing. He turned when he saw two other vehicles pull in. One was Deputy Halvorson, who got out, took one look, and swore.

"Good God. Damn it, Hulk. It is you. What were you thinking?" Halvorson asked him.

Hulk grumbled, "I didn't do nothing."

"Oh, hell yes, you did. Once I realized what the hell was going on, I just knew you would be involved somehow." He looked over at Delta. "This is my ex-brother-in-law. He's a well-known, useless, lazy-ass piece of shit."

"And now he can go to jail for it," Delta said, with pride.

At that, two unmarked vehicles pulled up. As soon as the plainclothes men got out, one looked over at Halvorson and said, "You might sweet talk yourself into the sheriff's position right now—at least on a temporary basis."

The deputy frowned at him.

The agent explained, "I know you're in the clear."

"How the hell did you know I was?" Halvorson blustered.

"I could see a man fighting the crooked system, struggling to stay loyal," he replied, and then smirked. "*That* and I also checked your background, and nothing popped."

"That's one of the reasons I was kept from promotions because of all this bribery shit and looking the other way, which isn't what I do." Halvorson shook his head. "My wife and I divorced because I wouldn't follow along with whatever the hell these guys were getting into. I knew it was a bad deal, and I wouldn't do it." He pointed to Hulk. "Are you taking this guy, or am I?"

Delta looked at the two new arrivals and smiled. "I think these gentlemen came to deal with all of it."

The two men never introduced themselves, but they shook hands, picked up their prisoner, and spoke to Deputy Halvorson one more time. "Be in the office tomorrow morning. We'll have a talk." And, with that, they left.

"Who the hell are they?" he asked, turning to look at Delta.

"People who specialize in dealing with crooked law enforcement," Delta replied. "Just be happy you're not on their list."

"Shit," Halvorson muttered. "Do you always deal with such scary-ass people?"

"Yeah, I do. Makes life pretty simple."

Halvorson snorted. "Now … what about you guys?"

"We'll need to write out our statements, clear up all the paperwork that goes along with dealing with this kind of garbage," Delta replied, "and then we're getting out of here. As a matter of fact, we might just leave first and send all the paperwork back later."

"Can we do that?" Rebecca asked, reaching out a hand and sliding her fingers through his.

"Yes, we can." He looked down at Gracie. "Did she get hurt again?"

"No, she didn't, but Hulk said some really expensive technology was inside her that the boss lady was after, so that it didn't fall in the hands of the buyers or even the Chinese who made the patented prototype. Boss lady was cloning the device and hoped to sell it to the new owners of the company, keeping the Chinese from selling their own creation."

Delta nodded. "That's what I heard from Badger, so it's consistent with the intel so far. At least for now. More will be found, I'm sure."

"Gracie's been through so much—"

"We'll get somebody in New Mexico to check her out and remove it."

"Do we have to get it removed?"

"Yes, just in case it can be used against her. Or us, for that matter."

"Oh, shit," she muttered, "maybe we should get it done here."

He shook his head. "No offense, sweetheart, but I don't really trust anybody here."

She smiled. "Especially not my girlfriend, Robin, *huh*?"

"Well, she might be capable of the surgery part, but I

would just as soon know that the people removing it care more about Gracie than that piece of technology."

"Good point," she whispered. She looked back at Deputy Halvorson. "So, you can contact us if you need anything, but I really hope you don't have to."

And, with that, they got into Delta's vehicle, and, Gracie at their side, they drove off.

"I COULD HAVE used some sleep," Delta muttered.

"I can drive," Rebecca offered immediately.

"No, it's fine. We'll check into a hotel or motel or B&B or whatever is up here in the next few miles and grab a few hours of sleep," he noted quietly, "and then we'll continue."

"Do you think that's okay? That we'll be safe?"

"I know it's okay," he stated, glancing at her. "It's all good." He reached out a hand to Gracie. "She really did have good timing, didn't she?"

"She also went to bat for you," Rebecca said, smiling at him.

He shrugged. "Animals like me."

"Yeah, I've noticed." Her lips twitched. "It's one of the reasons I thought you might be okay because her ears always lifted up whenever we talked on the phone."

"Yeah, about that. Grace never did go missing, did she? You had her the whole time, didn't you?" She looked over at him sideways, and he nodded. "I figured that one out pretty quickly. I just wasn't sure what I was supposed to do about it."

"Are you mad at me?" she asked in a small voice.

"No, sweetheart. It would be interesting to know how

you knew something was wrong though."

"It was just the way they treated her, and the way Gracie responded to them," she explained, waving her hands. "I couldn't stand it. Something was so underhanded about it all, so secretive. I figured there was a problem, but I didn't know what, didn't have evidence. And then, when I snuck her home that day, and the company asked me about Gracie, I lied." She took a deep breath. "Once I lied, I couldn't exactly keep her with me, like when I was at work, so Robin was keeping her part-time. I had Gracie back with me when I was kidnapped, and I guess they brought her with me." She sighed. "I lied hoping that it bring an investigation into the company."

"Well, I don't know what your long-term plan was for that," Delta noted, "but I don't have a problem with your keeping Gracie permanently." She smiled at him in delight. He shrugged. "They sure as hell aren't getting her back."

"Thank God for that." She started to laugh. "Jeez, I had no idea that keeping Gracie, trying to keep her safe, would bring you into my life."

"And now that you know?" he asked, turning to look at her.

She smiled. "I should have done it sooner."

He burst out laughing. "So, you're okay to see where this goes?"

"Yes. I'm absolutely okay to see where this goes," she confirmed, feeling something blossom inside her that she hadn't felt in a very long time. "I hadn't realized just how oppressed I'd been feeling and how upset I was getting every time I went to work. It feels like I have a whole new lease on life somehow."

When he yawned, she winced.

"Come on. Let's grab a room, sooner rather than later. You need to get some sleep," she said, "and I haven't had a decent night in forever."

They pulled into the next motel along the highway. When he parked around back, she smiled. "Do you think they're still coming after us?"

"No, I think it's habit at this point."

"And a good one," she whispered. Once they got into the room, she looked over at him and asked, "Shower or sleep?"

He thought about it and winced. "I want sleep, but a shower sounds too good."

Without even thinking about it, she started to strip off her clothes. When he stared at her in surprise, she looked over at him and added, "Hey, we save water if we shower together."

His eyes lit up, and he shucked his clothing faster than she thought possible. When it came to his prosthetic, he looked down at it and sighed.

"You take that off in the bathroom, I presume," she noted. "You really should get Kat to build you a waterproof one. Maybe we can get something out of titanium steel, maybe blue steel. … That would look awesome."

He looked at her, and he started to grin. "You definitely need to talk to Kat," he said on a laugh.

"You just want an in with the designer."

"Absolutely I do," he declared, as he walked toward her, nude except for his prosthetic. "And, yes, we'll take it off before the shower."

"Are you okay with a shower?" she asked him. When he just glared at her, she threw up her hands. "Fine. I'm saying though, you need to get a waterproof one."

"I'll tell her that you said that," Delta replied. "She'll love it."

Rebecca blushed. "Well, you don't need to tell her *why* I recommended it."

"Oh, I think I do," he teased, laughing as he bent over the bathtub to turn on the shower. Stepping back, he quickly removed his prosthetic and stood with his uneven gait.

"You can stand on it?" she asked.

"I can stand on the stump. I can't go far, but I can take a few steps if I have to."

"I love being able to talk to you and to get your feedback on this. The animals don't talk back when I ask them."

Delta chuckled, as he shook his head and smiled. Then he stepped into the shower, steadying himself on the wet floor.

She slipped behind him and grabbed the bar of soap. "I get to start." And, with that, she quickly turned, so the water sluiced over them both. Turning back to him, she washed him from head to toe, taking special attention as he rose to attention in front of her. She chuckled. "I can't say I've ever played in the shower before."

"I can't say I've ever played in the shower with some-body quite so deadly." When she reached for him again, he gasped. She wrapped her hand around his shaft and gently stroked him up and down. He shook his head. "You're quite deadly. You know that, right? I'm already unbalanced."

"Ooh, so what does that mean? I'm taking advantage of you, am I?"

He grinned. "That's okay. Believe me. When we get out of here, I'll be back on my home turf," he explained, in between waves of pleasure coursing through him. "So I'll give you as good as I get."

She wrapped her arms around him, sliding her slick skin against his, and whispered, "I'm counting on it."

He sucked in his breath, grasped the back of her head and pulled her tight, kissing her until she was moaning in his arms. He lifted his head and asked, "Are we finishing this here or going to bed first? We can finish the shower and then head to bed, or we can try it in here. What do you think?"

"I would love to try it in here but not right now." She laughed. "Besides, we still have to shampoo our hair." And, with that, she got back to the business of sponging down the rest of him and pouring shampoo onto her hand and working it into his hair. When she'd done his, she quickly did hers, and together they managed to rinse off.

When the water was off, she wrapped a towel around herself and eyed him with a teasing look. "I'm not really sure how you'll make it to the bed," she whispered, "but I sure hope you get there fast." Then, laughing, she raced out into the other room.

He had to grin. Not only had she not been turned away by his facial scar or his prosthetic, she was leaving it up to him to deal with it however he needed to. He quickly dried off, then realized he didn't want the prosthetic in bed with him anyway. So, he hopped his way to the bed a little slower, only to find her curled up on her side, waiting for him.

He stopped at the bathroom doorway, leaned against it, and whispered, "You know you're beautiful, right?"

Her eyes opened wide, and she stared at him in surprise, then smiled. "It's not something I ever really think about, but, as long as you're happy, I'm good with it."

He nodded. "I'm more than happy with you," he murmured, "because you really are truly gorgeous. Inside and out."

"That is something I'm very happy to hear." She opened her arms and asked, "Are you coming over here anytime soon?"

He made the last few steps in a half hobble hop, definitely awkward and lacking finesse, but he couldn't care less because nothing in her gaze changed as she watched him make his way to her.

She smiled at him. "It really doesn't matter how you get from point A to point B," she told him. "All that matters is that you make the trip."

As soon as he collapsed onto the bed, she wrapped her arms around him, rolled over so she was on top, and announced, "Besides, this way I get to be on top."

He groaned, as she once again wrapped her hands around his shaft and stroked him gently up and down, while she cupped his sac beneath and wiggled all along his hips and thighs. He sucked in his breath, his hands gripping the sheets on either side as he lifted his hips, not to shift her off but rather desperate to change the status quo.

She leaned down against him. "I don't suppose you like horses, do you?"

He opened his eyes, and, as she watched the light flare inside, he asked, "You do?"

"I'll tell you one thing," she whispered. "I love to ride."

And she slowly mounted him, then set a pace that had them both crying out. When she finally exploded above him, she held on, as he flipped her onto her back and drove into her, once, twice, three times. Then they both exploded together.

When he sagged down beside her, she chuckled, wrapped her arms around him, and tucked up close to him. She murmured, "If you're this good with a bad ankle, I can't imagine what you'll be like when that ankle joint is fixed."

He burst out laughing. "I think I'll tell Kat that's why we need you to work for her."

"Oh God. Just so you can get a working ankle joint, and we can test it out?"

"Absolutely," he murmured. Tilting her head, he kissed her deeply. "I'm so glad you decided to come to New Mexico."

"I still have a mess here to deal with at my townhome," she noted. "Still, I figured I should take a look at New Mexico and see if it's a place where maybe I would like to live and work." She batted her eyes. "I need to see for myself if there is a compelling reason for me to stay."

"Absolutely there is," he declared, pulling her close and kissing the top of her head, "and I'm just one of them. It's also a perfect place for Gracie."

She stopped and looked at him, then asked, "Do you have a house?"

"I have a house, I have a yard, ... a big yard, with acreage that backs onto a creek," he shared. "It's perfect for animals."

"What about a family?" she asked, looking up at him hopefully.

He nodded and smiled. "It was always part of the plan. Somehow the plan didn't quite work out."

"That's because it wasn't the right time," she stated, kissing his neck. "You know what the universe is all about, ... her time or no time."

He burst out laughing again. "Well, I'm really glad I'm on her time now."

"So you should be," Rebecca said, as she laid her head back down again. "I always wanted three."

"Oh, I was thinking more like five."

She stilled, kicked her head back, and repeated, "Five?"

"Sure," he agreed, with a grin. "Five dogs and three kids."

She smiled. "Oh, I can get behind that."

"Good, then tomorrow we start the first day of the rest of our lives," he proclaimed, as he pulled the blankets over them. "Our new life will be what *we* create. Exactly as we want it."

"That sounds perfect," she murmured, "especially if Kat is okay with having me working for her."

"We won't know until we ask. I suggest we do that as soon as we hit town. I need to report in anyway," he shared, "so you can come with me."

"I don't know," Rebecca replied. "That might be putting Kat on the spot."

"You don't understand. You don't put Kat on the spot. She's probably already figured out who you are and what you do, and she'll snag you as soon as you walk in."

Rebecca chuckled. "I wouldn't be at all upset about that either. ... Work for me has been an uneasy place for a long time now," she whispered. "Finding a place to call home sounds like just what the doctor ordered."

"And we'll get there," Delta said. "Let's just sort it out, get you there for a first look, take care of the rest of this madness, and get you moved down there. I'm ... I hope I'm not pushing you. Yet I am pushing," he admitted, with a smile. "So, I'll need you to tell me if it's too much. I'm just so excited because we have a chance now to create everything we wanna create."

And, with that, they closed their eyes, tucked up tightly together, and slept. They had a great future ahead of them, and they were both eager to get to it.

Gracie must have read their minds, as she gave a *woof* of agreement.

EPILOGUE

K AT GRINNED, WHEN she opened the door to see Delta standing there with Rebecca. "Now, don't tell me," she greeted them. "You need an ankle joint."

Delta smiled broadly, genuinely happy to see her, and beginning to allow himself to feel the effects of the past several days.

Kat continued. "You may be surprised to hear that I have some parts for you." Then she looked over at Rebecca, smiled, and nodded, "Hi, it's nice to meet you. I'm Kat."

"Hi," Rebecca replied shyly.

Kat studied the pretty woman, who looked as if her life had been flipped upside down. Yet somehow she'd landed upright. "Rough couple days, *huh*?" she asked Rebecca.

"You're not kidding," she murmured. "Yet it seems like all good things end well."

"And that's what we count on." Kat nodded and smiled as she eyed Rebecca. "I also hear that you've done some work on prosthetics."

"Yes, but on animals though," she clarified. "So I don't know how helpful that would be to you."

"Are you kidding? It's already helpful, especially if you know your way around a wrench, a screwdriver, a hammer drill, and a few other tools."

"Yeah, I do," she said. "All very necessary on the electronic circuit board side of things."

"Good," Kat declared, with a huge smile. "Are you looking for a job or just looking to take a holiday?"

"Well, a holiday for a little bit would be nice," Rebecca replied, "and I still have to get some of my stuff moved out."

"We can just hire a company for that," Kat noted, with a wave of her hand. "There are people in the world who do that sort of thing. We've got other things to do." She heard her husband coming to join them and looked over at Badger, a big smile on her face.

Badger walked up, introduced himself to Rebecca, and smiled. "How you doing there, Delta?"

"I'm doing great," he stated, as he wrapped an arm around Rebecca's shoulders. "If I'd realized this is the kind of shit you guys were handling—"

"You would have run in the opposite direction," Badger stated.

Delta laughed. "I might have run, but only because I wouldn't have understood." He shook his head. "Now I understand, and that's a whole different story." He leaned over and kissed Rebecca hard on the cheek. "This would have made any trip perfect."

Badger chuckled, looked over at Kat, and teased, "So, I guess you got another successful matchmaking feather in your cap. What will you do now?"

"Yep, I did, and I already know who I have in mind for the next job. But first things first." She looked over at Rebecca and offered, "Why don't you come into the office tomorrow, and we'll see if it's a match."

Badger's gaze lit with interest. "You guys think you can work together?"

Rebecca smiled. "I'm game, if Kat's game. All I've heard

about is this ankle joint of Delta's."

That set Kat off into giggles again. Badger just shook his head. "I swear to God, these two? All they deal with is that ankle."

"But I was thinking blue steel would be cool, maybe with some filigree metal all through it," Rebecca suggested. "That would be awesome."

At that, Badger looked at her with interest.

Kat's gaze lit up, and she nodded. "I really would like to get more artistic with some of this. That would be amazing." And, with that, the two women headed off to have a chat.

Badger called out to his wife, and Kat turned and looked at him. He asked her, "What about the next one?"

"That's all right," she said. "I'll get there. I already have Conall tagged for it."

He stopped, his hands on his hips, and asked, "Why him, for crying out loud?"

She smiled. "Because he'd be perfect for it." And, with that, Kat turned and walked into the kitchen, her arm wrapped around Rebecca, as they talked about ankle joints.

Badger turned to face Delta, shaking his head. "Well?"

"Yeah, *well*," he replied, with a knowing smile. "Outside of an ankle joint, I could really use a beer."

Badger chuckled and slapped him on the shoulder. "Out to the pool then. That's where the beer and the relaxation happens," he declared. "That was a job well done, by the way. Now, if only Kat wasn't thinking about Conall for the next one."

"Why is that?"

"Because he's big, a little on the rougher-built side. Yet he's all heart and a big marshmallow. If it's a bad case, he's bound to go to pieces."

Delta frowned at him. "I think you're considering that from the wrong angle. If it goes bad, his heart will hurt, and then he'll move on, stronger and better than ever. But that marshmallow? We need guys like that. Most of the world is too scared and too ashamed to show any emotions. Guys like Conall, they're all emotion, but they're also really good men to have behind you."

Badger nodded. "Agreed. So Kat was right, … once again."

This concludes Book 23 of The K9 Files: Delta.
Read about Conall: The K9 Files, Book 24

The K9 Files: Conall (Book #24)

Welcome to the all new K9 Files series reconnecting readers with the unforgettable men from SEALs of Steel in a new series of action packed, page turning romantic suspense that fans have come to expect from USA TODAY Bestselling author Dale Mayer. Pssst… you'll meet other favorite characters from SEALs of Honor and Heroes for Hire too!

Conall is more than happy to head out after a War Dog has gone missing, leaving a wheelchair-bound military war veteran lost and alone. Yet what seems like a simple job takes an unsavory turn, when Conall comes face-to-face with darker undertones in that town.

Bethany always wanted to have her own veterinary clinic, and she's been doing a decent job of it, until so much of the town died that she finds it hard to get and to keep decent staff. Her temporary help suddenly embroils her clinic in a mess involving a missing War Dog, and then Bethany uncovers what else this young lady is involved in. None of it's good.

Conall refuses to back down or to walk away from the sudden hell Bethany's life has become. No telling how ugly this can get …

Find Book 24 here!
To find out more visit Dale Mayer's website.
https://geni.us/DMSConall

Author's Note

Thank you for reading Delta: The K9 Files, Book 23! If you
enjoyed the book, please take a moment and leave a
short review.

Dear reader,

I love to hear from readers, and you can contact me at my
website: www.dalemayer.com or at my Facebook author
page. To be informed of new releases and special offers, sign
up for my newsletter or follow me on BookBub. And if you
are interested in joining Dale Mayer's Reader Group, here is
the Facebook sign up page.
http://geni.us/DaleMayerFBGroup

Cheers,
Dale Mayer

About the Author

Dale Mayer is a *USA Today* best-selling author, best known for her SEALs military romances, her Psychic Visions series, and her Lovely Lethal Garden cozy series. Her contemporary romances are raw and full of passion and emotion (Broken But … Mending, Hathaway House series). Her thrillers will keep you guessing (Kate Morgan, By Death series), and her romantic comedies will keep you giggling (*It's a Dog's Life*, a stand-alone novella; and the Broken Protocols series, starring Charming Marvin, the cat).

Dale honors the stories that come to her—and some of them are crazy, break all the rules and cross multiple genres!

To go with her fiction, she also writes nonfiction in many different fields, with books available on résumé writing, companion gardening, and the US mortgage system. All her books are available in print and ebook format.

Connect with Dale Mayer Online

Dale's Website – www.dalemayer.com
Twitter – @DaleMayer
Facebook Page – geni.us/DaleMayerFBFanPage
Facebook Group – geni.us/DaleMayerFBGroup
BookBub – geni.us/DaleMayerBookbub
Instagram – geni.us/DaleMayerInstagram
Goodreads – geni.us/DaleMayerGoodreads
Newsletter – geni.us/DaleNews

Made in the USA
Monee, IL
21 February 2024

53892381R00154